THE WEDDING PARTY

BOOKS BY LORNA DOUNAEVA

The Wife's Mistake
The Perfect Housemate

THE WEDDING PARTY

LORNA DOUNAEVA

bookouture

Published by Bookouture in 2025

An imprint of Storyfire Ltd.
Carmelite House
50 Victoria Embankment
London EC4Y 0DZ

www.bookouture.com

The authorised representative in the EEA is Hachette Ireland
8 Castlecourt Centre
Dublin 15 D15 XTP3
Ireland
(email: info@hbgi.ie)

Copyright © Lorna Dounaeva, 2025

Lorna Dounaeva has asserted her right to be identified as the author of this work.

All rights reserved. No part of this publication may be reproduced, stored in any retrieval system, or transmitted, in any form or by any means, electronic, mechanical, photocopying, recording or otherwise, without the prior written permission of the publishers.

ISBN: 978-1-83618-257-3
eBook ISBN: 978-1-83618-256-6

This book is a work of fiction. Names, characters, businesses, organizations, places and events other than those clearly in the public domain, are either the product of the author's imagination or are used fictitiously. Any resemblance to actual persons, living or dead, events or locales is entirely coincidental.

For Lizzy

PROLOGUE

Hours after sunset, a faint aura shimmers in the sky. The land pulses and shifts with the rhythm of the wind, and the waves crash against the shore with relentless fury, clawing at the sand before dragging it back into the depths with an almighty roar.

Two people walk along the beach. She is tall and graceful, dressed in a shimmering ivory wedding gown, while he is bald and broad-chested, his kilt swishing around his knees.

'Why did you invite them?' Gordon asks. 'They've done nothing but mock you since they got here. Not one of them strikes me as a true friend.'

Asha laughs. 'They thought they were going to play me, but I was ready for them. Turns out I'm a better actress than I realised.'

A deep crease forms between his eyebrows. His mouth tightens at the corners, and his eyes lock onto hers, puzzled. Sensing his reaction, she softens her tone, dropping her gaze for a moment before meeting his again.

'I invited them because I wanted to show them how lucky I am.' Her voice is steady but laced with defiance. 'Because I have you, and I'm so damn happy. I wanted to rub it in their faces.

They all think they're better than me, Gordon. I needed to prove how wrong they are.'

'By inviting them to our wedding?'

Asha stands on her tiptoes and presses her lips against his. This is what she always does when she wants to get out of something. But this time he is not having it. He needs to get to the bottom of this. What is this hold these people have over her?

'But why—' The words catch in his throat as a loud *pop* pierces the air. A strange sensation spreads through his chest, followed by a dull, searing pain.

He looks down. A vivid red stain blossoms across the pristine white of his shirt, spreading outward like spilled ink. The realisation of what is happening hits him slower than the pain. There is a second *pop*. This one punches through his chest, the force tearing his flesh, a white-hot agony that radiates through him.

His legs falter, and he staggers, knees buckling. His breath comes in shallow, ragged gasps.

Reaching out, he grabs onto Asha, his fingers curling tightly around her arm for support. She stares at him, her eyes widening in shock, her voice rising in panic, but he can barely register her words over the rushing in his ears.

He fights to stay upright, but his vision dims at the edges. Out of the corner of his eye, he catches a movement, a dark figure emerging from the shadows, purposeful and steady. He sees the rifle, sees how the barrel is now trained on Asha, the moonlight glinting off the cold steel.

Asha is so shocked she can't speak. He falls from her arms like stone, landing hard on the rocks. But his pain doesn't matter. Nothing matters at that moment but her.

He looks up at the clouds in the sky, the water, the land. This incredible island.

'I... love you!'

Asha stares into his eyes, and he sees wild, unadulterated fear.

Something is blocking his windpipe and his next word almost chokes him.

'Go!'

She leans in and gives him one last kiss. 'I love you so much.'

'I... love you too. Now go!'

Another bullet rips through the air. And Asha is gone.

ONE
DIANE

The sun is a fiery blob on the horizon, like melted butter dripping over burnt sienna mountains, with little wisps of sea mist floating about like cotton wool. The water churns with small waves crashing against the dock. The faint smell of diesel and fresh seafood drifts through the air. Diane watches as fishermen unload crates of crabs onto waiting lorries. A seagull gives her the side-eye as it whips right by her face, then soars up into the sky, white wings glinting in the sunlight.

Her heart leaps as she spots Pete and Sarah. They appear to be engrossed in conversation, their bodies slightly angled away from each other. She takes in the soft curve of Sarah's smile and the deep furrow of Pete's brow. His hair has receded, and there are intricate worry lines etched around his eyes and mouth. Sarah, by contrast, positively glows with good health.

Her phone pings. It's Asha, the bride to be:

Well? Are they a couple or aren't they?

'Diane!' Sarah breaks away from Pete and runs along the pier.

'I missed you!'

'You too. It's been too long.'

Sarah flings her arms around her and Diane feels the bond that ties them together, despite the eight long years that have passed since they all last met together like this. An archive of memories floods through her mind. When Pete comes to take his turn, she holds onto him for so long that he breaks away from her and peers into her eyes.

'You all right, Di?'

'Yes, yes of course. Just so excited to see you! It's been so long!'

'Too long!'

She looks from him to Sarah. 'So, you two are living together now?'

'It's just a temporary arrangement,' Sarah says. Her dirty blonde waves are now streaked with pink and she's sporting a blunt fringe that adds a touch of edginess to her appearance. She wears a tight white vest under the same old denim jacket and a long red skirt that is fraying at the bottom.

Diane's eyes skid back to Pete. He was thin back at uni, but now his eyes have sunk into their sockets, making them look like the marbles in a pinball machine. His jaw is clenched but he says nothing as he looks towards the sea.

'No Cameron?' Sarah asks.

Just hearing his name sends an electric charge right through Diane's heart.

'No, he couldn't.' Diane has her lies prepared, but they won't trip off her tongue. Cameron won't be joining her on this or any trip from now on. The enormity of her situation settles in her chest and she delves into her handbag, hoping to find a painkiller to numb the ache.

Pete excuses himself to go to the gents, and Sarah leans closer, all conspiratorial. 'Pete really needs this holiday. It's not good for him, being stuck at home so much. He needs to get back out there. He's lost his confidence.'

'Why, what's happened?'

To her shame, Diane has not made much effort to keep up with Pete. She'd heard something about him being in the army, and then later, that it hadn't gone so well. He couldn't handle it. Was that why Sarah has taken him in? Is he a lost cause?

'Pete's fine,' Sarah backtracks. 'He's just a bit self-limiting right now, you know?'

Diane doesn't know. She doesn't have a clue.

'Do you mean he's got…?'

'Has anyone heard from Ethan?' Pete asks, returning too quickly, before they've had a chance to get to the bones of the matter.

Cameron has this knack too, always interrupting the conversation at the wrong point. But she can't think about him now. She tries to focus on the original purpose of this trip, the reason she agreed to come. For weeks, she has wrestled with her conscience, debating whether to go ahead with her plan. The guilt has gnawed away at her, pulling her in two directions. But she has nothing left to lose now. She might as well let all hell break loose. Misery loves company. And soon there'll be plenty of it.

'So how long have you two been living together?' she asks, returning her attention to her former housemates.

'Almost a year now,' Pete says. 'Sarah has been my rock. I don't know what I'd do without her.'

Sarah nods but the smile doesn't reach her eyes. 'Pete's helped me out a lot too. He's great at fixing things. If you need any decorating done, he's your man.'

'Cameron's pretty handy too,' Diane says. 'He installed our kitchen all by himself.'

She doesn't know why she's talking about him like this. Perhaps it's because she's not ready to deal with reality. They've been married almost eight years. Their next anniversary is at the end of the month. It's unimaginable to think that she will be spending it alone. She presses her lips tightly together. She's not ready to tell them the relationship is over. Not yet. They will all find out eventually, but she needs to wrap her own head around it first, before she shares her pain with the world. Besides, she's always had a nagging feeling that deep down, they prefer Cameron to her.

'Pete cooks a great stroganoff too,' Sarah is saying.

'He sounds like the perfect houseguest,' Diane says.

But surely she's over-egging it? Diane remembers what he was like, back in the day. A bit of a slob, as she recalls. She'd have to remind him when it was his turn to take the bins out, and he always left his dishes to fester in the sink instead of rinsing them. Still, a whole decade has passed since then. It sounds like he's a reformed character.

'So what about Gordon?' she says. 'What's he like?'

Sarah and Pete both shake their heads. 'Haven't had the pleasure,' Pete says, 'but I hear he owns a massive cattle farm. There's a shop as well. Must be doing all right for himself.'

'Well, that explains the whirlwind romance,' she says with a smile.

She's being unfair to Asha. Her parents own a popular fusion restaurant in Edinburgh, so she imagines she's fairly comfortable. She's had a successful career of her own too. Opportunities fall into her lap.

She looks at Sarah. 'What do you make of him?'

'I haven't met him yet.'

Diane does a double take. 'Really? I'd have thought she'd be desperate to show him off.'

She really is surprised. Sarah and Asha are still close. So why is this the first time she's meeting Gordon?

'Asha sent me some pictures,' Sarah says. 'He looks how

you'd imagine a farmer to look. He's older. Quite ordinary looking, big and bald.'

'Nothing wrong with being bald,' Pete says, running a hand over his own thinning scalp.

'He's not who I would have picked for her,' Sarah says. 'But she was always keen to get married, wasn't she? So, they must have the same life goals.'

'I suppose. But this whole Orkney wedding! I couldn't imagine a less Asha place to get married. Edinburgh Castle would be more her speed.'

'He's from Orkney, isn't he?' Pete says.

'Well, what about the cathedral?' Sarah says. 'There's St Magnus, this ancient Viking cathedral with incredible acoustics, and yet she wants to get married in some field.'

'Maybe Asha is humble now,' Diane says.

They all laugh heartily and, all at once, the years collapse in on one another, and it is as if no time has passed at all.

While they wait for the rest of the wedding party to arrive, they walk down to the visitors' centre. She takes a look at the big map on the wall. The island Asha and Gordon have chosen for their wedding is so secluded it doesn't even get a mention. It's just a tiny green dot in the sea. She waits while Sarah and Pete stock up on snacks, then they head back to the dock. There's no sign of the other guests yet, but she's heard it will just be a select few. She supposes she should feel honoured to be included.

She looks out at the water and a shiver runs down her spine. The inky depths reflect the old stone buildings and sloping hills that overlook the town. Red and blue fishing boats sway lethargically, their vibrant hulls standing out against the muted tones of the quay. Her heart lifts as she glimpses a yellow kayak, just for a moment, but then it's gone.

The minibus arrives with the rest of the wedding guests

onboard. Asha is the first to jump out, a gentle breeze playing with the strands of her hair. She raises a hand to wave, and it's like the world slows for a moment. She never has to try to get anyone's attention. No one could miss her, with her alluring dark eyes and endlessly long legs. She steps forward and hugs them each in turn.

'It's been too long,' she tells Diane, a little crossly, as if this is her fault. It isn't. In fact, if Diane remembers correctly, the last time they were all together was at her own wedding. If Asha hadn't invited them all to Orkney, she's not sure they would have ever seen each other again.

'No sign of Ethan?' Asha says.

'He's stuck in Glasgow,' Sarah says. 'I don't think he's going to make it.'

Asha pouts. 'What a shame! It would have been so nice to get all the gang back together.'

'Maybe he couldn't hack the thought of a week on a remote island,' Diane murmurs.

She had wondered about it herself. Originally, it was only going to be a weekend, but Asha persuaded them they should make a proper holiday of it.

It will do you all the world of good, she'd said. *There's something about spending time in nature. It's very good for the soul.*

Of course, Asha has always enjoyed telling others what to do. She and Gordon will be off on their honeymoon as soon as the wedding is over.

Now she pulls Diane to one side. 'So what do you make of Sarah and Pete?'

'I don't think they're a couple. In fact, I'm not even sure she likes him at all.'

Disappointment flashes through Asha's eyes. 'Why are they shacked up together then?'

'I'm not sure. I haven't got to the bottom of it. Anyway, never mind them. I want to meet Gordon. Where is he?'

'You'll meet him in a minute. He's helping with the bags.'

They both look over at the minibus, where a large muscular man is offloading boxes and bags. Presumably these are their provisions for the week, since there won't be any shops on the island.

Once he has finished, he comes over and Asha makes the introductions.

'Everyone, this is Gordon. Gordon, meet Sarah, Diane and Pete.'

'Hi,' Diane says, adjusting her scarf against the breeze.

'Great to meet you!' Sarah nudges Pete, who remains silent.

Gordon smiles at them. 'I've heard a lot about you all.'

Sarah giggles, but Pete still doesn't respond. His entire body stiffens, and he takes a half step back.

Gordon pretends not to notice. 'Well, I'll go and see if they're ready for us.'

They watch as he strides towards the boat.

Sarah looks at Pete. 'You all right?'

He shakes his head slightly, as if to clear it. 'Yeah. Fine.'

There's the rumble of an engine as a taxi pulls up.

'Cheers, mate!'

She turns at the sound of his voice.

'Ethan! You made it!'

'Of course. Wouldn't miss it.'

He's smiling as he saunters towards her. He hasn't lost his swagger. His jeans hang loose from his hips and he wears a brown leather jacket, with the collar pulled up against the wind.

'I thought you were stuck in Glasgow,' she says, stepping forward to hug him.

'I managed to get a connecting flight through Aberdeen. My luggage, unfortunately, is currently circumnavigating Greenland. I've been tracking it through the AirTags.'

'Lucky luggage! I always wanted to go there.'

'Me too.'

'Do you think you'll get it back?'

'Maybe, but not till after the trip. I had to buy a few things at the airport. I'll be wearing tourist shirts all week.'

He unzips his jacket to reveal a sequined Loch Ness monster, with the words 'Scotland', emblazoned over the top.

Diane bursts out laughing. The sound is strange to her own ears.

His eagle eyes land on her bandage. 'Hey, what happened to your hand?'

'I... shut it in the front door.' She forces a laugh which comes out as a whimper.

He looks at her closely. 'Was it Cameron?'

She doesn't know how to answer that.

'I wondered why he wasn't coming. You two were always attached at the hip.'

Her head dips, her gaze fixed on the bandage. 'Well not any more.'

'Good.'

He looks over at the boat. 'Did you hear about the one that sank just outside the Pentland Firth? I wonder if it was the same model?'

There's an impishness to his smile, and Diane knows he's winding her up.

She might not be worried, but Asha's dad is standing by the boat with a concerned look on his face. His frown deepens as he walks along the pier, inspecting every detail. The sides are streaked with rust, and a few patches of seaweed cling stubbornly to the hull, swaying with the motion of the water.

'Honestly, it's fine,' Gordon says, catching his expression. His tone is calm, reassuring, but Asha's dad doesn't respond. His attention remains fixed on the ferry as it bumps gently against the side of the pier.

Gordon puffs out a breath of air, then puts on a smile and

goes to speak to the crew. A few minutes later, they lay down a gangplank, and the guests gingerly cross it to get onboard.

Ethan leans close to Asha. 'Are you sure it's seaworthy?'

'The crew know what they're doing. They wouldn't set foot on this boat if it weren't safe.'

The other guests have started to board.

Diane smiles at Ethan. She really is glad to see him. 'Come on, we'd better board the deathtrap.'

The boards shift beneath her weight as she steps onto the ferry. A crew member offers her a reassuring smile which she does not return.

There's no room in the cabin. The bags are placed in the hold and they have to sit out on deck. Everyone turns and faces the water. The engine starts with a deep rumble. Then they are off, going faster than she would like. The boat hops over the waves and she feels her stomach contents swirling about. She looks back at Kirkwall, at the lights of the buildings and the early morning tractors at work in their fields. It's not a large city, but it's huge compared to the place they're heading to.

Goodbye, civilisation. Good riddance.

Asha switches places with her dad so she can be next to them. She looks around at them all: Ethan, Pete, Diane and Sarah. All the housemates back together.

'We should get a picture!' Sarah says. 'Damn, my phone's dead.'

'Use mine,' Ethan says, handing it over.

They all gurn for the camera. Then laugh as Sarah shows them the resulting pictures.

The ferry slices through the water. Diane pulls out her binoculars as they tour past the island of Hoy. She watches as great skuas circle above, their sharp eyes scanning for prey. She has read about these 'bonxies', as they are known in Orkney.

The pirates of the sea. These birds are bold, brutal and breathtaking. They watch as other birds catch fish and squid, then swoop down and snatch them away. They'll eat other birds too. Even the larger ones, like herons and gulls.

They pass a wall of sheer cliffs and, as the boat turns, a spectacular sea stack rises out of the waves.

'That's the Old Man of Hoy,' Pete says.

He puts out his hand for the binoculars, but Diane bats him away, intent on watching puffins burrow into its rugged surface. Beyond the shore, Orkney's two highest peaks stand tall against the sky.

'Give us a look,' he pleads.

'In a minute.'

Through the binoculars, she sees the vibrant colours of the moorlands, dotted with primroses and clovers, adding bursts of colour to the muted greens and browns.

Pete leans towards her. He's outgrown the cheap aftershave he used to douse himself in, and she gets a whiff of him; a combination of sweat and grease. She wrinkles her nose and wonders, not for the first time, what the hell happened.

The boat makes an abrupt change of direction. She gazes into the water. It's a deep, oily green, with little bubbles of foam dancing on the surface. She looks out for the seals and orcas she's heard so much about but there is no sign of them. She pictures herself falling overboard, tumbling down into its depths.

'Look at the horizon,' Cameron used to say, whenever they went on a boat trip. But then Cameron was raised on boats. He has always had good sea legs and a cast-iron stomach. Diane has neither.

As her nausea wells up, she crawls to the edge of the boat, leans over and dry heaves. She remains in that position for much of the journey, her head bobbing as she falls asleep then jerks awake again. Sarah slips a comforting arm around her.

'It won't be long now. You're going to be okay.'

Will she? Diane isn't so sure.

'Is Pete... bothering you?' she asks, once the waves become a little gentler.

Sarah lets out a surprised laugh. 'Bothering me? What do you mean?'

'I mean, is he leeching off you? I saw you both in the shop earlier. He didn't even try to get his wallet out. You paid for everything.'

Sarah screws up her eyes, the way she always did when she was formulating a lie.

'You don't have to explain,' Diane cuts in before she can say anything.

She turns her attention to the water. The sun is like a beam, exposing smaller islands in the distance. They rise out of the sea; dark green lumps of land. They look empty and almost entirely treeless. There are few buildings or houses that she can see and she wonders how many of these islands are truly wild. Most of them have little puffs of vapour floating around them. But as they continue onward, it begins to feel as if they might sail over the edge of the world. The sky around them becomes murkier, until they are engulfed in a thick sea mist that clings to her hair and makes her nose tingle. And then, out of the mist, rises a new lump of land. It is almost triangular in shape and darker than the ones that came before it, with jagged grey cliffs that jut out around the edges like teeth. A flock of crows circle overhead, their caws echoing through the air.

'This is it,' Gordon says. 'Haarlorn, the island of mist.'

TWO
DIANE

Haarlorn

'Does anybody live here?' Diane asks, looking out at the island.

'Just the caretakers,' Asha says. 'It's private land, so no one can come here without prior arrangement. They have holiday cottages specially built for hunting parties and suchlike. But it's really beautiful too. The perfect setting for a wedding.'

Everyone strains to get a better look. Dozens of people, all jockeying for position. Gordon takes a step towards Pete, who pitches forward and stumbles towards the edge.

'Sit down!' Sarah shrieks.

Pete regains his balance. He stays by the railing and stares out at the water.

'Hey, who are all those people?'

He points into the distance.

Gordon laughs but does not reply.

At first, Diane can't see who he's pointing to but then she notices a row of figures on the shore. They stand completely rigid and one looks as if he is pointing a rifle straight at them. As the boat drifts closer, she sees that they are merely scarecrows, fashioned out of straw and cloth. They have been artfully made. The faces have a lifelike quality, with penetrating eyes and long, pointed noses. Their mouths hang open displaying bright red tongues and their false teeth rattle in the breeze.

The ferry glides into a small inlet. The crew members extend their hands to help the passengers off. Diane is the last to disembark. Her knees have turned to water, but she's grateful to make it safely on to dry land.

'Diane?' Sarah says.

'Just give me a minute.'

She still feels the tipping motion as she stands on the dock. She gazes out at the vast expanse of water, squinting to see if she can make out any islands in the distance. She knows that somewhere beyond this island lies Orkney's capital, Kirkwall, and further still, mainland Scotland, and yet all she can see is the yawning abyss of the sea.

She watches as the ferry makes a sharp turn. The water churns and splashes the wooden posts. She feels the vibration in her bones as it roars away.

'What's their rush?' she asks.

Gordon shakes his head. 'They probably got word that there's going to be weather.'

He turns his attention to the stacks of boxes and bags piled on the dock and calls out to the rest of the group.

'Wait! Everyone grab what you can!'

There is muttering from some of his friends and relatives, but gradually, the pile grows smaller until there is just Diane's backpack left for her to carry.

She doesn't look too closely at the scarecrows as they pass. There is something disconcerting about the way they have been posed, as if they were once real people who have been frozen in time.

Two figures trek up the hill towards them.

'Ah, here are the caretakers,' Gordon says, sounding relieved.

Broderick and Judith are both short in stature, with weathered faces and calloused hands, and even though she is accustomed to Scottish accents, Diane has to listen carefully to catch what they are saying:

'Welcome to Haarlorn. How was the crossing? A bit choppy, or nae too bad?'

She lets the others drift ahead, hanging back as they climb the hill to the level ground beyond. The holiday cottages are small stone buildings. The end strip of each roof looks pixelated, as if it has been built out of Minecraft blocks. Diane noticed this feature on some of the houses in Stromness and Kirkwall. She imagines it provides protection from the wind and rain. Each of the cottages is identical apart from the names painted on the doors: Skylark, Oystercatcher, Hawk, Hen Harrier, Arctic Tern and Red-throated Diver.

Diane will be sharing Red-throated Diver with her old housemates, except for Asha. She and Gordon will have Oystercatcher all to themselves.

The doorways are so low they have to duck their heads as they enter. Inside, it all looks really cosy. There is a small fireplace surrounded by comfy chairs and sofas. The air is a little stale, and she guesses it's been a while since anyone stayed here.

She takes the room at the back of the house. It has a stunning view, looking out to sea. She stands at the window and thinks that she could look at this all day. It would never get old.

'It's quite homely, isn't it?' says Sarah, interrupting her chain of thought. 'I'm in the room next door.'

Diane offers her a sly smile. 'Not sharing with Pete then?'

'Hardly.'

They've barely had five minutes to settle in when Judith appears in the living room. There are no locks on the doors. No need for them, she supposes. The wedding party are the only people on the island. And yet, she doesn't like the way Judith has walked in without knocking.

This would never work back in Inverness. She would hate to have people wander into her flat unannounced. She always locks the doors at night and Cameron leaves his golfing umbrella in the hallway, just in case. Or at least he did.

She swallows bile and forces herself to pay attention. Tries not to think about the good times, when Cameron would pull her out into the rain. Just for the hell of it. They had some good times under that golfing umbrella. Some really good times.

'I'll take you for a tour now,' Judith announces.

Pete and Ethan emerge from their rooms. No one wants to miss this. It's not a large island. But they're still keen to see the lay of the land. After all, this is going to be their home for the week. From what Asha was saying on the boat, it sounds like the four of them are the only ones staying on after the wedding. Gordon's family and friends need to get back to their farms, and Asha's parents have their restaurant to run. She's surprised they haven't retired by now. She supposes they've got no one to hand it down to, now that Asha's marrying Gordon.

They step outside and find the other guests already waiting. Judith leads them down a narrow path, pointing out the native flora and fauna. As they walk along the shore, she explains that there is no internet or phone signal on the island. Sarah pulls a face but Diane is happy about this. She wanted to get away from it all, and now it seems she won't have a choice.

They arrive at the lighthouse – a towering white structure that stands tall against the waves. There is a spiral of steps that leads all the way to the top.

'I'll leave that for another day,' Judith says. 'But take my word for it, there's a bonnie view. You can see for miles around. On a good day, you might even see all the way to Kirkwall.'

'How does it work?' Ethan asks. 'Do the lights go on automatically?'

'No, someone has to go up there to operate it.'

He tilts his head. 'I thought they were all automatic these days?'

'Most of them are, but no one bothered to automate this one. We don't get many visitors, but if it's misty out, we come up here and switch it on. There's also a foghorn that helps the boats work out our position.'

They leave the lighthouse, and she makes them squelch through a path of thick mud that clings to their boots. Brambles scratch Diane's legs, making her regret her decision to wear shorts.

'Right then, I'll show you the circle,' Judith says.

Diane is already picturing a roundabout as they trudge further down the path and climb over a rickety stile, into a large field of grass which, unlike the surrounding area, has been carefully mowed and maintained.

She blinks in delight at the sight of an ancient stone circle. The stones are worn and weathered and not as tall as those she has seen at Stonehenge, or even at the Ring of Brodgar, but there is something magical about them, all the same.

Her mind reels at the thought that this monument has stood here for centuries. There is a moment of silent reverence, and she can't resist the urge to reach out and touch the stones. She imagines a surge of energy coursing through her fingertips.

Asha smiles. 'This is where we're getting married. I'm very spiritual these days.'

Ethan snorts, but even he admits it's a cool location.

'Very Instagrammable,' he says, 'just as long as the weather cooperates.'

Asha meets his eye. 'Let's hope it does.'

They continue with their tour, walking up a long road, alongside which they find the remains of a petrol pump. It's very old, judging by the petrol prices. It seems incongruous with such a quiet island.

'Did people actually live here?' Pete asks.

Judith nods. 'There were over a hundred residents at the turn of the last century. You'll see the graveyard just over that hill.'

'What happened to them?' Diane asks.

'Well' – Judith glances over her shoulder – 'some of the men died in the two world wars. There was a lot of jealousy and infighting. The deaths fell unevenly, you see, with some families dropping like peats in the fire, and others surviving more or less intact. Then came The Great Winter. It was a gey rough year. It was so bad no ships could get through with deliveries. Folk started to lose it and a sort of madness set in. They had to ration everything, and it brought out all those old grudges. They started fighting, killing each other. Others became ill and couldn't get their medicines. There were even those who took to the sea and tried to fight their way through the waves but no good came of it. Their boats were smashed up on the rocks or else lost at sea. When the weather finally lifted it was spring time, and with it came the sea mists, the haars. When a ship from the mainland finally docked, they found the place strewn with bodies and those that had survived were scarcely speaking, or else blethering a load of nonsense. The last remaining family moved to Kirkwall in the seventies and that was that. The island was abandoned. The government sold it off, and it's privately owned now. Broderick and I stay here year round to mind the birds and animals, and in the summer months we get folk such as yourselves who come out here for a taste of island life.'

'Wow, don't you find it creepy, being all alone like that?' Sarah asks.

Judith eyeballs her. 'I'm not alone. I've got Broderick, haven't I?'

Diane pictures the long, dark winters. Just the two of them.

Then the ghost of a smile flickers across Judith's lips. 'Seriously. I'd find it creepier to live down south with all the soaks and junkies. Up here, it's just us, and it's fine.'

The island tour finishes up in the grounds of Judith and Broderick's cottage. The lawn is a large stretch of grass that's been left to grow wild. The paint is peeling on the chicken coops, and the fence looks like it will come down with the next gust of wind.

Pete has got a beer from his backpack. His fingers tap idly against the metal, but every few minutes, he lifts it to his lips, taking long, steady sips. He stands beside Sarah, so close you would be forgiven for thinking they were together, but she is starting to see that Sarah is his safety net, and the further apart they get, the more unsettled he becomes.

He stiffens as Asha and Gordon walk towards them, hand in hand. Asha is beaming, exchanging significant glances with Gordon.

'We have something to ask you,' she says, as she looks from Pete to Sarah. Diane moves a bit closer, curious to hear what she's going to say.

Pete takes another sip of beer. A long one.

Sarah forces a smile. 'We're all ears.'

'We want you to be our honorary bridesmaid and groomsman,' Asha says, with a dazzling smile.

'Oh!' Sarah glances at Pete, who tightens his grip on his can.

'What would we have to do?' Sarah asks.

'Not much. Just hand us the rings during the ceremony. It doesn't matter if your dress doesn't match the little ones. But you're okay to make a speech, right?'

Sarah nods. Pete still hasn't said a word. Sarah speaks for both of them. 'Thank you. We'd loved to handle the rings, wouldn't we, Pete?'

He nods mechanically.

Asha beams. 'Great! We'll drop the rings off to you before the wedding.' She leans closer and gives Sarah a hug. 'Thanks. It means a lot.'

Gordon nods. 'You'll have to excuse me. I need to go and speak to Broderick about this afternoon's entertainment.' He hurries off but Asha remains where she is.

'Whose idea was this?' Pete asks, finally finding his voice.

'Gordon thinks it would make the wedding more equal,' Asha says. 'He has a lot more family than I do, so he thought it would be good to redress the balance.'

Sarah nods. 'That makes sense.'

Diane watches with interest. She has noticed Asha has not invited any other friends to the wedding. Or perhaps she has, and they all declined.

Pete lets out a breath, his gaze still fixed on the spot where Gordon was standing. 'Is that a shooting range over there? Would it be possible to have a go?'

'Judith?' Asha calls out. 'Can we use the range?'

Judith huffs and turns away from them, so Diane thinks that's that, but then she goes to the lock-up and takes out a black rifle. It has a sleek, military look, and the barrel is long and narrow. She takes them through a short safety briefing, during which Pete closes his eyes and Asha examines her nails.

'Watch closely,' Judith says, her stance confident and practised. She raises the rifle to her shoulder with steady hands and takes aim. As she pulls the trigger, the gunshots echo through the air and the bullet strikes the target dead centre. Diane watches from the sidelines, noting Ethan's intense gaze. Then he looks over at her. A smirk crosses his face, and their old rivalry sparks back to life, as if they've never been apart. She doesn't have to be the best shooter in the group, just better than Ethan.

They each take a weapon and a pair of protective goggles and line up along the range. The guns are empty, so first they have to load the bullets into the chambers. Pete is the first to pull the trigger, setting off a resounding blast that pierces the air. As soon as he lets off his shot, there is a barrage of bullets as everyone else joins in. Diane watches as Ethan lines up his shot. He hits the target, not right in the middle. But he does a decent job.

She tries to block out all the noise in her head as she focuses on her own shot. Her hand shakes as she pulls the trigger. It goes slightly off target, leaving her even more determined to get it right. They both fire again. Their next shots are worse, but on her third go, Diane hits the bullseye.

She jumps up and down, then realises Judith is waving at her because Ethan has yet to shoot. She steps back, and he gives her a wink. Then he gets into position and hits it right on the target as well.

He high-fives her and she forces herself to smile. Then she turns to see what Asha is giggling at. Asha points out her own target. From the look of it, she hasn't hit it once.

'If that was a deer, it would be gone,' Ethan says.

'Then it's a good job there are no deer in Orkney.'

Gordon drapes an arm around Asha and peppers her neck with kisses.

Ethan's gaze hardens, unable to conceal the annoyance rising inside him. Diane isn't sure if it's the public display of affection he finds objectionable, or the fact that Asha has chosen this oafish-looking man when she has repeatedly rejected Ethan over the years. Regardless of the reason, she likes it when he's angry. It adds an edge to everything. Makes the game more exciting.

With a jolt, she remembers her plan. She knows she should

keep Asha's secret, but why should she, after everything that's happened? She rubs her hands together, a sly smile creeping across her face as she glances at Ethan. Her eyes shine with an unspoken promise. It's the kind of smile that says:

Wait till you hear what I've got planned.

THREE
DIANE

2011, Aberdeen

The cool, crisp air numbs the tip of Diane's nose. She zips up her coat as she follows a guided tour around the grounds of Aberdeen University. They stop in front of a large lecture theatre that looks more like a Gothic church. Boston ivy swarms the front of the building, and she pictures it overgrowing completely, like Princess Aurora's castle in *Sleeping Beauty*.

The student leading the tour pauses to see if anyone has questions. A tall girl with glossy black hair raises her hand, as if she's in school.

'Yes, I'm sure we were all wondering if there's a set number of clubs we should join?'

She looks a little too pleased with herself and smiles around the group, like she's just asked a really intelligent question. She's flanked by a man and woman, clearly her parents, who beam and nod their encouragement.

The tour guide squints at her. 'You mean like... the social clubs?'

'Yeah, like the debate society and choir.'

'Well, no. They're really just for entertainment and networking. There's no expectation that anybody has to—'

'And what about the weekends? Is it okay if I go home? I live in Edinburgh and was thinking of commuting weekly.'

'Well, it's a free country, so...'

Diane swallows a laugh and catches the eye of the girl next to her, who has dirty blonde hair and a blue denim jacket. She grins back.

The tour guide glances furtively around the group. 'Does anyone else have a question?'

They exchange glances and shrug. No one else seems to notice the swirling mass above them, like dark clouds gathering. Diane watches, slightly unnerved, as a flock of chittering starlings descends onto the lawn beside them, all sharp beaks and iridescent feathers.

'Right, we'll move on, shall we? As you'll see, this is a small campus. Everything is pretty much walkable.'

They stop in front of an old townhouse.

'Now, this building is interesting. It used to be a prison, so it has cells.'

'There aren't any prisoners there now, are there?' the annoying girl asks.

'Er, no, it's actually a museum now.'

'How old do you reckon she is?' Diane murmurs.

The blonde sizes her up. 'Sixteen or seventeen. I'm not being funny, but they really shouldn't let these young ones in. It's not fair on everyone else.'

'I know. Who wants to get stuck babysitting some kid?' Diane says.

'She'd better not be on my course.'

'What are you studying?'

'Geography. You?'

'Engineering.'

'We're probably both safe then. She'll be doing media or some bollocks.'

'So, do you think you're going to choose Aberdeen?' Diane asks.

'All my friends are going to Glasgow, but sod that. The whole point of going to university is to get away.'

'Glasgow? Is that where you're from?'

'Yeah.'

'You don't sound Glaswegian.'

'My family moved around a lot, but we've been in Glasgow five years now. And I'm guessing from your accent you're from London?'

'Surrey.'

'Close enough. I'm Sarah.'

'Diane.'

Sarah is easy to get along with; she has a sense of humour, and they both enjoy poking fun at the annoying girl and her ridiculous questions.

The tour ends right outside the pub.

'Do you fancy a pint?' Sarah asks.

Diane had planned to head straight to her hotel to relax. But hell, why not?

'Yeah, go on then. Just the one.'

They head inside, straight to the bar where they buy frothy pints and carry them over to one of the tables. Some old dude puts a few coins in the jukebox, and a seventies punk song starts to play.

'I bet some of them are lecturers,' Sarah whispers, nodding towards the people at the next table.

Diane feels a shiver of excitement. She can't imagine drinking at the same pub as the staff from her school. She takes a sip of her beer, sloshing a bit down her lap.

Sarah grimaces slightly as she swallows a gulp, and Diane gets the impression she's just drinking to fit in. The older crowd is having a rowdy argument about some poem, and the pub starts filling up, with more and more hot, sweaty bodies pushing to the bar.

'Hey, is anyone sitting here?'

She glances up to see two boys around their own age.

'No! Go ahead! Sit down!' Sarah almost falls over herself, moving their bags and coats out of the way, while Diane takes her time, sizing them up.

The blond one has a big friendly grin. He reminds Diane of a golden retriever, the way he bounces around. The other is altogether cooler. He wears a brown leather jacket and has tousled hair and high cheekbones like Ewan McGregor. There's mischief in his eyes, which appeals to Diane. Here's someone she could have fun with.

'I'm Ethan,' he says, spreading himself out on one of the stools. 'And this is Pete.'

Sarah looks at Diane. 'We aren't going to tell you our names. You'll have to guess.'

Ethan grins wider. 'You're Sarah, and you're Diane.'

Sarah gasps. 'How did you do that?'

Ethan shakes his head. 'I'm a man of many talents.'

Diane eyes Ethan. 'Seriously?'

His eyes drop to her chest. 'You're still wearing your name badges.'

Diane cringes and rips hers off. Sarah does the same.

Ethan settles himself in the chair beside her. 'You know, my mum and dad went here, and this was their local. Of course, it was men-only back then, so Mum and her friends had to cross-dress to get in.'

Sarah laughs a bit too loudly. Pete laughs too, rocking back and forth.

Ethan leans back in his chair and directs his gaze at Diane.

'You're English, right? Long way to come for uni.'

'That's kind of the point.'

'You just want a taste of our Scottish shortbread, don't you?'

She smirks. 'We'll see.'

'She does! Look at the dirty glint in her eyes!'

'Leave the lass alone,' Pete says. 'You're embarrassing her.'

'Don't worry, I'm not easily embarrassed,' Diane says, taking a big gulp of her beer. 'And for the record, I prefer wafers to shortbread. I like the way they snap in half.'

Ethan shrinks back in his seat, and Sarah giggles.

'So, tell me, what do I need to bring for this climate? Do you recommend a waterproof jacket or a big winter coat?'

The others all look at each other.

'You've been wrong-footed by this fine weather we've had today,' Ethan says. 'You should go out there and take a picture, so you remember what the sun looks like. It won't be like this tomorrow or the day after that.'

'Come on, it's not that bad,' Sarah says.

'Says the lass in waterproof boots.'

'Ordinarily, Diane, the sky is so grey that when the clouds finally part, everyone rushes outside to gawk at the gaps in the sky. The air is so damp it permeates your very soul, and there's a special kind of howling wind that blows into your face and seeps into your very bones. And don't even get me started on the rain. You can set out and it's a fine, bonnie day, and the next minute it's pissing it down. Some days, if you don't have a hat, your ears will fall off. You'll need layers, love. Layers upon layers just to survive, and maybe a brolly.'

'Oh, give over,' Pete says. 'A brolly will do you no good; it'll just snap in the wind. And while we do get four seasons in one day, you won't be that bothered by the weather, walking around campus. Everything's close together.'

'Don't listen to him,' Ethan says, his eyes boring into her. 'On the really cold nights, you'll be casting around the place, desperate for someone to keep your bed warm.'

He wiggles his eyebrows suggestively, and everybody cracks up.

They keep drinking, clinking their glasses together and toasting everything under the sun, the beer loosening everyone's inhibitions. After a while, they head into town for food, followed by a nightclub. It's not really Diane's kind of music. Too techno and not enough tune.

'I don't dance,' she says uncertainly as they queue to get in.

'Me neither,' Ethan says.

She feels her shoulders relax. 'Oh, okay. Good.'

They find a table, where they sit and watch. Pete is an amazing dancer. His body is like liquid, undulating and contorting as if he has no bones. His limbs flow effortlessly to the rhythm; it's almost unnerving, the way he bends and twists in ways that seem to defy gravity.

'He's got to be double-jointed,' Ethan shouts over the music.

Diane shakes her head and takes another sip of her drink.

'I'm not even sure he's human.'

'What is he then, some kind of demon?'

'More like some kind of wood sprite or something.'

Ethan snorts. He seems to think that's really funny.

There are no trains or buses running by the time they all stagger out of the club. No one cares. They queue for kebabs and head back to Diane's hotel, where everyone crashes in her room.

Sarah and Diane take the double bed, while Diane finds extra blankets for the boys on the floor. They don't stay there long. Within minutes, all four are sprawled out on the double bed, minds intoxicated, limbs intertwined. Somehow, they manage to sleep like that in one chaotic heap, giggles quickly fading to snores as they drift off one by one.

. . .

In the morning, they go their separate ways, but they keep in touch. Diane speaks with Sarah several times over the following months, and when their results come out, they look at them together over the phone.

'I got in!' Sarah shrieks.

Diane looks at her computer screen and clicks on her own email. She expects to get in, so her results are just a confirmation, but Sarah's enthusiasm is contagious.

Her phone beeps. 'That's Ethan. I'll hang up and see how he did.'

'Okay, I'll call Pete. Talk to you in a bit.'

'I passed!' Pete's even more excited than Sarah. She can picture him twirling around the room, moving that incredibly bendy body of his in ways no one else can. She can't help but wonder if he's more suited to becoming a contortionist than an economist.

'Hey, Ethan thinks we should all get a house together. What do you think?'

Diane considers. She assumed she'd stay in halls, but the idea appeals to her. The four of them, living it up like they did on open day.

'Yeah! Let's do it.'

'Are you nervous?' Pete asks. 'About leaving home?'

'You've got to be kidding,' Diane says. 'Freedom, baby! I've been waiting for this my whole life!'

Pete laughs, then starts coughing; a loud, honking sort of cough that makes him sound like a Canada goose. Soon Diane's laughing too.

Diane's parents aren't thrilled about the shared house, but she talks them around, especially when Ethan's parents offer to buy him a house that he can rent out to them.

'What are you then, a millionaire?' Diane says in wonder.

'Hardly. This is what my parents do. They buy houses and rent them out.'

It's nerve-wracking, turning down her place in halls and waiting for confirmation they have a house. The first place they want falls through, and they end up with a five-bedroom.

'There's a girl on my course who wants the other room,' Ethan tells them a few days after they've moved in. 'Her name's Asha. You'll like her. I said she can pop over later, so we'd better tidy up a bit.'

'Cool,' Diane says, casting her eye around the place. It's already getting untidy, with plates and cups on the table and random hoodies slung over chairs. She and Sarah do a quick clean-up while Ethan looks at his phone and Pete washes a few dishes.

'Who's cleaning the loo, then?' she asks.

Ethan snorts. 'Don't look at me.'

'I'll do it,' Sarah says, rolling her eyes.

'Thanks.'

Asha arrives at five on the dot, her parents in tow. It takes Diane a moment to place her, then she remembers—the annoying girl from their university tour. She exchanges a look with Sarah, who shrugs.

Ethan can't take his eyes off Asha as she breezes around the house, asking endless questions about the heating and the light switches.

Ethan answers them all patiently, going into excruciating detail about the boiler.

'It's a nice neat home you have here,' Asha's mum says respectfully.

'Thank you,' Ethan says, running a hand through his hair.

Diane subtly mimics him, making Sarah smile.

Pete puts the kettle on, making them all a cup of tea, and they sit down together.

Asha's dad rises to his feet, a wistful smile on his face. 'I am so honoured to be here with all of you as you embark on this journey into adulthood.'

Diane sets her cup down. Is he seriously making a speech?

'The days ahead will be some of the best of your lives, and I hope you'll all make the most of them. And remember, not only should you focus on your studies but also on the friendships you make along the way. You'll be living side by side, like a family. So, make sure you cherish this experience, and each other.'

She presses her lips together to keep from laughing, but when she notices the crinkles at the corners of his eyes, she softens a little. Her own father isn't given to such serious speeches. When he dropped her off at uni, he merely told her to keep her head down and stay out of trouble.

She drinks her tea in silence. Then Sarah takes Asha and her mum for a look at the garden. Diane begins clearing away when Asha's dad suddenly says, 'I can see you're an intelligent young woman. Sensible too. You'll be a good influence on our daughter.'

'I hope so,' Diane croaks.

It's strange, the way his words affect her. Does he mean what he says, or has he picked up on her attitude towards Asha? She finds herself fumbling with the cups and saucers as she carries them into the kitchen.

When Asha returns, she smiles brightly, and Diane promises herself that she'll at least try. The girl really does need to get out from under her parents' feet. Maybe, once she and Sarah knock some of those smug edges off her, she'll be all right. It's not her fault she has parents who spoil her rotten.

She glances at Sarah to communicate her feelings, and Sarah seems to get it. The boys, of course, are blissfully unaware of Asha's faults. All they see are her dark, alluring eyes and impossibly glossy hair. Asha could tell them the earth is flat and they'd be nodding along like lunatics. Anyway, Ethan is clearly smitten, and so Asha becomes the fifth member of their household. And for a while, at least, they all get on like... well, a house on fire.

FOUR
DIANE

Judith provides a satisfying lunch of thick crusty sandwiches made with sweet, tender crab meat, pulled straight from the cold waters surrounding the island. After, Broderick offers to take the men over to the north side of the island for a hunting expedition. Ethan waves as they pile into a van, and Diane feels a bit put out that she hasn't been asked to join them. She and Sarah remain behind with the rest of the women and the many boisterous children. Because, of course, the men aren't expected to take them hunting.

They all cram into Asha's cottage, which is really not equipped for so many people. Asha pours glasses of wine and juice, while her mum picks up a book from the shelf and tries to read to the children. The book is about Orkney folklore. She turns to a page filled with pictures of selkies, mythical creatures who shift between seal and human form. They live as seals in the sea but can shed their skins to become human on land. The story takes on a dark side as one of the selkies' skins is stolen by a man, trapping her on the land. The selkie has no choice but to live as a wife and mother, yet she continues to yearn for the sea, and the story ends with her finding her skin and returning to her true home in the ocean, leaving the humans behind.

Diane quite enjoys the story, but none of the children will sit still long enough to listen. Most likely, they've heard it all before. Eventually, Asha's mum gives up and opens the front door, letting them all out like you would a restless cat. Diane watches them go, wondering what will happen if they run off into the wild, never to be seen again.

Reluctantly, the other women pick up their wine glasses and venture outside to keep an eye on them. Perhaps Asha's mum isn't as daft as she looks. She leans back in her chair and closes her eyes, enjoying the peace and quiet, while Diane and the others look at each other.

'It's been so long!' Asha says for the millionth time.

'Too long,' Sarah agrees.

They sit in silence for a minute before Asha jumps up and grabs a game from the sideboard.

'A friend gave me this. Shall we try it?'

The game consists of answering a series of awkward questions.

'How long has it been since you last had sex?' Diane asks Sarah.

Sarah glances over at Asha's mum, who is only pretending to be asleep. 'A few months,' she says, lowering her voice.

Asha leans closer, eager for details. 'Was it Pete?'

'God no.'

Diane takes a card. She ignores what is written there and formulates her own question instead.

'If you had to cut out one member of our friend group, who would it be?'

'Pete,' Sarah says.

'I'm asking Asha.'

Asha thinks for a moment. 'Oh, that's too hard. You can't ask me that.'

'I answered,' Sarah says.

Asha's mum is very still in her chair.

'Ethan,' Asha says. She meets her eye, then looks fleetingly away. 'I don't want to play any more. Let's just talk, shall we?'

'Can we?' Sarah looks like she hates the game as much as Diane does.

Diane looks down at her lap and sees pus leaking through her bandage. She hasn't got around to changing the dressing yet, what with the rush to get to the pier this morning. Her thoughts drift back to Cameron. She misses him so much. Will she ever stop feeling guilty for leaving him like that?

'So, tell me. How did you and Gordon meet?' Sarah asks Asha, taking Diane out of her thoughts.

A smile appears on Asha's face.

'I was helping out at my parents' restaurant one night and there were a load of farmers in. They'd been to some kind of protest thing against the government. Anyway, one of them asked if the meat on the menu was Orkney beef and I said it was. He told me it probably came from his farm.'

Diane snorts. 'As chat-up lines go, I've heard better.'

'Oh, he was so lovely though. His mates left, but he hung around until—'

The door bursts open with a violent crash, shaking the entire room. Diane looks up in surprise as five men in dirty overalls storm inside. They sweep the room, searching for something, or someone. Every muscle in her body tightens as, one by one, they turn and look at her. Then one of them grabs Asha by the arm. The others get her legs and Asha's screams ring out as they carry her away.

FIVE
DIANE

Diane leaps to her feet, unsure what to do. A crowd is gathering outside. Everyone is there, the whole wedding party, egging the men on. Their laughter rings in her ears.

'Here he is!'

She turns and sees Gordon being marched towards them by another group of men. He looks bigger and stronger than his assailants, but he lets them bully him along, and he is alternately grimacing and mugging for the camera as a young woman films it all on her phone.

'It's a blackening,' Pete says as he and Ethan fall into step beside her.

A lightbulb goes off in Diane's head. She was warned about this pre-wedding tradition back when she and Cameron got married, but their wedding was held in the city, and this is a rural tradition, popular in the north of Scotland.

She smiles and waits for her heart to return to its normal rhythm.

Asha is given an all-in-one coverall to put on, while Gordon is stripped down to his jocks.

'Close your mouths!'

The warning comes too late. Someone empties a bucket of filth over the bride and groom to be. It is black and gloopy. Diane takes a step back, retching because the smell is so bad.

'What's in that stuff?' she calls out.

'Oh, the usual. Molasses, porridge, rotten eggs, fish guts and eyeballs. Bit of seaweed.'

An older woman turns round and looks at her. 'You're English?'

Diane blanches. She's lived in Scotland since she was eighteen. She *feels* Scottish, but she never could shake the accent.

'Right, well it is supposed to bring them luck.'

Another woman shakes her head. 'It's to show them how tough marriage can be. If they can stand this, they can stand anything.'

Gordon is coughing and spluttering as a fresh bucket is tipped over him. He's got the worst of it. There is gunk dripping down his forehead, and you can no longer make out the colour of his skin. He shouts and swears. Diane is picking up a whole new vocabulary as bucket after bucket reduces him and Asha to human blobs of muck.

She turns to see two people carrying huge bags of feathers, which they tip over the happy couple. The feathers stick to all the tar and goo, and Gordon hops around like a large flightless bird. Asha dances around, lying on the ground and rolling about to pick up as many as she can. Then she and Gordon hug, and their tar and feathers stick together. They break apart, and Gordon walks towards one of his assailants and tries to share the muck, but the man leaps out of his reach.

A man with a thick red beard ventures closer to take pictures with what looks like a professional camera.

'That's Gordon's mad uncle,' Sarah says. 'He's going to be doing the wedding photos.'

'Why "mad"?' Diane asks.

'Don't know. That's just what they call him.'

Diane watches him as he lines up his next shot. If anything, this man looks the most sane of all of them.

'You have to make some noise,' one of the cousins tells Diane as she clangs pots and pans together. Diane claps her hands a couple of times, then gives up on account of her injured hand.

'This stuff is drying like cement,' Asha complains, trying in vain to peel the feathery tar from her arms.

'Better than a facemask!' Sarah says.

Asha is finally released at the beach, where Gordon is already in the water, washing off all the gunk. His uncle films her running down the beach to join him, pulling off her shoes as she goes. She plunges into the waves.

'Agh! It's freaking freezing!'

'Keep going! You get used to it,' Gordon yells.

Diane looks out to sea. The rusting hull of a ship sticks out of the water, presumably abandoned there since the war. No one takes any notice of it. It's just part of the scenery, like the islands in the distance.

She spots a lone kayak on the horizon. As it gets closer, she sees that it's yellow, and for a moment she can believe it's Cameron. He would definitely be out on a day like this. Never one to waste good weather. But she knows she's kidding herself. There is no way that could be him. She needs to stop these obsessive thoughts.

'Let the celebrations continue!' Pete whoops.

He sounds a little drunk. Sarah walks away from him, purposely heading up the beach to speak to the other guests. She is good at mingling; in a way Diane and Pete have never been. They both jump as a plane swoops over them, flying impossibly low over their heads. Pete bursts out laughing, then turns and looks at her.

'Some people say I'm a good listener,' he says.

Diane's stomach clenches. The pity in his voice twists something inside her. Her throat tightens, threatening to choke her.

'Don't.'

He doesn't back off. He just stands there, silent, waiting.

Anger flares inside her, but then something shifts, something she can't control. The walls she built crack open. Her whole body trembles, her breath hitches and then she's sobbing onto his shoulder. He wraps his arms around her, and she finds him surprisingly solid. His chest feels firm and steady, like he's been here before.

She hates herself for breaking in front of him. But she can't stop the flood. She doesn't have it in her to push it all down any longer.

He doesn't try to fix it. He just holds her, a quiet presence, offering nothing but his humanity. And that's what kills her. It makes her feel small, vulnerable and helpless. Everything she's sworn she'll never be again.

She pulls out a tissue and wipes the tears from her eyes.

'Can you give me a minute?' she asks.

'Whatever you want,' he says.

He touches her lightly on the shoulder and she takes a few steady breaths before she goes to look at the barbecue. They are cooking the birds the men shot on their hunt. Another blackening, of sorts.

'Diane?'

She jumps as someone lays a cold hand on her shoulder. It's Asha. She's wrapped in a towel and shivering slightly. A strand of seaweed sticks to her hair like a slimy green highlight.

'Are you okay?'

Diane forces a smile.

'I've never seen a blackening before. It's all a bit pagan, isn't it?'

'Ha! Ha! That guy who tipped the first bucket over our

heads is Gordon's neighbour. They've been scoring points off each other their whole lives.'

Diane shakes her head. She can't imagine what it would be like, living in the same place your whole life. She scrutinises Asha closely. She is remarkably unchanged by the passing years. Tall and lean as ever. No sign of crow's feet, although her stomach is slightly rounder.

'Things are really happening for you,' she says. 'You must be excited?'

Asha beams. 'Finally! You have no idea how long I've waited.'

'I know you always wanted to get married before you turn thirty.'

They look at each other for a moment and Diane fights the urge to say more. She wants to ask Asha why she invited her. They haven't seen each other in so long. Was it guilt that made her add her name to the guest list? Or was it Sarah's idea? Perhaps she really does want all her former housemates to be there, to witness her big day. To see that she has succeeded, where most of them have failed.

'So, you and Gordon. Is it true you've only met him a handful of times?'

Asha purses her lips. 'So what? We speak nearly every day on the phone.'

'But you don't really know him, do you?' She looks over at Gordon, who is now talking to Sarah. She is doing all the talking and he's just watching her, the way you might watch the weather, weighing up its strength, gauging whether a storm is coming in.

'We've only been together a short time, but he gets me. Really gets me. Like no one else ever did.'

'You know Ethan would have married you in a heartbeat.'

Asha pulls a face. 'I'm surprised he came.'

'Well, he needs to see you and Gordon together. Then he can move on with his life.'

'He was never serious about me, anyway. He just couldn't accept I wasn't interested. Having said that, I was impressed when he said he wanted to spend the week.'

Diane shrugs. 'The weekly rate wasn't much more than the weekend one.'

'You do know there's no Wi-Fi up here?'

'We'll be fine. we're going to fish, hunt and hike. And Broderick is going to take me game shooting, since I didn't get the chance today.'

They both watch as one of Gordon's relatives chases her two children up and down the garden.

'Are you planning to start a family?' Diane asks.

Asha smiles. 'I don't know. Looks exhausting!' She drops her voice. 'You know, I was talking to Pete before, and I'm pretty sure he's hot for Sarah.'

'Really? That's not the vibe I've been getting.'

Asha doesn't like to be corrected. She folds her arms.

'Don't you think it's time they settled down?'

Diane smothers a laugh. Asha can be so old-fashioned at times. 'I think they're just fine as they are. Marriage isn't for everyone.'

'I never said anything about marriage. I just think it would be nice if she had someone. Some people aren't meant to be on their own. Did she tell you about the calls?'

'What calls?'

A smile flickers across Asha's face. She loves to share a secret. 'She's been getting weird phone calls. Some pervert doing this heavy breathing nonsense down the line like some bad eighties film.'

Diane blinks. 'She never said anything to me. How long has this been going on for?'

'I don't know – a while?'

'Perhaps that's why she asked Pete to move in? As a security measure.'

They walk down the beach, closer to the barbecue. Pete doesn't take his eyes off her the whole time.

Asha might be right, Diane thinks. Maybe he does like her.

Ethan stands close by. He smiles at Diane, then turns to Asha. 'Hey, can I have a quick word?'

Asha nods, her expression unreadable, and they drift a few metres away, leaving just enough distance to talk privately. Ethan's arms flail as he speaks, his voice too low for Diane to catch, but his body language screams frustration. His shoulders stiffen, his gestures sharp. Intriguing. She leans casually against a nearby wall, angling herself closer.

'...reputation...' Ethan's clipped tone cuts through the air.

'I wouldn't—' Asha's voice is soft, almost pleading.

'Good,' Ethan snaps. 'Because it would be a very bad idea.'

Before she can edge closer, Gordon strides over to them. Ethan freezes mid-sentence, his face darkening. Without another word, he turns on his heel, storming back towards Diane.

'What was that about?'

His jaw tightens. 'Just reminding Asha where her loyalty lies,' he says, reaching for his beer.

'Okay, now you have to tell me.'

'Another time if you don't mind. I need to calm down. This is supposed to be a party.'

Diane shrugs. 'If you say so.'

Everybody is wired after the barbecue. The children are high on toasted marshmallows. The adults have drunk their way through a keg of beer. Lord only knows what they're all going to be like tomorrow, she thinks. The sun lowers in the sky, but it never gets truly dark. Finally, Asha's mum sends her daughter off to bed.

'You need to get a proper night's sleep or you will have bags under your eyes,' she says sternly. 'And I will not have you ruining the wedding pictures.'

Asha submits and Gordon leaves with her. Judith gives a few loud hints that it's time they all vamoose back to their cottages. The children are herded off the beach.

Asha's parents stay to help clean up the mess, so they all sneak away. Ethan slings a friendly arm around Diane's shoulder and she doesn't shake it off. Old friends are just what she needs right now when her whole world is falling apart. She gets a flashback to the good old days, stumbling back home from a night out on the town. If they were particularly drunk, Pete and Ethan would try and get her and Sarah into bed, but their hearts were never really in it because secretly they both preferred Asha.

When Sarah gets back, she is still mucking about with her phone, despite the fact that Judith and Broderick told them repeatedly there's no signal on the island.

'Has anyone seen my charger?' she asks.

'Yeah, I borrowed it,' Ethan says without apology. 'Mine was in my missing suitcase. You can have it back when my phone's charged.'

Sarah narrows her eyes but doesn't object. Just like old times.

It's going to get really quiet, Diane now realises. Once the wedding is over. Are they mad to stay on, just the four of them?

They have a couple more drinks and fall into the usual banter, but the rhythm feels off. Ethan is telling a joke and Pete always used to jump in and steal the punchline. But he doesn't do that tonight. And Sarah doesn't laugh. She used to laugh so easily, but the years have hardened her, made her less eager to please. She keeps glancing down at her phone, even though there's no reception. Perhaps she's thinking of those hoax calls Asha mentioned. Perhaps she misses the attention.

After a while, they all disappear off to their rooms, one by one, until Diane is the last person standing. Sarah has left her phone on the coffee table. Diane reaches for it and switches it off, then slips it into her pocket.

There. Sarah won't have to worry about troublesome phone calls any more.

In the kitchen, she pours a generous measure of whisky into a tumbler, then sidles off to her room with it. She sips it, feeling the cold, empty space in the bed beside her. She swallows the rest down in one and waits for the warmth to spread through her body. The curtains hang open, giving her a bird's eye view of the moon. She shuts her eyes and tries to relax. She's still too tense, still waiting for the trauma to subside, but gradually, her mind drifts away.

She wakes with a jolt.

What was that?

A sound, like a wounded animal, pierces the night. Except it isn't an animal.

It's human.

And it's coming from inside the house.

SIX
SARAH

2024, Glasgow

It's around a year before Asha's wedding when Sarah finally sees Pete again. She stumbles outside one lunchtime after a particularly long and boring meeting about the council's new housing project. She leaves the stuffy conference room and heads outside into the rain. Being Glasgow, it's sideways rain – the kind you don't really notice until you feel the icy cold droplets trickling in through the collar of your jacket, working their way down the front of your top and pooling at the bottom of your bra.

Sarah isn't thinking about anything of consequence that day. She thinks she might like to see a film after work, but she's currently single, and her friend Millie has just moved down to London, so she finds herself without anyone to go with. She isn't adventurous enough to go out on her own, convinced people will stare at her, as they did the one time she took herself out to dinner.

She heads for a small sandwich shop tucked away in a row of old tenement buildings. Fellow office workers stream around her, clutching sandwiches in cheap plastic packaging that will soon be added to the city's landfill. Still, the smell of fresh bagels and doughnuts is enticing.

Just in front of the shop, she pauses. Partially hidden between two overflowing bins, a homeless man sits in a khaki green sleeping bag, his shoulders hunched against the chill of the wind. His eyes are alert as he scans the flow of people walking by. She glances down at the hat in front of him on the pavement, weighed down with pennies, then back at the man. His face is covered with a thick, bushy beard. She fumbles in her pocket and finds a pound coin. She tosses it into the hat, and he acknowledges her with a nod. She is about to walk on by when he coughs. It is a loud, honking sound, like a goose.

She stops in her tracks. She'd know that cough anywhere. Disbelief floods through her.

'Pete? Oh my god, it is you, isn't it?'

When he doesn't reply, she keeps talking, berating him.

'Why didn't you call me? You know I would have helped. We all would.'

He finally looks up at her with sunken, world-weary eyes. She gets the impression he has given up on life.

Well, Sarah Lambkin does not give up on anybody.

She's due back at work, so she gives him the keys to her flat, plus money for the bus fare, and tells him she'll see him later.

Her colleagues all tell her how lovely it is that she is taking him in. All except her boss who calls her into her office.

'I'm sending you home early,' she says with a frown.

'Oh, but why?'

'You need to get home and check what that young man's up to.'

'Pete's fine. He's an old friend.'

'When was the last time you saw him?'

'Well, it's been a few years.'

'People change, Sarah. This man's been living rough. He

may have picked up some bad habits. He could have cleaned you out by now.'

'Oh, but I really don't think—'

'Just put my mind at rest, all right?'

Sarah nods and gathers up her things. She isn't worried. She knows Pete. She knows he can be trusted, but she heads straight home, all the same. Without stopping to pick up her dry cleaning.

She walks in to find Pete's disgusting boots and clothes piled up by the door. He's taken a bath and is now sitting at the kitchen table, peeling neeps and tatties for their evening meal, dressed in her T-shirt and jogging bottoms. She looks at him and smiles, pleased to see that her faith wasn't misplaced. Her boss is way too sceptical. She should take a leaf out of her book and try trusting people for a change. She might be pleasantly surprised.

She sets her bag down on the counter and pops open a bottle of wine. Pete still isn't ready to talk, so she chats about her day as the two of them work side by side, preparing a simple dinner of veggie mince and mash.

Afterwards, she goes into her box room and shifts some of her books and other items up into the loft to make room for the sofa bed. She puts out fresh covers and adds some air freshener to make the room smell nice. Pete's face lights up when he sees it.

'You're an angel, Sarah, always have been. I'll never forget this.'

She leaves him to sleep and heads downstairs to take care of the dishes. She's dying to know how his life has veered so horribly off course, and a sick, selfish part of her is glad she isn't the only one wasting their education. But she knows better than to force it out of him. He'll open up when he's ready.

At this point in her life, she's just ended things with her

boyfriend, Todd, so she's glad to have Pete stay with her for a while. They'll heal each other, she tells herself.

They soon settle into a routine. Pete cooks dinner while she's at work, and she arrives home to find a ratatouille or a mushroom stroganoff waiting for her. He's keen to get back to work himself, but it's clear he isn't ready. In the second week after he's moved in with her, she notices how badly his hands are shaking while he's chopping carrots, and that night, the screaming starts.

She has no idea what's going on at first; she almost dials 999, convinced there's someone in the house, attacking him. It's only when she dares to peer into his room that she sees it's merely Pete, fighting with the bed covers, and she begins to realise how serious his problems are. There's no way he is ready for work yet, no way he's ready to move on.

She tries contacting his family to see if anyone can help, but they don't want to know. Nor does the council. It seems that young single men slide to the bottom of the waiting list, veteran or not.

He tells her a little of what happened to him. She sees the pain in his eyes as he talks about the conditions he's endured, sleeping side by side with men who took their trauma out on him.

'You don't want to hear the worst of it, Sarah. You'll never understand the manipulation, the mind games. Those guys were deeply disturbed, damaged predators, and I was their plaything. They tore me apart. Not just physically, but in here.' He points to his head. His hairline has receded so badly, it's almost unrecognisable, leaving a patchy crown where his white-blond hair used to be.

'Oh, Pete!'

From then on, she never pushes him for more details, understanding what it must have taken for him to share as much as he has. She feels protective of him, determined that nothing so terrible will ever happen to him again.

Cooking continues to be Pete's main contribution to the household. Sarah is earning all the money and doing most of the housework, though he occasionally fixes things.

Then one morning, her car won't start. The ignition clicks, but the engine doesn't even try to turn over. She leans her forehead against the wheel and groans.

She catches the bus to work and phones the garage, holding her mobile tight to her ear as she waits for an appointment.

'Earliest we've got is Friday,' says the mechanic. 'Could be the battery, but if it's the alternator...'

Sarah doesn't hear the rest. She's thinking about the overdraft she's already dipped into this month when her washing machine broke. For goodness' sake, why does everything always have to break at once?

When she gets home, Pete is outside, crouched next to the car, a dab of oil smeared across his cheek.

'Where did you get the tools?' she asks.

He stands up, wiping his hands on his jeans.

'I borrowed them from one of the neighbours.'

She raises an eyebrow. Pete hates talking to the neighbours. He's really gone out on a limb.

'How's it going?' she asks. 'Any luck?'

'See for yourself.'

He turns the key in the ignition. The engine grumbles, then roars to life.

'You got it working!'

She runs her hand along the bonnet, feeling the vibration and it's like a huge weight has lifted off her chest.

She pulls out her phone and cancels the garage. Then she dashes down the road and buys a bottle of wine to celebrate. It's a Portuguese red, more expensive than the wine she usually buys. The rich, velvety liquid slides down her throat, warming her insides. Pete seems to like it too.

'This is lovely,' he says with a grin.

They drain their glasses and reach for the bottle at the same time. Laughing, she pulls away and lets him pour. They polish it all off, and she opens a bottle of Merlot. His lips become dark, like a vampire's, the red wine staining his mouth. His eyes sparkle, and she sees a glimpse of the old Pete. It's as if the fancy wine has brought him back to life.

'Do you remember that time someone switched Asha's shampoo for mayonnaise?' she says as they sit side by side on the sofa.

'I'm pretty sure that was Ethan.'

'I thought it was Diane.'

'Maybe it was both of them?'

'Nah, they were always at each other's throats.'

'Except when they weren't. They always had a spark, those two. Don't you think?'

Sarah shakes her head. 'They were always arguing, if that's what you mean.'

'Do you think he was jealous? When she got together with Cameron?'

'Nah, he didn't want to be tied down.'

'You mean he's a total commitmentphobe.'

'Yeah, I suppose.'

'Then why was he always propositioning Asha?'

'Because he's Ethan.'

He gazes into her eyes, and she becomes deeply aware of his breathing. Their faces grow closer, more serious. She feels the softness of his lips on hers and there's a rush of heat through her body. She isn't sure if it's him or the wine. But it feels good. She feels his arms snaking around her, and her body responds. Their kisses grow deeper, and before she knows it, he's leading her up to the stairs to her bedroom.

He's still there when she wakes up in the morning, and she's mortified. Pete is a friend in need. She's never, ever considered him boyfriend material, not now, and not back in the old days when they lived together.

She works late that day, staying at the office until the security guard comes around to tell her he's locking up the building for the night. Reluctantly, she gathers up her things and follows him out.

When she gets home, Pete is sitting in the kitchen, waiting to eat dinner with her. She hasn't told him what time she'll get in, only that she'll be late, which means he's been waiting there for hours, like a lovesick puppy.

'I'm not hungry,' she says, instantly averting her eyes. 'I'm going to go upstairs, take a shower, and then I'm having an early night.'

He rises from the table. 'Do you want me to come up with you?'

'No! God, no, Pete. Last night was just a one-time thing, okay?'

'Okay.' He looks so sad, she almost wishes she could take it back.

It's so awkward after that. Pete seems to get the hint. There's no suggestion that he expects to get back into bed with her, but the air between them is uncomfortable now. Instead of bringing them closer together, their brief encounter has soured their relationship once and for all.

This makes for a very difficult living situation. There's no way she can chuck him out on the streets; even she isn't that heartless. The only solution is to get some other poor sucker to take him in.

SEVEN
SARAH

Sarah knows this sound all too well. Her feet hit the floor and she stumbles out into the hallway. Ethan snores contentedly as she passes his room. He always did have the ability to sleep through anything.

She turns left, stopping in front of Pete's door. She throws it wide open and watches for a moment as he thrashes about in the bed, his body drenched in sweat. He cries out again, so loud that she wants to pour cold water over him.

'Pete?'

She finds the lamp at the side of his bed, flicks it on and shakes him gently, the way she has learnt. He continues to sleep, but his body releases some of the tension. He turns towards her, eyes still closed, and lets out a longer, quieter moan.

'Pete? Pete! It's okay. It's just a dream.'

Diane appears in the doorway, watching with morbid fascination as Sarah soothes him.

'What's happening?'

Sarah is still watching Pete, looking to make sure he's really settled.

'He has night terrors,' she says in a low voice. 'PTSD from something that happened to him in the army.'

Diane blinks, and Sarah gets the impression she's freaked out. The sounds Pete makes used to frighten her too. But it's not his fault. He's just a frightened, traumatised man. Sometimes she forgets that. She promises herself she will be kinder to him, more patient. It's not for much longer, after all.

'Let's get back to bed,' she tells Diane gently.

Wind rattles the window as Sarah rolls out of bed the following morning. She heads to the kitchen to find Ethan frying bacon, and she can almost imagine they are back in the house share. Ethan often used to cook a big fry-up on the weekends. Back then, he declared himself the resident chef. Actually, Sarah was more skilled at cooking, but she was happy for someone else to cook for a change since she always ended up doing the lion's share of the housework. Diane did her part, but Asha was too much of a princess. Ethan was a useless mama's boy and Pete was just plain useless.

Pete bounces into the room. As always, he seems totally oblivious to the state he got into last night. He plonks himself down at the table next to Sarah and pulls out his phone, then curses under his breath when he remembers there's no Wi-Fi.

'Have you seen my phone?' she asks. 'I could have sworn I left it right here.'

Her whole life is on that phone. All her messages. All her secrets. It makes her uneasy just thinking about it.

'Sorry, haven't seen it,' Pete says.

She pops her head into the kitchen.

'No, sorry,' Ethan says, reaching for the sugar.

Oh yeah, that's right. He used to add sugar to the bacon. What's wrong with him? She's so glad she went vegetarian.

'Are we out of milk?' Pete asks, opening and closing the fridge.

Sarah bites back her annoyance. 'Are you seriously expecting me to come and look for you? If there's no milk in the fridge, we're out of milk, Pete.'

'But we had plenty yesterday. Someone must have drunk it all.' He glances from Diane to Ethan, but no one owns up.

'All right, I'll go over to Broderick's and see if he's got some more. Or I could just go next door and ask Asha?'

She and Sarah exchange a look. 'Asha will be getting ready for the wedding.'

'Sure, but it won't take a minute.'

He hurries out the door.

'Hey, have you seen my phone?' Sarah asks.

Diane nods. 'I think I saw it on the coffee table.'

'Well, someone's moved it.'

She glances at Ethan. He's looking out the window, watching as Asha comes out of her cottage to talk to Pete. Sarah notices Asha is wearing nothing but a tiny pair of pyjama shorts and a lacy vest.

Diane leans forward conspiratorially.

'So, are we ready to take her down?'

EIGHT
DIANE

One Month Earlier, Inverness

'What are you up to?' Diane asks, mixing herself a drink as she talks to Sarah on the phone. They haven't spoken in weeks, but Cameron is finishing off something for work, and she is bored.

'Nothing much.'

'Are you looking forward to Asha's wedding?'

'I am – assuming it's still going ahead.'

'What do you mean?'

Sarah falls silent.

'What? Tell me.' Diane draws a breath. 'Let me guess – she's pregnant?'

Sarah lets out a little gasp but she says nothing. She's still holding something back. Diane can sense it. She racks her brain, shuffling through as many possibilities as she can think of.

'Are you saying it's not Gordon's?'

'What are you, a bloody mind reader?' Sarah says with a sigh.

Diane is amazed at her own brilliance. 'It's true, isn't it?'

'Asha called me late last night. I think her conscience was bothering her.'

'Holy hell!' Diane sets down her drink and performs a little pirouette. She feels all tingly. Finally, she's got one over on Asha. 'Gordon doesn't know, I take it?'

'He doesn't have a clue. They've only been seeing each other once a month, so Asha's absolutely sure it isn't his.'

'Whose is it, then?'

'She'd been seeing another guy before she met him. It was just a physical thing. They hooked up every once in a while when he was in town. She hadn't seen him in months, and then he turned up at her flat, and she felt like she owed him... just one last time before she got married. She thought she needed to get him out of her system.'

'Bloody hell. I never would have thought of Asha as a player. She's always been so picky. She must have got more desperate in recent years.'

'Loneliness can do that. But you mustn't say anything,' Sarah warns.

'Of course not. Wouldn't dream of it.' Diane swirls her drink around in her glass, her synapses sparking like fireworks.

Sarah starts waffling on about something else, but Diane isn't really listening. All she can think about is Asha's wedding day, and how much better it's going to be now that she knows this juicy little secret.

As she sets down the phone, she turns to look at Cameron. He has a regretful expression on his face, and she can tell he's about to say something she won't like.

'Di?'

'Yes?'

'I'm really sorry, but the boss wants me to go on the Stavanger trip.'

'Oh, okay. No bother. I'm sure I can cope without you for a few days.'

'It's more like a week.'

'Okay.'

'It's going to clash with Asha's wedding, Di.'

'You're kidding!'

'I wish I was. I was looking forward to going to Orkney.'

Diane chokes down her anger. 'I thought George was going to Stavanger?'

'Yeah, well, the boss took me to one side and said he doesn't have confidence in him to do a good job.'

Diane's jaw drops. 'He said that?'

George is senior to Cameron, so it seems almost inconceivable that the boss would say such a thing. 'Do you think he's going to get the sack?'

'I doubt that's—'

'Think about it. If they want you to go to Stavanger instead of him, this could mean good things for you, Cam. If you do well on this trip, you could get promoted.'

'I'm not so sure.'

'Well, I am. It's about time they rewarded you for all the hours you've been putting in.'

His blue eyes flick from left to right. 'You'll tell Asha I'm sorry, won't you? For messing up her seating plan. Let's make it up to her with a good present.'

'Like what?'

'I don't know. What does she like?'

'She's basically Cleopatra. So anything bright and shiny.'

He smiles. 'Gold candlesticks it is, then.'

'Gold-plated. She'll be divorced within a year. We don't want to go overboard.'

'What makes you so sure?' he asks, pulling her into his arms.

She gives him a devilish smile. 'I have my intel. Trust me, it'll be over before it starts.'

'What if he's really good in bed? This new man of hers?'

'Doesn't matter. She's impossible to please.'

His eyes narrow. 'Have you ever tried... satisfying her in bed?'

'Yuck, no! Don't be gross!'

She may have experimented a little in her student days, but never with a friend. And certainly not Asha.

'It's just, you all seem so close, the five of you. It's hard to believe you've never got hot and heavy with any of them.'

'Cameron, my darling. You know my full, unadulterated history. Besides, if I was going to go for any of them, it would be Ethan.'

'Ethan? I thought you hated him.'

Diane smiles. 'Oh, I do, but if you're going to make me choose.'

'I'm really not.'

'Well, all right then. I suppose I'm stuck with you.'

NINE

Other people sleep at night.

I don't know if I dream, or if my mind just buffers.

All I know is that it feels strange to be here, with them.

It's triggering.

These people are my friends, I know them inside out. At least, I know the people they used to be. But they've all changed. It's like someone took a magnifying glass and ramped up all their worst qualities, making them clearer, brighter, louder.

I don't know what to make of them any more.

And I hope to God they don't know what to make of me.

TEN

SARAH

'Where did Pete get that suit?' Ethan says as they walk down to the stone circle.

'Shh, he'll hear you!'

'But seriously. He looks like a lamp.'

Sarah glances guiltily over at Pete, who is walking with Diane. It's true his bright blue jacket is way too big for him, and the yellow shirt is a bit much, but it was the best she could find, without splashing a load of cash. Actually, both their outfits came from the charity shop, because she found her red dress while she was in there buying Pete's suit.

Diane is wearing sunglasses, even though it's overcast. Perhaps she had too much to drink last night. She looks like she's dressed for a day at the office. Sarah guesses she hasn't splashed out either. Ethan, in his black jeans and t-shirt, still somehow manages to look smarter than the rest of them. There's just something about the way he holds himself, his confidence that makes him look put together no matter what he wears.

This road route is a lot easier than the shortcut Judith dragged them down yesterday. Even so, when they reach the field, the grass is damp and slippery, and she pictures Asha slipping in her wedding dress and face-planting down into the mud. Of course, Asha being Asha would just brush herself down and laugh. In fact, she'd probably make the mud work for her. When you're that beautiful, anything looks good.

She looks around at her old friends. She can't help thinking how different this is from Diane's wedding, which was far more traditional, far more... predictable. Asha's wedding feels more unconventional. Rebellious, even. There are no fancy cars or posh officials. The ground has an earthy smell from last night's rain, and Sarah has a sense that anything could happen. The air feels electric, charged with something primal and untamed.

'So what's the plan?' Ethan asks as they approach. 'When are we going to start throwing mud?'

'I didn't mean literally,' Diane says, pulling up her sunglasses so they sit on top of her head.

She looks at Sarah. 'I think we should tell them.'

'Pete already knows.'

The group closes in.

'Tell us what?' Ethan says.

Sarah shakes her head imperceptibly.

No, don't do this.

But Diane being Diane will do what the hell she likes.

They hunch together like a wake of vultures, heads low and tilted with anticipation.

'Turns out Asha's pregnant. That's why they're getting married so quickly.'

Sarah watches as Diane's eyes sweep over the group, clearly savouring the shock on Ethan's face. She grins proudly, like she's just provided him with a delicious treat.

His eyes widen. 'Who told you that?'

'Asha did,' Sarah says in a small voice. 'But you can't say anything! This is her wedding day for God's sake! She's supposed to be our friend.'

'That's not all,' Diane says, as if Sarah hadn't spoken. 'It's not even Gordon's!'

Sarah closes her eyes. This is all her fault. She has to do something, anything, to stop this. But Diane is a dog with a bone. She takes a deep breath and looks at the others. Maybe they can talk some sense into her?

Ethan is rubbing his chin. 'Nah.'

Diane looks at him. 'What do you mean, "nah"?'

'I'm not buying it,' Ethan says.

Diane's face falls. 'What, you think she made it up?'

'She's always been full of it. Anything for attention.'

Sarah and Diane exchange a look. Diane kicks a stone, sending it scuttling to the side of the road.

'So, this is some kind of joke?'

She rounds on Sarah, glaring at her as if she's in on it. 'That explains why she told Sarah. Everybody knows she's a blabbermouth. Couldn't keep a secret if you paid her!'

'Hey!' Sarah objects.

But Diane is too caught up in her own thoughts to care. 'She knew Sarah would tell at least one of us, especially since she and Pete live together. Oh, she's played us!'

Sarah shakes her head. 'I still don't get it.'

Ethan looks at her. 'It's a joke, isn't it? Look at the way she's been putting away the booze. There's no way she would be drinking if she really had a baby on board.'

'Maybe she's bluffing?' Diane says. 'For all we know, that's non-alcoholic wine she's been drinking.'

'Do you really think so?' Ethan looks at Diane. 'Face it, she's played you.'

Diane covers her face with her hands. 'I can't believe I fell for it!'

'What were you planning to do?' Ethan asks with interest.

'I was going to let it casually slip out at the reception. You know, just a few words with a couple of the cousins, or better still, their children. It would have spread like chicken pox.'

'You would really have done that?' Pete says, shocked.

'I thought Gordon had a right to know.'

'Well anyway, it's obviously bollocks,' Ethan says.

Sarah's shoulders sink with relief. She feels like she's been let off the hook.

They start walking again. Pete has a disgusted expression on his face.

'I can't believe Diane was going to ruin Asha's wedding like that,' he whispers. 'That's just... evil.'

'That's Diane for you.'

'But is it? She was never that bad.'

Ethan and Diane have fallen behind, but Sarah still hears her emit a loud, dramatic sigh. 'God, what am I even doing here?'

She glances back, and sees Ethan take her arm. 'Don't worry. I'm sure we can do something else to spice up the proceedings.'

'Pack it in, both of you. This is Asha's wedding day, and I won't let you spoil it.'

'I'm going to need a lot more booze,' Diane says.

'I'm sure that won't be a problem.'

As they arrive at the stone circle, Sarah spots Gordon in a red kilt. He is a bundle of energy, pacing around, talking and joking in a loud booming voice. Every so often, he sneaks a glance at his watch, no doubt wondering where Asha has got to. If he knows her at all, he ought to expect her to keep him waiting. His friends and relatives are doing their best to keep the children in line, but it's too much fun to race each other round and round the circle, and Sarah wonders if this might have been the stones' original purpose, to keep a bunch of kids entertained.

Asha's parents stand a little apart from everyone else. Her mum looks beautiful in an intricately embroidered sari. Her dad has his head bowed, as if they were attending a funeral.

The celebrant arrives, a woman who was on the boat with them, whom Sarah had assumed was another relative, but now she's dressed in long, billowing robes and she's speaking in a soft, reassuring voice to Gordon, reminding him that it's the bride's prerogative to be late. She turns and smiles around at the assembled guests.

'Thank you all for coming on this beautiful, joy-filled day. Please can everyone take their places now?' Her voice drops. 'And I mean everyone.'

All the children freeze, like she's turned them to stone, their eyes wide and unblinking.

Then they do as they are told and go and stand with their parents. Sarah looks at the celebrant with admiration and decides she must have been a teacher in a previous life.

As they take their places on the outside of the circle, the sky darkens and Sarah feels the first few drops of rain on her skin.

'That'll be the gods, demanding a human sacrifice,' Ethan says with a smirk.

Sarah eyes the children. 'Plenty of possibilities here,' she whispers back.

Raindrops tap rhythmically on her shoulders as they wait for Asha to make her entrance. Everyone falls silent as the minutes tick by. Asha's dad keeps his head bowed, hands clasped behind his back, while Gordon shifts from foot to foot.

All at once, the rain stops and the music starts. Everyone seems to be able to play something, even the children; cello, drums, bass, accordion, pipes and fiddle. They play in perfect harmony, and after a few beats, she recognises the wedding march, although she's never heard it played quite like this before.

The sun peeks through the clouds, and Asha appears,

splendid in a long white gown with a lace collar. Her hair hangs loose down her back, her face covered by a simple veil. Her little bridesmaids walk behind her; four little girls in matching blue dresses. Their hair is so violently red, the way it catches the sun, it looks like it's on fire.

When Asha reaches the centre of the circle, Gordon pulls back the veil and they look at each other like there is no one else in the world. Tears prick Sarah's eyes. She looks at Pete and sees that he feels it too. He reaches for her hand. She quickly sticks it in her pocket.

She leans over to Diane. 'She looks beautiful.'

'I know. Don't you just hate her?'

The celebrant goes ahead with the ceremony. It's more pagan than Christian, as she waffles on about the earth and its elements. As the vows are exchanged, Pete and Sarah step forward with the rings. They are such dazzling gold rings. They clearly haven't scrimped on that part. Sarah hands hers to Gordon and waits while Pete hands his to Asha. His hands are shaking badly. He's clearly in need of a drink.

'In the presence of those who know you best, and with these ancient stones bearing witness, Gordon and Asha, you have declared your love and commitment to one another. It is with immense joy that I now declare you husband and wife. May you remain as pure and faithful as you are today and may your bond stay as strong as these stones. Your journey through the mists of time has been blessed by the wind, the sand and the sea. Gordon, you may now kiss the bride.'

The kiss seals it. It's not a demure peck or a shy brush of lips, but something fierce and unrestrained. Gordon sweeps Asha into his arms, dipping her low and kisses her deeply, passionately.

The congregation erupts into cheers and whistles, the sound swelling like a wave. Sarah's breath catches as something stirs low in her belly, a flicker of heat she tries to smother.

She looks at her friends and takes in their reactions. Diane stands at the edge of the group. Her lips are pressed into a tight line, her gaze fixed on the couple. If Sarah had to guess, she'd say she was bored, eager to get this over with and move on to the reception. She turns to look at Pete. He has gone very still, but his eyes shimmer with unshed tears. Then there's Ethan, arms crossed tightly over his chest and jaw clenched as he scowls openly at the newlyweds.

And then there's Asha's dad. He stands a little apart from the rest, his back to the couple, shoulders rigid. It's sad, the way he can't let his only daughter go.

The kiss finally breaks, and Asha's laughter rings out, bright and jubilant. Gordon pulls her upright, spinning her briefly before they both turn to face the cheering crowd. Asha's dress flutters with the movement, and their pure joy sweeps through the gathering like wildfire.

Pete sniffles softly beside her, then he catches Sarah's eye with a sheepish shrug.

Gordon's uncle takes a few pictures seconds before the rain chucks it down again.

'Everyone inside!' Broderick bellows.

He waves his arms like he's herding sheep, guiding the guests towards the large barn in the next field. Fairy lights glow faintly through the rain. It all looks snug and warm.

Sarah moves with the throng, surrounded by damp, chattering guests who laugh and shout as they hurry to get out of the rain. As she reaches the entrance, something makes her pause. A prickling sensation crawls up her spine, and she glances back at the ancient stone circle.

Pete is standing there in the rain. His hair is plastered to his forehead, his jacket soaked. His eyes are fixed on Asha and Gordon, who have broken away from the group.

Sarah's gaze follows his line of sight.

The newlyweds aren't heading for the barn like everyone

else. Instead, they're making their way towards a small outbuilding. Asha laughs, her dress swirling around her as she leans into Gordon, who has his arm protectively around her waist. They disappear from view, their laughter fading into the rain, and Pete just watches, his body unnervingly still.

'Pete?'

He jerks his head in her direction.

He looks like a startled rabbit. His lips part like he's about to speak but can't find the words. She wants to ask what's wrong, but something in his posture, in the rigid line of his shoulders, tells her to leave him alone, so she turns and follows the others into the barn.

ELEVEN

SARAH

Sarah weaves her way round the tables, looking at the hand-carved nameplates until she finds her seat, in between Diane and Ethan. She glances up as Pete finally enters, looking more composed. She drops her gaze, and he walks right past her, heading straight to the bar.

She grins as she realises Asha has complied with her request and seated Pete with some of the cousins. She rubs her hands together. This will give her the opportunity she's been looking for to talk to Diane.

Before she can breathe a word, Ethan reaches across her for the water jug and proceeds to fill his glass, dripping water onto her lap in the process. Being Ethan, he doesn't apologise.

'You know that's not vodka?' she says crossly, wiping herself down with a napkin.

He exchanges a look with Diane, and instantly she is transported back to the last time they were all together, at Diane's wedding... There had been plenty of vodka then. Diane had quite a bit before the actual ceremony. Sarah had wondered about that. She'd never known Diane to be nervous about anything.

'I can't believe how lucky I am,' she had said, her voice giddy with excitement. Asha had insisted on doing Diane's make-up for her, and she'd taken the job seriously, so they were surrounded by tissues, make-up brushes and bottles of perfume.

In those final moments before leaving for the church, Diane had grabbed Sarah and pulled her into a tight hug. Then she'd turned to Asha, enveloping her too.

'No more vodka,' Asha had said sternly. 'You need to pace yourself. You don't want to pass out on the wedding cake.'

Diane had burst out laughing, tears streaking her eyes.

Asha had expertly wiped them away. 'You see? This is why you need the waterproof mascara. Seriously though,' she'd said, her voice softening, 'I'm really happy for you.'

'Me too,' Sarah had added, placing a hand on Diane's arm. 'Cameron is a lucky man...'

'Ladies and gentlemen, Mr and Mrs Gordon Kirkness.'

Asha and Gordon make an entrance. She's changed into a different gown, Sarah notices. A shorter, ivory one that shows off her gym-sculpted shoulders. She's redone her lipstick too; a bold shade of red that she will no doubt imprint all over Gordon's neck. Asha's mum looks on proudly. Her dad has tears in his eyes.

The musicians take up their instruments. Asha and Gordon dance, their feet moving in perfect sync. Soon, others join them, twirling and swaying to the beat. One of the little bridesmaids skips up to Ethan and tugs on his sleeve.

'You have to dance with me.'

He arches a brow. 'Do I?'

'Yes. I need to dance with every man in the room so I can find out which ones are princes and which ones are toads.'

'The toads are more fun,' Sarah says.

Ethan chokes back a laugh, but he rises to his feet, even though he hates dancing.

She glances over at Pete, sitting alone at his table as the

cousins hit the dance floor. He glugs back his wine and watches them with mournful eyes. Then he takes a crafty swig of his neighbour's drink.

She turns to Diane who is watching it all with a distant expression. 'Are you having fun?'

'Are you?'

Sarah shrugs. 'It's always good to see old friends.'

'What's the deal with Pete?'

'He's no good on his own. He needs his hand held, just for now at least.'

'So I gathered.'

Sarah takes in a breath of air. Might as well go for it. 'Actually, I was kind of wondering.'

'Yes?'

'Maybe you could take him in for a bit? Just for a couple of weeks? Give me a bit of... respite.'

Diane folds her napkin. 'Is he that bad?'

'No, it's just...' Sarah looks across at the dance floor, where the little girl is dancing on Ethan's feet. They look adorable.

Diane closes her eyes for a moment. 'I don't know... I'd have to ask Cameron.'

'Of course.'

'Do you think Cam—'

A teenage boy stops at the table in front of them. 'Which of you ladies would like to dance with me first?'

Diane bursts out laughing. 'I thought you'd never ask!'

Sarah watches in astonishment as Diane rises to her feet. The Diane she knew hated dancing as much as Ethan. She watches as they glide onto the dance floor and swallows the urge to scream. Why the hell did she come to this bloody wedding? She should have said she had too much work on. She should have said she was broke.

She grits her teeth. Never mind, Asha and Gordon leave for their honeymoon tomorrow. And most of the others have to get back to their farms. She will catch a lift back with them. There's no way she can stomach a whole week with her former housemates. She thought she could, but she was wrong.

She accepts a glass of champagne from a passing waiter and sips it angrily.

'Sandwich?' Ethan says, appearing in front of her with a platter.

They're all meat and he knows it.

Sarah pushes past him and goes to find Asha. She can't stay here another day. She'll do the right thing by Pete and leave a bit of money in his backpack, but he'll have to find his own way home. Ethan and Diane will help him if need be.

'What time does the boat leave in the morning?' she asks one of the other guests, who is wrangling a half-naked toddler into his pyjamas.

'First thing, Gordon says.'

'Well what time's that?'

'I don't know, nine? Ten?'

The toddler twists about and manages to get one arm out of the top she's just put on him. Sarah sighs. Asha will know, but every time she tries to get her attention, someone gets there first. Asha is still the queen bee, still in charge of everything even after all these years. But Sarah is too damned old to be anyone's sidekick.

She finally manages to draw Asha off the dance floor, but that's when Gordon's uncle claps his hands.

'If everyone could return to their seats, the speeches are about to begin.'

Asha shakes her head with regret, and Sarah heads back to her table with a sigh.

Gordon speaks eloquently.

'Hello, everyone! Can I just say what a privilege it is to be here today, surrounded by all of you. I want to say a big thank you to both our families, and friends who have travelled so far to be here, but most of all to the person who makes it all possible – my wife, Asha.'

He pauses to look at Asha. There is such tenderness in that look that Sarah feels her heart melt.

'Those of you who know Asha will already be well aware of what an incredible woman she is, and I have to say it's a bit intimidating, marrying someone like her. Asha knows what she wants, and she goes after it. She's not afraid to fight, and when things don't go so well, she bowls me over with her willingness to move on and forgive.' He looks directly at Diane at this point, and Sarah wonders if he's in on it, this story of Asha's. Her cheeks burn and she wishes more than anything that she had stayed away.

Gordon is smiling again, looking over at Asha's parents now. 'I hope, over time, I can prove to all of you how much I love this beautiful, funny, intelligent woman. I know I'm not perfect, far from it, but I can promise you this. That I am, and always will be completely devoted to Asha.'

'To Asha!' the best man echoes.

Everyone raises their glasses, and even Asha's father musters a smile.

When the hush has died down again, the best man is clamouring for their attention. 'And now a few words from the father of the bride, Vikesh.'

Asha's father takes a deep breath and clambers to his feet. He looks around the room.

'They say a father's job is to protect his daughter, but at some point, you have to step back and let her make her own decisions – especially when the daughter in question is as headstrong as Asha. She's always gone after what she wants and this is no different. I can only hope that Gordon knows just how lucky he is. So, here's to my daughter and her new life.'

For a moment, there is complete silence, followed by a polite burst of applause.

THE WEDDING PARTY

Once the noise has died down, one of the cousins claps her hands for attention.

'And now, one of Asha's oldest friends, Sarah Lambkin.'

The announcement prompts a ripple of applause as Sarah rises to her feet. She clears her throat, and begins, her voice steady but warm. 'Thank you. I just want to say a few words. I've known Asha a long time. She is lively, fun, and entertaining. Back when we lived together, there was never a dull moment. But Asha has other qualities too. She is fiercely loyal, thoughtful and kind.' She swallows hard. 'Best of all, she can take a joke.' At least, Sarah thinks she can. She looks at Asha now, looking so lovely and serene in her wedding dress, and it's hard to believe she set her up. Why would she feed Sarah lies like that? It seems incredible that she would do such a thing, to test her old friends on her wedding day of all days. What on earth was she trying to achieve with that stunt? Deep down, she supposes she already knows the answer to that. After everything that's gone down between them over the years, all the ribbing and joking around, perhaps Asha wanted to know once and for all if they are really her friends, or if it's time she put these old friendships to bed. Sarah has been having similar thoughts ever since she arrived in Orkney. She wonders if Asha has come to the same conclusion she has... Everyone is looking at her and she realises they are expecting more.

She glances towards Gordon, and her smile widens. 'And now, she's found someone who matches her in every way. Gordon. Gordon, my first impressions of you are that you're perfect for her. I've never seen Asha so happy, and that's all anyone could wish for their... for their friend.'

For some reason, she can't quite get her tongue round that last word.

Raising her glass, she finishes on a toast, 'To Asha and Gordon, may your life together be as bright and wonderful as this day.'

The room cheers, glasses clink, and Sarah collapses back into her chair, glad to be done with her speech. But before she can relax, Ethan pushes to his feet, grinning like he's been waiting for this moment.

'Wait, wait, wait!' he calls, silencing the room. 'I think we can top that.'

Sarah groans under her breath, but Asha is laughing, so she leans back and lets Ethan do his thing.

'Now, I'm not here to outdo Sarah, but I do have a few things to add,' Ethan begins, his grin widening. Everyone is listening now. He's got their full attention. He glances over at Diane, then locks eyes with Asha.

'I see the bride has changed her dress again. What did you get up to out there in the woods, Asha?'

He gives her a sly wink, and Sarah cringes. She can't even look at Asha's parents.

Ethan doesn't care. He's still talking, drawing everyone in.

'Back in the day, Asha wasn't like the other girls at uni. She had this air about her – like she was way above all of us immature guys. She wasn't one to fall for the usual lines or flattery. In fact, she was so up herself that a bunch of us made a bet to see who could get into her knickers.'

There is a ripple of laughter, mainly from the children but Ethan keeps going:

'Me and my mates, we pulled out all the stops, I can tell you. We tried smooth talk, party tricks and all the dance moves. Especially my mate Pete over there. He was quite the showman.'

There is a smirk on his face as he jumps to his feet and demonstrates, thrusting his pelvis and gyrating his hips in a crude approximation. Pete glowers. He lifts out of his chair a little, and for a moment, Sarah thinks he's going to get up and wallop him.

'We offered her chocolates, flowers, romantic dinners, the

whole kaboodle. But Asha wasn't having any of it. I never thought anyone would be able to thaw out the "ice princess". But here we are, and I have to hand it to you, Gordon. You've done what the rest of us couldn't. Looks like we've finally got our winner! But seriously, folks, here's to Asha and Gordon. May today be just the beginning of a beautiful partnership.'

Asha has been leaning on her elbows, shielding her face with her hands the whole time he's been talking. But now the speech seems to be over, she finally lets down her guard, only for Ethan to pull a pair of knickers out of his pocket and fling them at Gordon, clearly expecting him to catch. From Asha's mortified expression, Sarah guesses they are actually hers. They look like the type of things she would wear too, fussy and lacy.

Gordon swipes them off the table and shoves them out of view while Asha turns her head away, cheeks flaming.

There is a smattering of applause as people don't quite know how to react.

'There's no way Ethan's getting an invite to my wedding, if I ever get married,' she whispers to Diane.

It's not even true, what Ethan said about Asha. She had her share of men. She just didn't brag about it.

Diane twiddles her wedding band.

'It doesn't matter, they won't last five minutes anyway,' she predicts.

'I don't know. I think they're really in love.'

'Yeah, for now they are.'

Diane watches them as she takes a sip of her champagne.

She looks over at Pete. He's had too much to drink. It's a shame he can't dance it off the way he always used to but his eyes are glassy, and he keeps leaning on people, making a nuisance of himself. She'll have to take him back soon, before he gets so inebriated he can no longer walk. She readies herself for the task, but Diane has noticed too.

'Pete's pissed. We need to take him home.'

Ethan rises from his seat. 'Okay.'

Sarah is impressed. Her former housemates are constantly surprising her. Diane glances at her, but she purposely hangs back. Lord knows she's done her share. Let them deal with Pete for once.

She stays a little longer, chatting with Asha's parents. Her father still has that stern, serious look on his face. Probably because he hasn't drunk anything stronger than water, or perhaps because he's made it abundantly clear he feels like he is losing a daughter, rather than gaining a son.

She spots Gordon standing on his own and goes over to speak to him.

'Lovely wedding. The ceremony was beautiful.'

'Thank you for your lovely speech, Sarah. And I'm so glad you were able to come. It means a lot to Asha. She talks so much about you all.'

You all? Sarah isn't sure how she feels about this. Does Asha see her as part of a set? Her old housemates. She is nothing like the rest of them.

'Yeah, well sorry about Ethan. And Pete.'

He shrugs it off. 'Well, they certainly livened things up a bit.'

'You're a bigger person than I am. Honestly, I wouldn't hold it against you if you decided to spike Ethan's slice of cake with laxatives.'

'Well, I'll leave that to my wife,' he says with a smile.

Asha floats towards them, her dress shimmering in the light.

'Asha, you look stunning!'

'I know,' she says with a grin.

Sarah smiles. She'd forgotten about this, Asha's willingness to laugh at herself. It makes all her perfection a little easier to stomach. Asha's hand finds Gordon's, as if they can't bear to be apart for more than a few minutes. Sarah starts to feel like a third wheel, so she makes her excuses and steps outside, into the cool night.

It's just a short walk back to the cottage. She heads down the road, marvelling at how quiet it is, in the total absence of traffic. She is completely alone in the twilight, the moon glinting off her silver clutch bag, but she tells herself not to be afraid. After all, they are all friends here. There is no one to fear on this island.

The cottage is quiet when she arrives. The only sound is her own footsteps on the creaky wooden floorboards. She heads into the kitchen and pours herself a glass of water to starve off the inevitable hangover. She gulps it down and rinses the glass, placing it upside down on the draining board. It's only then that she realises she never did get the time of the ferry. Never mind, she can ask Asha in the morning.

As she enters her room, she notices a strange shape on her bed. She flicks on the light and shrieks at the limp bird splayed across her pillow. There are feathers everywhere, bloodied and muddy, and its beady eye seems to stare straight at her.

TWELVE
SARAH

Sarah stares at the dead bird. It's horrible. There is blood and guts all over the sheets. She looks up at the window. It's closed, just as she left it. She stalks straight to Pete's room, since the drunk bastard is the most likely culprit, but when she gets there, she finds him fast asleep, sucking on his knuckles like a baby. She backs away, turning to find both Ethan and Diane in Ethan's room. They are lounging on his bed, listening to music and drinking, just like they did all those years ago. They look up, startled, as she bursts in.

'What's the matter?' Diane asks.

'See for yourself.'

Sarah leads them back to her room, and Diane slaps a hand over her mouth.

'Oh gross! That's nasty.'

Sarah eyeballs Ethan.

'Pete picked up some roadkill on the walk home,' he admits, shaking his head. 'I thought he got rid of it. For goodness' sake!'

Sarah tilts her head. 'Roadkill? There's hardly any cars on this island.'

'Yeah. Must have been Broderick or Judith who ran it over.'

He stifles a yawn, and Sarah feels a fresh stab of anger.

'Well, clearly I can't sleep here!'

Diane lays a hand on her shoulder. 'We'll deal with it. We'll get these sheets in the washing machine. You can bunk in with me for tonight. Mine's a double.'

She nods wearily. She doesn't want to share with Diane. She wants to sleep in her own bed, but what choice does she have?

Ethan's eyes glint with a perverse delight.

'Hey, come to that, mine's also a double.'

Sarah forces a smile. 'Thanks. I'll bear that in mind.'

He looks at Diane. 'If you're putting a wash on, I've got some dirty clothes that can go in with it. They're at the foot of my bed.'

Sarah cringes. She's forgotten how bossy he can be. But this is standard Ethan. Barking instructions and expecting people to follow as if he's some kind of unelected leader. This is how it was in the shared house, but back then, they had a reason to put up with him. Ethan's parents owned the house. That isn't the case now. Nobody owns this place; they're all renting it equally. There's no reason to go along with anything he says, no reason to suck up to him, no reason, even, to be his friend.

The more she thinks about it, the more she wonders why she has been his friend for so long. It comes down to some misplaced sense of loyalty, she supposes. She's romanticised the past; she doesn't like to think of all the time they've spent together as meaningless. But the more time she spends with these people, the less she likes them, the less she feels like they're people she would actually choose to know. If she had met them in her current life, she wouldn't have chosen a single one of them to be her friend. They're all so messed up, so selfish, so fatally flawed.

And yet, unironically, she feels a certain kind of love for them. They're like a family. They know each other in a raw, rotten way that nobody else does. They know each other's vulnerabilities, each other's weak points, each other's failures. And there's something about that that makes her care, at least a little. She could throw Pete out onto the street anytime she likes, but she doesn't. She could stop replying to Asha's messages. And as for Diane – well, she doesn't have to follow her any more either. She thinks of how she planned to ruin Asha's wedding day. Sarah should never have gone along with it, not even for a minute. She isn't at uni any more.

She goes and lies down in Diane's room. She hears Diane and Ethan talking to each other. Laughing. Did they do this? she wonders. Is this their twisted idea of a joke? But if they did, surely they wouldn't offer to clean up afterwards.

She wishes she had her phone. She closes her eyes and thinks about the last time she saw it. She recalls checking it, and setting it down on the coffee table. Diane said she saw it there too, and she was the last to go to bed last night. So why wasn't it still there when she got up in the morning?

Unless it was Diane?

She pushes the thought away. Diane may be many things, but she's not a thief. She has a strong sense of right and wrong. There is no way Diane would ever steal from her.

Not unless she knows.

She sits bolt upright, her heart racing. She runs over to the door and looks out. Diane and Ethan are in the kitchen. Diane is putting the sheets in the machine, like she promised.

She shuts the door and rushes over to Diane's bag, digging through the side pockets until she finds a phone. Her heart drops as she pulls it out, but it's not hers. It's Diane's, and it's out of battery. She replaces it and searches inside the bag, running her hand between rolled-up sock bombs, jeans and shirts. It's not there. If Diane took it, she must have hidden it somewhere.

But where?

THIRTEEN
DIANE

Two Hours Earlier

Diane and Ethan walk back from the wedding, supporting a swaying, slurring Pete between them. Pete is babbling incoherently.

'...no justice in the world... not fair. Not fair at all. Should've done something. Should've stopped him.'

'What is he going on about?' Ethan asks.

Diane shakes her head. 'No idea.'

Pete always liked his drink, but not like this. This is on another level.

'He's really different, isn't he?' Ethan is shaking his head like he's pulled up a rock and Pete's the insect writhing beneath it.

If Pete were a woman, people would say he'd really let himself go. Diane can't think of the equivalent way to describe a man. But that's what has happened. It's as if he's lost all self-preservation. All dignity.

'He's an embarrassment,' Ethan says.

Pete mutters something, but Diane still can't make out what

he's saying. He never used to be this bad. His time in the army has clearly taken its toll on him.

Ethan watches her closely. 'And what about you? You're different too, Diane.'

'Thanks a lot!'

'I don't mean in a bad way. You're still classy, and feisty as hell. That's what I always liked about you.'

Ethan is pretty feisty too, but she doesn't tell him that. He has a fragile male ego to go with it.

'Oh no, I'm the same as I always was,' she says as they head past the scarecrows.

'You're not, though. You're more quiet, detached. We haven't argued once.'

She bursts out laughing. Her arguments with Ethan were legendary. They used to argue over anything and everything. Asha used to say they were like an old married couple. She enjoyed those arguments, though. She used to get off on them. Ethan was always a worthy adversary.

His face becomes serious. 'It's because of Cameron, isn't it?'

She swallows hard. It's as if all the air has been sucked from her lungs.

'I can't talk about that right now.'

His lips tighten. 'I'm not asking for details, Di. But if he doesn't treat you right, don't go back to him. He doesn't deserve a second chance.'

Diane is listening vaguely. She is thinking about her wedding day. She remembers how great she felt in her vintage satin gown. She recalls her dad whispering to her to slow down as they entered the church. But she couldn't. It was all she could do not to run down that aisle, straight into Cameron's arms. She thought that happiness would last forever.

They stop abruptly. Pete has dropped to his knees. At first, Diane assumes he is going to be sick, but instead, he is holding something that was lying in the road. It's a dead pheasant.

'Look at this poor creature,' he says, stroking its feathers.

Diane bursts out laughing. 'Oh my god, drop the roadkill!'

But Pete will not put it down. He swings it about by the wing, pretending it can fly.

'What did they put in that booze?' Ethan asks. He tries to get him to drop it, but Pete is enjoying himself too much.

'Tweet, tweet,' he chirps.

'For goodness' sake, leave the poor thing alone.'

They haul him to his feet, but since neither Diane nor Ethan wants to touch the bird, he hangs on to it, the carcass swinging from his hand as he stumbles along.

When they reach the cottage, Diane turns to look at him.

'You'd better leave that thing outside. I mean it, Pete. I'm not having it in the house. Lord knows what germs you've caught off it. In fact, I suggest you go and wash your hands. Right now. Use the antibacterial handwash.'

To her surprise, Pete drops the bird and heads straight for the kitchen sink.

He washes his hands and pours himself another drink. Ethan intervenes, guiding him towards his bedroom.

Diane pours him a pint of water, which she takes into him a couple of minutes later.

'Thanks, Di! I love you, Di!' Pete says.

He's absolutely wasted. She shakes her head and turns to go. He reaches out and grabs her. His grip is surprisingly strong. 'You okay?' she asks.

He doesn't say anything, but he doesn't release her hand either. She settles down on the floor beside him. 'I suppose the wedding went quite well in the end,' she says. 'I mean, you didn't lose the rings.'

His mouth twitches. 'Might have been better if I did.'

'Oh. You don't approve?'

'It's not for me to judge.'

'Pete? Can I ask you something?'

'Hmm?'

'When we met Gordon for the first time, you looked like you recognised him. Do you know him from somewhere?'

His jaw tightens, and he shakes his head. 'I thought I did, but it's not him.'

'Not who?'

His eyes flicker a little, and for a moment, Diane thinks he's going to fall asleep.

'He reminds me of someone. Someone I never want to see again.'

'Oh! Who?'

Pete shakes his head. 'This guy I... used to know.'

'In the army?'

'Yeah.' He grinds his teeth. 'He made my life a living hell.'

'But it wasn't Gordon?'

'No.'

'You're sure about that?'

'Positive.'

'Glad to hear it. Goodnight now.'

She leans down and kisses the apple of his cheek.

He falls asleep with a smile.

FOURTEEN
SARAH

The morning light streams through the window, casting shadows on the bed. As she emerges from a deep sleep, Sarah feels Diane's breath against her neck. She watches for a moment as her former housemate shifts about. Her face is contorted as if she is in pain. Sarah slips quietly out of the bed, trying not to disturb her. Diane immediately rolls over onto her back, taking up the space Sarah has just vacated.

'No, Cameron!'

Sarah watches with concern, but Diane is still asleep, drool dripping from the corner of her mouth. She heads across to her own room and finds the bed stripped bare. There is an ominous stain on the mattress. It's hard to imagine a bird would leave that much blood.

She shudders and grabs her dressing gown off the hook on the door. She pulls it around her, tying it at the waist before padding out to the living room. Her bare feet sink into a gooey brown substance on the carpet. With a grimace, she grabs a tissue from the coffee table to wipe it off. She recognises Asha's velvet chocolate wedding cake. It appears someone dropped their slice and left it on the floor.

The entire room is a mess. There are empty bottles strewn about, candles still flickering with light, and a dirty boot sits on the table. All at once, she is back in the shared house. They were all such pigs back then, and she was such a doormat, constantly cleaning up after them. A surge of anger washes over her. No one ever appreciated her, not then and not now. She shoves the boot off the table and that's when she notices Ethan sprawled on the sofa. He's fast asleep with Asha's wedding veil draped over his face. Her blood boils as she walks over to him and rips it off. He continues to sleep, or at least pretends to.

Pete stumbles out of his room, his bony frame only just holding up a loose dressing gown that hangs open to reveal his naked emaciated body. A wave of disgust washes over her.

'Cover yourself up!' she barks.

'Whoops, sorry.'

She doesn't think he is sorry. Perhaps he thinks he can seduce her this way. Like those pathetic men who send women unsolicited dick pics.

'Did you put that dead bird in my bed?' she asks once he's decent.

'What bird?'

She sees the hint of amusement in his eyes.

'You're sick, you know that?'

'Sarah!'

She ignores him and pulls on her coat and boots, then she rushes back to the bedroom and stuffs all her possessions into her backpack. Everything but her missing phone. Diane is still asleep, so she takes her bag and dumps everything on the floor, rummaging around in the mess of clothes and accessories. Her phone is not there.

She stuffs it all back in and scribbles a quick note for Pete. He can let the others know. She should probably tell them in person, but they might try to persuade her to stay. No, persuade is too polite a word. Demand is a much more accurate term for what Diane and Ethan would do. They would demand she stay. But Sarah doesn't have to listen to their demands any more. Besides, she needs to get going. She lets the door close behind her with a resounding slam.

Outside, she takes a deep breath of fresh air. She doesn't know what time she needs to be down at the pier, but she's willing to sit there all day if necessary. Anything to get off this godforsaken island.

The hard earth shifts beneath her boots as she stomps down the long, winding road. She still can't believe Asha lied to her about being pregnant. What was that about? She could understand it if they were still back at uni. Back then they were always pranking each other, constantly trying to trip one another up. But they are grown women now, older, wiser. She had thought they'd grown out of all that childish nonsense. She'd thought their friendship had matured into something worth nurturing. It seemed she was wrong.

After a few minutes, she hears the rumble of an engine. She turns and squints against the bright sun to see a dirty green four by four driving down the road. The vehicle slows to a halt beside her and Judith leans her head out the window.

'Where are you off to then?'

'I'm going to catch the ferry,' Sarah tells her, adjusting the backpack on her shoulders.

Judith shakes her head. 'You're too late. It's away.'

Sarah eyes her with horror. 'When's the next one?'

'The boat comes at the end of the week. As was asked.'

She exhales.

'Well can you not request that it comes sooner? I'll pay them for their trouble.'

Judith laughs. 'And how do you think I'm going to do that? I've already told you, there's no phone signal on the island.'

Sarah sees the flicker of defiance in her eyes. Judith is being difficult, she is certain. If she wanted to get the boat back, she would. There has to be a way.

She hurries on, hoping the ferry will still be there, but when she reaches the pier, she sees it pulling out to sea, leaving behind a foamy white trail. Tears spring to her eyes.

She waves her arms in the air.

'Wait! Wait for me! Please come back! I want to go home!'

She watches the water, but the ferry continues to chug along, heading further and further into the distance.

And now she is stuck here for the rest of the week.

With them.

FIFTEEN
SARAH

Sarah decides to walk off her frustration. She aims for the circle, feeling drawn to its ancient energy, but somehow she ends up lost in a maze of narrow paths and overgrown shrubbery. She hears the sound of crashing waves and follows it down to the sand. She keeps going, letting the coast path lead her around the island until she reaches the lighthouse.

The white tower stands tall against the blue sky. She gazes up to the top and wonders how long it would take to climb up there. She goes inside and looks up the spiral staircase. It looks such a long way but she puts one foot in front of the other and keeps climbing, all the way to the top. She enters the lantern room, a little dizzy from the exertion. She goes to the window and the view takes her breath away. It really is an amazing vantage point. She sees the holiday cottages, and Judith and Broderick's place. The stone circle. She even sees a lone figure swimming in the sea. Whoever it is, they are a lot braver than she is.

She heads back down the stairs and manages to find her way back to the cottage after a couple of wrong turns. She does not intend to say anything to the others about missing the boat, or about getting lost. They will only rib her for it. Her dire navigation skills were a running joke back when they were at university, in sharp contrast to Diane's, with or without the help of a map.

'Remind me again why you're doing a geography degree?' Ethan asked her one night, when they were up late, studying for exams.

'I want to save the environment,' Sarah had replied.

Ethan had smirked. 'That's quite a lofty goal for one person.'

Sarah had felt her cheeks flame. 'I mean, I want to help save it,' she had corrected.

She didn't even get close. After uni, she ended up in the council's planning department. The work does not pay well and is not particularly stimulating, but Sarah doesn't have the drive to look for anything else. Her ambitions are crumbling, and she has to accept that what she's doing is 'fine for now'. But deep down, it's profoundly disappointing. Nothing in her life has gone quite the way she planned.

When she returns to the cottage, it is looking a bit better. The mess has been largely cleared away and Ethan is in the kitchen, stirring a large pot of porridge, while Diane sets the table. Without a word, Sarah heads straight to her room, feeling humiliated by her failure to leave. She stares out the window, wondering how such a beautiful, wild place can be all at once suffocating.

'Breakfast!' Ethan yells a few minutes later.

Sarah would rather stay in her room, but she knows they'll only come and drag her out and she doesn't want any of them in here. She feels violated enough after finding that bird in her bed. It has served as a timely reminder of what her ex-housemates are capable of. A reminder of their moral ambiguity. She shudders as she thinks of the way they always tested each other, their little cruelties disguised as amusing pranks. It's all fun and games as long as no one gets hurt, but that's the trouble with this lot. You never quite know how far they're willing to go. She still can't quite believe that Diane was willing to wreck Asha's wedding.

She trudges out to the kitchen and drops into a seat. Pete is already at the table, fully dressed, thank goodness. He's buttering a stack of toast. Diane is pouring the coffee.

Ethan slops scorching hot porridge into four bowls. Diane takes one mouthful and pushes it away. Sarah moves hers around with her spoon. It is thick and fast-setting, like concrete. She reaches for the saltshaker. It squeaks with each twist, the sound amplified by the silence in the room.

Everybody watches her, especially Ethan, and she remembers now how much he hates people adding salt and pepper to his cooking. She gives the shaker an extra twist, just to wind him up. God, she's turning into Diane.

'What are we doing today?' Pete asks.

'We could go to the beach,' Sarah says. 'There's a nice sandy one next to the pier.'

'It's a bit cold,' Diane says. No one argues. It's just like old times. Her word is final.

'Is it just us now?' Pete asks, reaching across her for the jam.

Sarah nods miserably. 'The rest of them left this morning.'

'Asha and Gordon will be off on their honeymoon, lucky sods. Riding motor bikes across Cambodia.'

Sarah can't imagine a less Asha activity. She's always been more of a spa girl than an adventurer.

'Can Asha even ride a motorbike?'

Diane shakes her head. 'She says she's going to learn when she gets there.'

'Typical Asha,' Ethan mutters. 'Always expects everything to be easy.'

There's some truth in what he says. Asha does always expect everything to fall into her lap, but that's because it does. She only applied for one job after leaving uni, and she got it. Then she got headhunted every few years, allowing her to rise up in the ranks with minimal effort. It's so bloody unfair.

As they are clearing away the breakfast things, someone hammers on the door. Sarah jumps up to answer it, but there is no need. Broderick shoves the door open and barges in.

'Who took it?' he demands.

Sarah exchanges a glance with the other housemates, then looks back at Broderick.

'Who took what?'

'My best hunting gun. It's gone from the lock-up.'

He looks accusingly from Pete to Ethan, then his gaze drifts to Diane and finally back to Sarah.

'Not me,' Ethan says.

'Nor me.'

Everyone is shaking their heads.

Broderick stares at them all a little longer, his face growing hot with rage.

'Whoever took it, you have one hour to return it or you won't know you're born.'

He turns and storms off again, leaving them all staring at each other in confusion.

'He's off his rocker,' Pete says.

'Bloody lunatic,' Ethan agrees.

Diane shoots Sarah a look, and she sees a flicker of fear in her eyes.

'It must have been one of the other guests,' Pete speculates. 'There were a dozen of them on the hunting trip. Any one of them could have taken it.'

'They've all left now,' Diane says quietly.

'Then they must have taken it with them.'

'Wouldn't they have noticed a big hunting rifle on the ferry?'

She catches Diane's eye again, and a telepathic message passes between them. Diane remains in the living room, arguing with Ethan and Pete, while Sarah heads to the bedrooms to search each one in turn.

SIXTEEN
DIANE

'I checked under all the beds and in the wardrobes. The gun's not there,' Sarah says.

'Good,' says Diane. 'I checked in here and in the kitchen. Not that there's much place to hide it. But you know. I thought maybe Pete...'

Sarah shakes her head. 'Pete's harmless.'

'What about last night? That thing with the bird? I can't believe he did that. I told him to leave it outside.'

'Yeah, well he has a weird sense of humour.'

'Maybe someone hid the gun to piss off Broderick?'

They both glance at the door. 'If so, they've succeeded.'

Pete is down on the ground doing push-ups. He raises himself on one arm and then the other, does some kind of complicated plank.

'Isn't that bad for your back?' Diane asks.

'I have to exercise to keep it strong,' he says.

She watches him for a moment.

'If you took the gun, now is the time to put it back.'

He looks up at her with bewildered eyes. 'I haven't got it. You know I haven't. I've been here all morning.'

She glances at the kitchen, where Ethan's scrubbing away at the dried porridge on the hob.

'One of you took it.'

Pete shrugs like it's not his concern. Diane leans closer. Then regrets doing so when she sees the state of his teeth.

'He could report us to the police,' she points out.

He doesn't look the least bit perturbed. 'He's not going to.'

'Are you sure about that?'

'Too much hassle. He'd have to get over to the mainland first.'

'Well, he might take matters into his own hands then.'

'What's he going to do, shoot us?'

'He's got the guns.'

'Well, we've got one of them, allegedly. You know what I think?'

Diane shakes her head. God knows what's going on in that bird's nest brain of his.

'I think he's scared of us. If one of us has really got the gun, then he's got to be wondering, what's our next move? What are we going to do with it?'

Laughter bubbles up from her insides and overflows like the mess in Ethan's porridge pot. 'You're probably right,' she decides, turning her back on him.

She walks through to the kitchen and takes the sponge from Ethan. 'Here, I'll do that. You cooked.'

'Oh, cheers.'

She watches as Ethan heads back out to the lounge.

Pete has finished his exercises. He clambers to his feet and takes a seat as far away from Ethan as he can. Ethan is reading and doesn't seem to notice the way Pete keeps looking at him.

Diane rinses the last few items and sets them on the draining board. She turns in time to see Ethan glance over at Pete. Pete smiles at him. It's a knowing smile. An expression that ought to put him on the alert, but Ethan doesn't seem to notice. Diane always thinks of Asha as being the self-obsessed one, but in truth, Ethan is just as bad. She's guilty of a double standard, she supposes. Asha gets stick for it because she's a woman, whereas men are often arrogant, and it's just considered part of their masculinity.

She wonders if Ethan is getting worse. More than once, he has said something that makes her grind her teeth. Like when Pete stung himself on the nettles yesterday, she distinctly heard Ethan telling him not to be such a 'girl'. And she recalls the way Ethan talked to Asha at the barbecue. That didn't look like a friendly chat. He had looked nervous, as if he was worried about something. Worried about something Asha was going to do. Or say?

'Get your dirty feet off the sofa!' Ethan barks at Pete.

Pete growls at him in response. He acts like a little terrier at times, but Ethan is a Dobermann. He would tear Pete to pieces if they got into a real fight. Sarah senses it too. She's quick to plant herself between the two of them when they sit down on the sofa.

An hour passes before Broderick returns. He's calmer now. His jaw is unclenched, and she notices a shift in his demeanour. What is that? Acceptance? Resignation?

'Whoever took it, just put it back,' he says sternly. 'Guns are no toys. Judith and I hold the licences. They should only be used when we are there to see to it.'

'Could someone have taken it on the boat?' Diane asks.

'No. You know yourself, there's nowhere to hide on that boat. I'd have noticed.'

'Right, well I'll see if I can get to the bottom of it.'

He gives her a curt nod. 'You need to watch yourself,' he says in a low voice. 'Don't let them drink too much. You hear me? Guns and booze don't mix.'

She nods ruefully. 'I'm sorry about all this.'

'Right, well. When you find it, just drop it back over. And make sure it's not loaded. I don't want any of those fools shooting holes in their feet.'

'Okay.'

She watches him leave. There is a slight hobble to his walk she hadn't noticed before and she can't help but wonder if he was speaking from experience just then.

Sarah comes out of her bedroom.

'Well?'

'Well, nothing.'

'So much for consequences,' says Ethan, flinging the soggy tea towel at Pete's head. Pete grabs it and flings it back.

'Who wants to go for a hike?' Diane asks.

'I'm good here,' Pete says, indicating the can of lager he's just popped open.

'Me too,' Ethan says, taking up a book. It has an intriguing title: *Never Back Down: The Art of Winning by Default*.

'I'll come,' Sarah says. 'I just need a minute to get ready.'

Diane eyes Pete and Ethan. 'What's the point of being here if you're just going to hang around the cottage? We're meant to be getting out there and exploring.'

Pete rubs his stomach. 'Exploring will have to wait. I've got gut ache.'

'Me too,' Ethan says. 'Do you think it's something we ate?'

Diane snorts. 'Something you drank, more likely.'

She laces her hiking boots while Sarah sprays herself with insect repellent, then faffs about filling her water bottle. Bored of waiting, Diane throws on her jacket and steps outside. The sky is clear, with a light mist, but the weather is so changeable that it can be sunny one moment and rainy the next.

As she checks her watch, she sees that her hand has finally stopped bleeding. She unravels the bandage and finds the wound has turned every colour of the rainbow. She must remember to change the dressing when she gets back. Sarah's good at that sort of thing, but she'll have to deal with it herself. Sarah asks way too many questions.

'Which way do you want to go?' Sarah asks when she finally makes it outside.

'I was thinking we'd go that way,' Diane says, pointing towards the north of the island. Sarah nods her head, but Diane can tell she's not really paying attention.

Diane leads the way. The path she's chosen is quite overgrown, but she enjoys whacking the branches and stomping through the dense vegetation. Sarah is as slow as ever, moving along at a snail's pace.

'Diane!'

'What?'

'You're going too fast. Wait a minute.'

Diane stops altogether and lets out a yawn while she waits for Sarah to catch up. She turns and sees the sheep grazing in the fields, and beyond that, the deep greyish-green of the sea. Then she catches a whiff of seaweed. It smells gassy today, sulphuric, like boiled eggs, or her grandmother's vitamin supplements.

Sarah catches her up, and they walk together in familiar silence. They never did this when they lived together, despite the numerous nature trails available in Aberdeenshire. They didn't care much for the tranquillity of nature back then. Instead, they were drawn to the allure of the Granite City, and all the various pubs, clubs and bars it had to offer.

'Can you picture Asha living on a farm?' Sarah asks after a while.

'It's hard to picture her mucking out pigs.'

'Asha is not going to muck out the pigs. At most, she will stand nearby and shout encouragement while Gordon does it.'

They both titter, then they fall silent again, but Sarah keeps looking at her, as if she's working up the courage to say something. Finally, she clears her throat.

'Have you thought any more about asking Pete to stay with you? I really do need a break.'

Diane grits her teeth. 'Like I said, I'd have to ask Cameron.'

She rubs her throbbing hand. What is she even talking about? It's not like she's ever going back there. 'Does Pete even want to live in Inverness? All his family are in Glasgow.'

'Like they give a toss. Haven't seen any of them offering to take him in.'

'Well, why can't the army house him? It's not right, the way they treat people. The system is all wrong. They screw them up and toss them out.'

'I know. It totally sucks.'

They continue along the footpath until they come to a fork in the road. Diane instinctively chooses the route that heads down towards the sea. Her footsteps speed up again, because she can only walk slowly for so long. They stop at the top of a cliff and look down at the cove below. Sarah points out a little motorboat sitting on the shore, and Diane raises a brow.

'It must belong to Broderick and Judith,' Diane says.

Of course they have a boat of their own. They need to be able to travel back and forth to the mainland. They would hardly want to rely on tourist boats and occasional deliveries.

'Judith told me there was no way off the island!' Sarah sounds so indignant Diane doesn't know what to say.

'You wanted to leave?' she asks.

Sarah doesn't answer. Her face is very pinched. Diane gives her a moment. It's not like Sarah to lose her cool.

'Why did you want to leave?' she asks after a bit.

Sarah looks at her.

'What, the bird?'

'Amongst other things. It's just... getting to me, that's all. I thought I could hack it but now I'm not so sure.'

Diane tilts her head. 'I never realised you were such a townie. But if you want to leave that badly, I'm sure something can be arranged.'

'I'll ask Judith again,' Sarah says, nodding. 'I'll offer her money. Everyone has their price.'

Diane doesn't get it. Sarah is not in the habit of being melodramatic. At least, that's not how she remembers her. She turns abruptly, heading right at the end of the path, so as to take a different route back to the cottage. They round the corner and keep walking towards an old stone bothy. Diane grinds to a halt in front of it, stopping so suddenly Sarah ploughs into her.

'Sorry,' Sarah says automatically.

Diane does not apologise in return. She is staring at the crumbly old building.

'What?'

'Hello?' she calls into the echoey darkness.

Sarah swallows. 'Is there someone in there?'

Diane steps inside. There is no electricity inside the shelter, but the large window brings in natural light, enough that she can look around. She sees the remains of a fire in the hearth and holds her hand over the embers.

'It's cool.'

'So what?'

Sarah is still hanging about in the doorway, as if she's afraid of invading someone's home.

'Look at that!'

Diane lifts a rock and reveals the packaging from a caramel wafer bar. On the windowsill sits an empty tin of baked beans. There is also a rolled-up blanket on the bed. It is the exact same design as the one on her own bed, back at the cottage.

'You see that? Someone's been sleeping here,' she says.

'Those beans must have been opened recently. Look, there's no mould on it yet. It has to be fresh.'

Sarah shakes her head. 'But no one's allowed on the island. No one but us and the caretakers. Don't you think it was probably one of them?'

'I hardly think so. Not when they've got a perfectly good cottage to sleep in.'

'Perhaps they watch birds in here or something?'

'That doesn't explain all this stuff. The blanket. The beans.'

Sarah's eyebrows narrow. 'Shall we go and tell Judith and Broderick?'

'Yes, I think we'd better.'

They take the coast path, which leads them all around the outside of the island, back to the caretakers' house.

Diane knocks on the door, but there is no answer. She tries the handle and the door opens. 'Hello? Anybody home?'

Her voice echoes around the empty kitchen. She listens, but she can't hear any sound from the rest of the house. Curiosity leads her to keep exploring. She ventures down the hallway, noting the framed pictures on the walls. They are all old and faded, but it's clear that these must be Judith's ancestors. They all share the same pointed chin. Although the pictures are in black and white, she can see that they have been taken here on this island, and it occurs to her that Judith must be a descendant of the original inhabitants. How curious that she has chosen to return and take up the caretaker position on the very island that drove so many of her ancestors to the brink of madness.

'Diane!' Sarah yells. 'Out here! In the garden!'

Diane turns and heads back out.

'Over there,' Sarah says, pointing.

'Hello?' she calls as Judith emerges from the chicken coop.

Judith does not react. Perhaps she is a little hard of hearing.

'Judith!' Diane yells.

At the sound of her voice, Judith raises her head. Irritation distorts her features as she stares at the pair of them.

'Now what do you want?'

Diane takes a step towards her. 'Did you know somebody's been sleeping in the bothy? The one on top of the cliffs?'

'What are you harping on about?'

'It's true. We were just there,' Sarah says. 'Someone's been cooking food there. Are you missing any chickens?'

Now she has Judith's attention. 'Of course not. There's nobody else on the island. Nobody gets here but by boat, and it's a tricky route. You'd need to know what you were doing.'

Sarah glances around. 'Is Broderick about?'

'No, you just missed him.'

'When will he be back?'

'He'll be a few days. He's gone to Kirkwall to get his messages. And he'll be visiting the family while he's at it.'

Sarah gapes. 'What, just like that?'

'He was supposed to be taking me hunting!' Diane says. She eyes Judith curiously. 'Did you two have an argument or something?'

The old woman's nostrils flare, and her ears flush at the tips. 'He wasn't in the best of moods, if you must know. It's not good for his heart, all this tension. I told him he'd be better off keeping clear. I can handle you lot.'

'Wh... when did he go?' Sarah asks.

'A little while ago.'

'In the speedboat?'

'Aye.'

Sarah's mouth drops open. 'Why didn't you tell me? You knew I wanted to leave!'

'He did knock on your door, as it happens. Your friends said you'd gone for a hike.'

Sarah lets out a ragged breath. 'I don't believe this!'

'But what shall we do about the intruder?' Diane says.

Judith's brows knit together. 'There's no intruder, I've told you. Nobody comes to this island, except by the ferry. We have never had an unexpected visitor. Not once. We're too out of the way. Do you understand me?'

'But someone's been there.'

'It would have to be one of you lot, mucking about. Anyway, I've got my guns. If anybody comes near here, I'll give them what for.'

Diane purses her lips. 'Can I have a gun? Just in case?'

Judith lets out a laugh. 'According to Broderick, you've already got one.'

'That wasn't us.'

'Do you think I was born yesterday?'

She strides past them, towards the house.

'Stupid bitch!' Sarah says under her breath.

Judith does not react, but Diane has a feeling she's heard perfectly. She looks at Sarah.

'Now what?'

'We'd better go back and warn the others about the intruder.'

SEVENTEEN
DIANE

Little puffs of wool poke out of a barbed wire fence. A herd of sheep grazes on the other side, white fleeces blending with darker ones. As Sarah and Diane approach, the bleating grows louder and quicker, rising in pitch. The sheep raise their heads, ears pricked, eyes locked on the two women. Then one of them moves, causing a ripple of woolly bodies as they all adjust their positions.

Diane swings one leg over the stile, but Sarah doesn't follow.

'What?'

Sarah nods her head at the sheep.

'They're just sheep. They're harmless.'

Sarah pulls a face. 'They're staring at me.'

'Okay, we'll go the long way round,' Diane says with a sigh.

She heads back to the road, but a few minutes later, Sarah stops again.

'What is it now?'

Sarah is pointing, her mouth open wide. Diane follows her gaze.

'They're just scarecrows.'

'No, look, they've got holes in them.'

Diane looks more closely. Sarah's right. One scarecrow is missing its shoulder, another has a big hole through its chest, like it's been shot right through the heart.

'Why would anyone do that?' Sarah asks.

Diane shakes her head. 'Damned if I know.'

They increase their pace. Sarah is practically jogging as they head back towards the cottage, the wind blowing down their backs. There's a listlessness to the island today. The air has a smoky aftertaste and there is a flurry of activity in the bushes and in the sky.

Sarah streaks past her and bursts into the cottage. Diane follows at a more leisurely pace, glancing all around as she does so. Pete hasn't moved from his position on the sofa.

He looks at Sarah. There is a question in his eyes but she doesn't answer it.

Ethan sets down his book. 'I was just going to make some coffee. Do you want one?'

'Yes, please,' Diane says. She follows him into the kitchen while Sarah paces around the living room.

'What's with her?' he asks.

She fills him in on what they discovered at the bothy, and the state of the scarecrows.

'Are you sure it wasn't Pete?' he says in a low voice.

'How could it be?'

'Sarah found him sleeping rough,' he explains. 'That's why she let him move in with her. He had nowhere else to go.'

Diane's heart aches. 'I didn't realise. Poor Pete.'

'I feel for the guy, but he's a bit of a headache,' Ethan says. 'I wouldn't put it past him to wander off at night and go and sleep somewhere else. I mean, maybe he likes roughing it outdoors or something.'

They watch Pete closely, but he looks content, relaxing on the sofa, drinking. Beer cans litter the floor by his feet, but he doesn't appear drunk so much as blissed out. His eyes are fixed on some invisible point in the distance. It's as if he's looking at something no one else can see. But for the first time on this trip, he looks truly at peace.

'He's not really doing any harm, if it is Pete,' Ethan says, opening the cupboard to get out the coffee cups. 'I mean, it's a bit unorthodox, but maybe he just needed the quiet.'

'What about the gun, though?'

'There was no sign of it in the bothy,' Sarah says, coming over to join them.

'No, but he must have stashed it somewhere. I wish I knew where. I don't like the thought of him having it.'

'Maybe it makes him feel safer,' Ethan suggests.

'Well, it scares the hell out of me,' Sarah says.

'We need to keep a close eye on him,' Diane agrees. 'I told Broderick I'd get the gun back to him. We just have to work out where he's stashed it.'

'How are we going to do that?' Sarah asks.

'Well if he keeps drinking the way he has been, it should be easy,' Ethan says.

He pours the coffee and they sit down at the table. Pete's head lolls to one side.

'I'd better go and save that beer can before he spills it all over the floor,' Sarah says.

She jumps to her feet and walks over to him. But as she tries to take the can from the sleepy man, he jerks awake and grabs her wrist. He has a strong grip, and Sarah whimpers, causing Ethan to rise from his seat.

'It's okay,' she says, extracting herself from his hold.

Pete immediately flops back against the sofa. He lets out a soft moan, but then he is silent, his chest rising and falling in a steady rhythm.

Sarah returns to the table and reaches for her coffee cup. 'I think I'll go and have a nap too,' she says with a little smile. 'You know what they say, "If they're sleeping, you should be sleeping."'

Diane forces a smile, but she is shocked at what Sarah has had to put up with.

'I don't know how she does it,' Ethan says once Sarah has left them. 'She's had him living under her roof for over a year now. I'd be losing my mind.'

'Me too,' Diane agrees. She thinks about Sarah's request. Under normal circumstances, she might have been willing to help, but that's not possible now.

Ethan yawns and stretches his arms over his head, displaying a bit of his tanned torso. 'I thought I'd go for a swim,' he says. 'Don't suppose you want to come?'

'I didn't bring my swimming costume.'

He grins mischievously. 'You don't need one. I'm just going to swim in my boxers.'

A smile flits across Diane's face. She feels a flash of her younger self. Student Diane was so much bolder and less afraid. She wouldn't have thought twice about swimming in her undies.

'All right then.'

She looks towards Sarah's bedroom. 'Shall we ask Sarah?'

'Nah, let her rest.'

She's kind of glad it's just the two of them. It adds a little to the excitement.

'Which beach do you want to go to?' he asks.

'There's a nice one in front of the bothy,' she remembers. 'It looked sandy.'

He smiles at her. 'Okay.'

They grab their towels from the bathroom and she shoves on a warm hoodie over her clothes. Together, they retrace the route she has just walked with Sarah. There is a different air to it now. The birds seem calmer, and she feels the sun's rays on her shoulders. She matches her stride to Ethan's and they break into a run when they see the sea.

'First one down to the beach!' Ethan says.

They sprint down the sandy dunes, pulling off their shoes and clothes as they go.

Diane sneaks a peak as Ethan's T-shirt comes off. He has a nice chest, muscular, toned. She feels a little self-conscious as she whips off her own clothes, piling them under a rock so they don't fly away. She is now wearing nothing but her black bra and knickers.

'Ready?'

He takes her hand again and they run towards the waves.

The water is a shock to the system. If he weren't holding her hand so tight, Diane would not venture any further, but as it is, he's pulling her into the icy water. She shrieks as she feels the coldness on her skin. Ethan breaks off his hold and then he's swimming, arms churning through the waves, out into the North Sea.

Diane swims after him. Her strokes are not as powerful, and her injured hand stings. Still, the salt water is probably good for it, she decides. He's swimming deeper, much deeper than she usually goes. She paddles after him, then gives up and turns on her back, allowing herself to drift.

She looks up at the clouds above and tries to empty her mind. There is so much going on up there. So much chaos. She wishes she could just stay in this moment, where she feels utterly invincible. She wishes she could keep the rest of the world at bay.

Ethan is paddling back towards her. She hears him powering through the foam, heading straight for her. She turns to look at him. Then he disappears underwater, and she feels a moment of panic because she has no idea where he's gone. She scans the waves, but there is no sign of him.

'Ethan?' she yells. 'Ethan!'

He pops up right in front of her, almost knocks her flat. He's grinning the way he used to whenever he thought he'd won a point.

'Having fun?' he asks, looking a little smug.

'I'm freezing my tits off.'

'Me too.'

'Hey, looks like we have an audience!'

She looks up at the cliffs above. Judith's car is there, and she's sitting at the wheel, watching them. She shakes her head with disapproval, as if she can read Diane's thoughts.

'Nosy old bat!' Ethan says.

The tide sweeps them back towards the beach, and he clambers to his feet, water dripping from his boxers. He stands there, hands on hips, and grins up at the older woman. Judith glares at him for a moment. Diane waits for the sound of her engine before she too emerges from the water. There is seaweed hanging from her bra. They walk up the beach and wrap themselves in their towels.

'Well, that was invigorating,' he says. 'We should do it again sometime.'

'Definitely,' Diane says, and to her surprise, she means it.

They walk back to the cottage, water sloshing in their shoes, and Ethan talks about how crazy Pete was the night before.

'I still can't believe he stuck that bird in Sarah's bed.'

Diane glances at him out of the side of her eye. It strikes her that it is no worse than some of the pranks Ethan used to pull when they lived together.

'He's driving her to distraction,' she agrees. 'She keeps on at me to take him in. But obviously I can't. Have you thought about it at all?'

'No.'

'Don't you feel for the guy?'

'I do, but I'm not having him in my house.'

'It just doesn't seem fair. Sarah shouldn't be his only option. I mean, I was wondering if it was worth contacting one of the military charities. Maybe they could help?'

'Military charities? Pete was never in the army.'

'What? But I thought...'

Ethan shakes his head. 'I know, he tells people that because he's embarrassed.'

'But what about the PTSD? Why is he so disturbed?'

'All that stuff that happened to him, that's all true. But it didn't happen in the army. It happened in prison.'

EIGHTEEN
DIANE

Diane stares at him.

'What are you talking about? Pete's not a criminal.'

'He didn't want people to know. That's why his family don't talk to him. Don't you think they'd have taken him in if he really was a vet?'

'Well, that depends. People suck. Okay then, what did he do?'

'He killed someone.'

Diane feels her pulse pick up. 'Now I know you're lying.'

'Wait a minute, it wasn't like that. Listen. His mum asked him to collect his stepdad from the station. He'd had a few beers. He was over the limit, but he thought he was still okay to drive. He managed to get there in one piece, but on the way back he drove the car straight into a brick wall.'

'Bloody hell!'

'I know. It was his own fault, but I really feel for him. He was a wreck before he made it to trial, couldn't eat, couldn't sleep. He'd lost like, two stone and his hair was coming out in clumps.'

'Why on earth didn't you say anything? We'd all have been there to support him.'

'Because he couldn't bear it, Diane. He begged me not to say anything to any of you. He thought if you knew you'd hate him. You know what he's like. Once he's got an idea in his head, there's no talking him out of it. Anyway, the trial was a total shitshow. His lawyer wasn't the best and Pete himself was a mess. I thought the judge might take pity on him and give him a community order but he sentenced him to eighteen months. Poor old Pete, he's really not built for prison. To be honest, who is?'

Diane wrapped her arms around herself. It didn't bear thinking about.

'So they put him in a maximum security prison with all these gang bangers and junkies. And on his very first night inside, a group of blokes threatened him. Fortunately for him, his cellmate stepped in and protected him. I visited him that first week. He thought he'd made a friend. He thought he was safe. But when I came back a month later, he was an even worse mess. Turned out his "friend" wasn't such a nice bloke after all. He made him do stuff he didn't want to do.'

Diane met his eyes. 'Oh hell!'

They were both silent for a moment, then Ethan continued.

'He pimped him out to others too. It was pure torture. He wasn't even safe in his own cell. He's out now, but he's still serving a life sentence. It never goes away. That's why you hear him screaming in the night, why he can never quite relax. They've ruined him for life.'

Diane puffs out a breath of air. She feels terrible for Pete, but at the same time, confused about the lie. If he could lie about the army, what else has he lied about?

She looks at Ethan. 'I didn't even know you and Pete were still in touch?'

'We're not. I mean, I tried to help him but he didn't want to take my advice, and then he started refusing my visits. I told him to contact me when he got out but he didn't bother. No wonder he ended up on the street. You just can't help some people.'

She sighs. 'I really wish you'd said something. I might not have chosen to share a cottage with him. And Sarah might not have taken him in.'

'That's exactly why I didn't tell you. He needed a place to stay, and I really wanted to see you, Di. You don't know what it's been like for me lately.'

'How do you mean?'

'We've broken up. Me and Charmaine. And she's caused me so much grief.'

'I'm sorry. I didn't know.'

He swallows hard. Diane has never seen him vulnerable before. She wants to reach out and take his hand, but she knows he'd hate that.

'It was a really bad break-up, Di. She ripped my heart out and stomped all over it.'

'I'm so sorry. But why didn't you say anything?'

'I didn't want to bring everyone down.'

Laughter erupts from deep within her belly. For some reason she finds this funny. They are all so incredibly, irreparably screwed up. It's like there's a giant X hanging over their heads or something.

Her brain is still processing everything he's told her. She tries to reframe Pete in the light of what she now knows, but it's hard. She can't get the image of him in combat out of her head. She thought he'd seen active service. She thought he was better than her. Now she knows he's just an unfortunate, undignified mess.

When they reach the cottage, she can't even look at him. She goes straight to her room and lies down on her bed, her mind whirring.

It would have been in the papers, Pete's court case. She could read about it online. She reaches for her phone, then remembers. No internet. It feels weird being so many days without it. She itches for it. She's beginning to understand Sarah's addiction.

She crosses the hall to Ethan's room. He's sitting on his bed, looking out the window at nothing in particular.

'Are you going to tell Sarah?' she asks.

He turns and looks at her. 'I don't know. If I do, then where's Pete going to go?'

'But don't you think she has a right to know who she's let into her home?'

'At the end of the day, he's still Pete though. He's still our mate.'

She's not so sure who he is any more.

She goes into the bathroom and takes Sarah's phone out of its hiding place under the sink. It's not a very good prank as they go. Sarah seems to have forgotten about it. She's probably enjoying the break. She looks at it for a moment, then tiptoes into Sarah's room and slips it under her pillow. The battery is completely dead and she still won't be able to get onto the internet, but Diane thinks it's about time she had it back.

NINETEEN
SARAH

Without warning, the living room grows darker and the sky rips apart in a violent demonstration of nature's wrath, unleashing a torrential downpour that pounds against the roof. Sarah longs for the weather app on her phone. She hates not knowing how long the rain will go on for. It feels as though it's never going to stop.

Diane and Ethan sit together on the sofa, whispering to one another in a way Sarah resents. Ethan appears fixated on the fire, constantly stoking it with more logs. The effect is smoky and toxic, setting Pete off. His cough is different this week, less honking goose, more death rattle, and every time she thinks he's stopped he starts up again.

She cracks open a window, but the bitter taste of ashes lingers on her tongue. Ethan and Diane are in the midst of one of their intense debates, their voices rising and falling as they argue about every topic under the sun. They seem completely engrossed in their own little world, oblivious to everyone else around them, and she is beginning to feel like a wasp trapped in a jam jar.

She sits by the window, her breath creating a small cloud on the glass. She watches as the rain falls in a steady rhythm. She feels a sense of urgency building within her as the droplets race each other, blurring and merging together at the bottom.

The moment it stops raining, she pulls on her coat and shoes, and barrels outside without a word to anyone.

Finally, a bit of peace.

She walks carefully. Bulbous clumps of slippery seaweed have been flung over the road by the wind, and she shudders as water drips on her from one of the few trees, but as she traipses through the mud, she is so grateful to feel the cool air on her face, and to have nothing to listen to but birdsong and the whistle of the wind.

The landscape has a newness to it, the colours more vivid after the rain. A rainbow peeks through the clouds then gradually fades as she walks, and she can make out a beam of sunlight. She will take it for now.

She looks across the land and deliberately heads in the opposite direction from the bothy, still wary of whoever is out there. She soon finds herself down on the beach near where they arrived. It's one of the larger beaches, with a swathe of dark grey sand and piles of rocks and pebbles arranged here and there as if by a film crew. The rocks here are curious, perfectly rounded, with fascinating colours and marbling. Little pieces of quartz sparkle in the sun.

She reaches the pier. The boards sag a little beneath her boots, worn smooth by years of tides. As she looks around, she spots something hidden under heavy tarpaulin, its edges stiff with salt crust. She pulls it back, the fabric crackling, and finds an old wooden rowing boat. The oars lie across the seat. Her breath catches. Another boat, she thinks. Another route off the island. Her heart lifts. She will show it to Diane later and see what she thinks.

She continues her walk, enjoying a flash of sun. She slips off her shoes, leaving them on a rock so she can feel the sand beneath her feet. She doesn't make it to the beach often. It never seems to be a priority in her busy life in Glasgow. But now she wonders why this is. The nearest beach is only a forty-minute drive. She just never thinks about it. It always feels like so much effort, managing her life. Managing Pete. Keeping all the plates spinning.

She heads down towards the water. The waves feel like ice as they lap at her toes. As she gazes out to sea, she spots a couple of seals paddling about like dogs. She stares in wonder and wishes she had her phone so she could take a picture.

She watches for a while, then walks on, enjoying the perfect, unspoilt beach. It feels incredible to be here, all alone like this. Looking around at the dusty sand and the huge boulders, she could almost believe she is on an alien planet, and just for a moment, she can understand why Judith and Broderick chose this life. She sifts the sand with her feet, searching for the groatie buckie shells Gordon's cousins told her about. The children consider these shells to be treasures mainly, as far as she can gather, because they are so hard to find.

Up ahead is a pile of rocks, and what looks like another seal. She quickens her pace. Is it all right there? It is a little far out from the shoreline. She doesn't know much about seals. How far can they waddle across the sand? She hurries forward, then lurches to a halt as she sees not a seal, but a creature in human form. She blinks, and the thought flashes through her mind that she has stumbled upon a selkie. Then her eyes focus more clearly, and a strangled scream erupts from her mouth. Lying across the rocks is not a seal, or a selkie, but Gordon, with a gaping wound in his chest.

TWENTY
SARAH

Sarah stares at Gordon's grotesque, bulging eyes. They seem to pulsate with a sickening energy, drawing her in and repelling her at the same time.

She stoops down and reaches out a hand, but she can't bring herself to touch him. There is no hope. She can see his body is as cold and blue as the sea. Tiny flies buzz around, and she wonders if there are maggots wriggling inside his decaying wound. A herring gull stands a few feet away, shifting on its pink webbed feet. Its beady yellow eyes are round and unblinking, flicking between her and the body. The sharp curve of its beak parts slightly and she notices a red smear on the tip. She shudders violently, and wrings her hands, her heart pounding in her chest.

She hasn't a clue what she's supposed to do.

On the mainland, she would dial 999 and call for help. But there's no possibility of that here, on Haarlorn.

Her mind races as she tries to piece together what happened. There is a clear bullet wound in Gordon's abdomen and another in his chest. Two dark sunken holes, the edges puckered and dry. There's no doubt he's been shot. Her mind flips to the missing gun, and she remembers Broderick's expression, angry and fearful. As though he sensed something bad was going to happen.

The intruder, she thinks. *The intruder did this.*

A flock of birds takes off from the nearby rocks, and she raises her head sharply, her senses alert to the danger she must be in. She wants to run, but instead she falls to her knees. She squeezes her eyes tight. Her body should have gone into fight or flight, but here she is, a blubbering, quivering mess. Her stomach is weak, her legs are jelly, and she has no choice but to sit here, sobbing over the corpse of the man Asha loves.

'Sarah?'

It is Diane. She's waving and jogging up the beach towards her. 'God, I thought I was never going to—'

Diane takes in the body, then immediately vomits uncontrollably onto the sand.

For a few minutes, neither of them says anything. Sarah waits until Diane lifts her head, then she leans over and rubs her back. Her knees are cold and numb.

'Where's Asha?' Diane asks.

Sarah's eyes widen, because Diane's right. If Gordon is here, then Asha must be somewhere close. She wouldn't just abandon him.

'Asha!' Sarah yells. 'Ash-a!'

Her voice echoes around the rocks, but there is no reply. They look at each other.

'Why... why would anyone shoot Gordon?' Diane says.

Sarah shakes her head. 'I don't know... I can't even...'

Diane's brain seems to click into gear. 'Let's go to Judith's.'

'You think she has a secret phone?'

'She must have something.'

Slowly, Sarah staggers to her feet. She is still wobbly, as if she's just climbed off a fairground ride. She takes one last look at Gordon.

'Are we supposed to close his eyes or something?' she asks.

'What difference does it make? He's already dead.'

Typical Diane, so blunt and matter-of-fact. She has no time for religion or superstition, but Sarah, who knows there is more to this world, wonders if he is still in there, or if his soul has already passed over, into heaven.

Assuming that's where he's going.

'I'm worried about Asha,' Sarah says.

'Me too.'

'Do you think she's—'

'Don't say it. There's no point speculating. We just need to find her.'

Sarah nods. She retrieves her shoes and they make their way up the beach, darting glances up at the rocks.

Did Gordon see the person who shot him? Was he even aware, or was it all over in a matter of seconds? She can't bear to think of the other possibility. That he lay there in agony, his heart pumping furiously as he called out in vain for help. And Asha, what happened to her? Could she still be here somewhere, hiding, waiting to see if it's safe? She remembers the person she saw in the sea. Could that have been Asha? She thought she'd seen a swimmer, but she isn't so sure now. Could it have been a body? Or perhaps Asha had dived into the sea to get away from her attacker. If so, she might have returned later. She might still be here, somewhere. Hiding, afraid.

They head up to the main road. 'It's just so surreal. I feel like I'm in a dream or something,' Diane says.

'A nightmare,' Sarah agrees.

They keep walking, eyes peeled for any signs of Asha or the shooter. Diane is shaking, and Sarah reaches for her arm. Her skin is almost as cold as she imagines Gordon's to be. She hopes she's not going into shock.

'Better stay off the main road,' Diane says. 'It feels safer.'

Sarah agrees, even though she hates getting her legs all

scratched up. They push their way along the overgrown footpath, ears pricked for the slightest sound.

'What do we do if we see the shooter?' Sarah asks.

'Make sure you don't run in a straight line. You've got to confuse them.'

Sarah nods, tucking this away just in case. They turn right and arrive at the bottom of Judith's garden.

The caretakers' cottage seems quiet. They dart across the lawn and peer through the window. There is no sign of anyone inside. Diane knocks on the door, and they wait a few minutes. They go to the chicken coop and look in there. The chickens cluck about. They've already had their feed by the looks of it. But no Judith.

They step out again, and Sarah shuts the gate. She tries the cottage door again, wishing their last exchange hadn't been so abrupt.

'Hello?' she calls.

'She might be tending to the sheep,' Diane suggests. 'Maybe we should wait inside?'

Sarah clutches her arm. 'What if there's someone else in there?'

Diane meets her eye. 'We'll have to be careful.'

She pushes open the door. The cottage smells of kippers.

'Hello?' Diane calls out. 'Judith, are you there?'

Sarah ventures into the kitchen and sees an old-style Aga. Dishes sit discarded in the sink, and there is a bottle of brown sauce on the table, along with a scattering of breadcrumbs and a gun.

They both stare at it for a moment.

'It doesn't mean anything,' Diane says. 'Country folk and their guns. It might be quite normal for her to leave it out.'

'Was there a gun here earlier?'

'No.'

She turns and notices a sheet of paper pinned to the board.

It has this week's date at the top, and the names of each of the holiday cottages. The top four are crossed out. Presumably, this means they've all checked out. The cottage they are staying in is not crossed out, which makes sense, seeing as they are still here. But Asha and Gordon's is not crossed out either. She stares at it for a moment. Has Judith forgotten to cross them off, or did they change their mind and decide to stay longer? It doesn't make any sense.

Sarah walks out of the kitchen and into the hallway.

'Judith?' she calls up the stairs.

She turns into the living room. It's cold in there. The fire is not lit.

'What do you want to do?' Diane asks.

'To go home.'

Sarah leans against the mantelpiece and sobs. She can't stop thinking about Gordon's face. He was so happy yesterday. He grinned all the way through the wedding ceremony. All the way through the reception.

And now he's dead and decaying on the beach.

Diane walks around the periphery of the room, peering at shelves and cabinets.

'We shouldn't touch anything,' Sarah says.

Diane stops in front of the old wooden desk.

'Look, they have ham radio. Maybe we could use this to get help.'

Sarah eyes a rectangular box with a number of dials and buttons on it.

'Do you know how to use it?'

Diane examines the controls. 'My grandad has one of these, but his is a bit different.'

She flips a switch and tweaks a dial, twisting it back and forth. After a moment, a crackly voice cuts through the noise. The sound is garbled.

'What language is that?'

'Sounds like Portuguese,' Diane murmurs, concentrating as she fine-tunes the dial. She continues to adjust it, and more voices emerge, some clearer, others barely audible, nearly all men, speaking in different languages.

Sarah shifts from foot to foot, anxiety prickling at the back of her neck.

'Come on, find someone who speaks English.'

Diane turns the dial again. Static crackles through the speaker, filling the air with a low, unsteady hiss. And then a nasal voice breaks through.

'That's English!' Sarah says her heart leaping.

Diane moves the dial back and forth until the voice becomes slightly clearer, though still faint, like they are speaking from the bottom of a well.

It's a clear day over here in Brixton, London. Your signal is five and nine. I'm going to head out for a mobile rally in a minute. Over.

Sarah frowns, glancing at Diane. 'What are they going on about?'

'It's a hobby. They just talk at each other.'

'Can we talk too?'

'Maybe.'

Diane picks up the headphones and slides them over her ears. She presses a button, her voice tight and uncertain as she speaks into the mic: 'Mayday! Mayday! Are you receiving me? This is Diane Lomax on Haarlorn Island, Orkney. There is an active shooter, repeat, there is an active shooter. Please send police. Over.'

Sarah leans in closer, straining to hear the reply. The static wavers, but the only response is a distant, garbled voice. Diane twists another dial, adjusting the frequency, but the voices keep on talking, and no one comments on what she has just said.

'I'll try another channel.'

She gives the same speech three more times, then sets the headphones down.

'I don't know if I'm doing this right,' she mutters, more to herself than to Sarah. She takes a breath and tries again.

Sarah grips the edge of the table, her nails digging into the wood. Her mind races, thinking of how many times Diane's voice has echoed into the void without answer.

'What if no one's listening?' she whispers.

Diane doesn't look up.

'We just need one person to hear us, Sarah. Just one.'

But all that comes back is the crackling hum of static. Finally, Diane lowers the microphone, shoulders slumped in defeat. She stares at the radio, as if willing it to give them the miracle they need.

Sarah bites her lip. 'What now?'

Diane glances at her and rubs her red-rimmed eyes.

'Now we head back to the cottage. We need to warn Pete and Ethan.'

Diane grabs the gun from the kitchen and they step outside, looking all around for any sign of a shooter. Sarah follows.

Diane takes a couple of steps towards the grass, then stops.

'Judith's car's not here.'

She's right. Sarah doesn't know how she missed it.

'Well, she must be back soon. Shall we wait?'

'I think we should warn Pete and Ethan,' Diane says. 'And we need to get a search party together to look for Asha.'

Sarah can't think of anything she'd like to do less. Of course, she wants Asha found, but she hates the thought of exploring this creepy island any further, and besides, she has a horrible feeling Asha is already dead.

They take a different route this time, an even more wild one, if that is possible.

'Do you think it was one of the cousins?' Diane asks. 'Some dispute about land or something?'

'No! They all seemed to love Gordon. Everyone was tearing up at the wedding. Didn't you see the way his uncle kept hugging him and patting him on the back? Anyway, Judith said they all left.'

Diane frowns. 'Hey, did you hear that?'

They stop, checking all around for any sign of movement.

'Probably a hare,' she says.

They walk on in silence, their eyes sweeping the surrounding countryside for any signs of the killer. As they walk, Sarah thinks hard, her mind flashing through the faces of each wedding guest. She immediately discounts the children. They were all under twelve. She doesn't think any of them would have got into the gun locker. Who does that leave? Judith and Broderick, the celebrant. Asha's parents. Gordon's uncle. Gordon's friends. The cousins. She didn't catch all their names. A lot of them looked alike, so they all blurred together. The person in the sea. Whoever it was in the bothy. And then, of course, her friends. If Judith's right, and they're the only ones left on the island, then it would have to be one of them: Diane, Ethan, Pete or Asha.

They reach the holiday cottages quickly and Sarah tries the door. It doesn't open.

She turns and looks at Diane. 'It's stuck.'

'Let me try.'

Diane hands her the gun and pulls on the doorknob until it comes off in her hand. She peers into the house, but there's no one in the living room.

'Now what?'

'We'll try the back.'

They walk around the house. The back has a better view than the front, overlooking some steep cliffs that lead down to the water. But Sarah is in no mood to appreciate the view. She goes to the door and this time, the knob turns easily. She's about to step inside when someone grabs her from behind.

TWENTY-ONE
SARAH

Sarah screams and lashes out.

'Ow!' says a familiar voice.

She swings round. It's Ethan. And Pete. She falls on them, telling them about Gordon. She's babbling so incoherently Diane has to repeat it.

'Gordon, dead on the beach. Looks like a bullet. Asha nowhere to be found.'

Ethan snorts. 'Yeah, good one.'

Pete's mouth twists into a half smile. 'I don't get it?'

'We're not joking,' Sarah says.

Pete grabs her by the shoulders, his eyes searching hers.

'Oh my god!'

Ethan looks from Sarah to Diane. 'What... you're serious?'

'Yes. Now can we please get inside. It's not exactly a good idea to stand out here yakking.'

Diane's voice is brittle, but she's still looking a bit green.

Pete takes the gun and leads the way.

'Maybe we should go down there,' Ethan says to Pete. 'Check it out.'

There is a voyeuristic glint to his eye. Not concern, or fear.

He's looking for a thrill. Most likely, Ethan has never seen a dead body before. He doesn't want to miss out. Or perhaps he's up for a little action. He wants to take on the murderer. Pete acts as though he hasn't spoken. Ethan tries again:

'Come on, mate. We should go down there!'

'You can do what you like,' Pete says. He sits by the door while Sarah and Diane huddle around the kitchen table.

Ethan's expression darkens. He's brave, but not brave enough to go it alone. He pulls up a chair.

'No sign of Asha at all?' he says once Sarah has explained in a little more detail.

'No.'

Dread gnaws at her heart.

'Why would anyone want to kill Gordon?' She can't help aiming this question at Ethan. It's hard not to think about his longtime crush on Asha, or that speech. He clearly didn't accept Gordon. And Ethan is nothing if not a loose cannon. But is he capable of murder?

'Where have you two been?' Diane asks, looking from Ethan to Pete.

Ethan avoids eye contact, his gaze fixed on his hands. 'You were gone so long we went looking for you, but then we heard you coming up the path, so we thought we'd make you jump. It seems so childish now.'

'Yes, it does,' Diane says. She turns to Pete. 'Could you do me a favour and check the bedrooms? Make sure no one's snuck in while we were out?'

Pete nods. He takes the gun with him.

'Do you really think someone might have got in?' Sarah asks.

'Better safe than sorry,' Diane says. She waits a beat, while Pete walks towards the bedrooms, then she leans forward. 'How certain are we that Pete is not the shooter?'

Sarah lets out a nervous laugh. 'You're kidding, right?'

Diane shakes her head. 'There are things about Pete you might not know, Sarah. I think we all need to be careful around him.'

Sarah can't take her seriously. This is Pete they're talking about. It took all his courage just to leave the house.

'What sort of things?'

Diane looks at Ethan, who gives her a small nod. 'Well, it seems he has not been entirely honest about his time in the—'

'All clear!' Pete says, striding back into the room. 'Your bedroom window was open though, Di.'

'That's how I left it.'

'Well I closed it. Best to block off all the possible routes in and out.'

'Thanks,' Diane says.

'Thanks,' Sarah echoes.

She's dying to ask Diane what she meant by her last comment, but she'll have to wait until Pete's out of earshot again. They look at each other, then at Pete and Ethan in turn. Someone knows who did this. Someone shot Gordon. And whoever it was, they might be coming for her.

She looks around the room again and studies each of them in turn. They all look stressed. Pete is drumming the counter with his fingers. Diane is still as white as a ghost. As for Ethan, he's building a fire.

He looks calm. Too calm? Diane flops down next to him. He stops what he's doing and slips his arm around her for a moment. They are comforting each other. She supposes that makes sense, but they seem very cosy with each other, all of a sudden.

She turns back to Pete. He's standing in front of the kettle, watching as it boils.

Whatever it is Diane thinks she knows, Sarah is certain that Pete, who has lived under her roof, is not a killer. He is not a threat to anyone. Except maybe himself. She has her own suspicions about why he may have taken that gun that Broderick was looking for, and it troubles her that he is holding one now. But at the same time, she feels better having someone who is trained to keep her safe.

Pete glances out at the living room, then leans in close.

'My money's on Ethan, if you really want to know. You saw him yesterday. That messed-up speech of his, and he was at it again just as we were leaving, getting in Gordon's face.'

She shakes her head. 'He might be hot-headed, but he's not a killer. Besides, he's been busy cosying up to Diane. Don't tell me you haven't noticed.'

Pete's eyes narrow. 'Yeah, because he doesn't want to look suspicious. But I see right through him. Always have.'

She opens her mouth to respond, but then Ethan steps into the room. His presence is like a cold gust of wind. They both pull back instinctively. Sarah looks out the window, as if suddenly fascinated by the view.

Ethan grabs a packet of peanuts from the cupboard and heads back to Diane.

'How do we know it wasn't Diane, for that matter?' she says. 'I mean, look at how she was planning to sabotage the wedding. What kind of friend does that?'

They both glance into the living room and back again.

'She looks pretty shaken up,' Pete says.

'Or guilty? Maybe she killed Gordon to spite Asha. Or maybe she was going for Asha and he got in the way.'

Pete shakes his head. 'I always thought her rough edges could be rubbed off, but now I'm not so sure.'

'Rough edges?'

'You know, she told me once about what she went through. With her brothers.'

'Did she?'

Sarah isn't sure what he's talking about. All she knows is that Diane grew up in a house full of boys, and that she doesn't like them very much. But it's not something she ever cared to talk about.

'They bullied her mercilessly,' Pete explains. 'They wrecked her childhood, and her parents never did anything about it. And I'm not talking your common or garden sibling teasing, I mean these boys were mean. They would punch and kick her when no one was looking. They put chillies in her food. They rubbed literal salt in her wounds. They set light to her homework. She could never have anything nice because they would steal it and break it. They were a bunch of thugs.'

'She told you all that?' Sarah is stunned. She prides herself on being a good listener. And honestly, she's a bit put out that Diane never said anything to her about all this. She and Diane were so close. Sarah always asked her about her home life, back when they lived together. And she told her all sorts of stuff about herself. She regrets that now. She probably overshared. She's not sure she likes Diane knowing quite so much about her. It feels as though she can see right into her brain.

'She told me one night when we were both drunk,' Pete says. 'She never brought it up again. I think she was embarrassed. Or maybe she doesn't remember.'

'I did notice her brothers weren't at her wedding.'

'Yeah, she'd cut them loose by then.'

'Well, I suppose that does explain a bit about why she is like she is.'

'You'd have thought she'd be nicer to Asha after all she went through.'

Sarah shakes her head. 'Victims make the worst bullies.'

'In that case, I wonder what happened to Ethan?'

'That's easy. Mummy issues.'

'I don't think I've ever met his mum.'

'Exactly.'

She slides open the drawer and pulls out a notebook and pen.

'What are you doing?'

'Making a list of everyone who was here yesterday.'

'You can't possibly remember them all.'

'There weren't that many.'

She sits for a few minutes and scribbles down all the names she can remember, and descriptions of the ones whose names she didn't catch. She counted seven couples with children, one couple without. Plus Asha's parents, Gordon's uncle and the celebrant.

'Didn't Asha mention Gordon had a rival?'

'Did she? I don't remember.'

'And what about the four of us? We must have been in bed when it happened – some time between the end of the wedding and the boat leaving early in the morning.'

But they had all been drinking. Was it possible one of them got up in the night, stole a gun and shot Gordon?

Ethan pokes his head into the kitchen again. It's like he can't bear to leave them alone. Perhaps he's paranoid they're talking about him.

'We need to go back to Judith's,' he says, leaning over Sarah's shoulder to get a look at her list.

'We've just come from there. She wasn't home.'

'We need her to help with the search for Asha. She can cover more ground in the car. Plus she knows the island better than we do. She can tell us where to look.'

'So we should break into two groups, one in the car and one on foot?'

'Isn't there a chance Asha left on the boat?' Pete says. 'They could have had a lover's tiff.'

'I doubt it,' says Ethan. 'You saw the two of them yesterday.'

'And I saw the look her dad gave him,' Pete says. 'Do you think he might have shot Gordon and sent Asha home?'

'Asha's dad has never been violent,' Diane says, 'and

besides, if he'd tried to get Asha to leave without Gordon, she'd have told him where to go.'

Everyone is nodding.

'So, back to the search,' Ethan says. 'I suggest we split into two groups. We'll cover the ground quicker that way.'

They all look at each other. Sarah eyes Diane.

'Are you all right?'

'I'm fine.'

She's not though. Sarah doesn't think she's ever seen her so pale.

'Are you sure?'

Diane lets out a puff of air. 'Actually, I think I need to lie down.'

Ethan shoots her a bemused look. 'Surely you don't want to be left on your own?'

Diane rests her head in her hands. 'I don't care. I just want it all to be over.'

'Maybe you should stay with her, Sarah,' Ethan says. 'You two have already had enough of a shock.'

Sarah shakes her head. 'No, I want to find Asha.'

'I'll stay with her,' Pete says.

Sarah bites her lip. She'd feel a lot safer if Pete came with her. But she can't say so because Ethan will get insulted. She swallows hard, thinking of all the mean things she has ever said and done to Asha. She owes her.

The others are arguing over whether they should take the gun with them or leave it for Diane and Pete to protect themselves.

Sarah leans over to Pete. 'Tell the truth,' she says in his ear, 'our lives could depend on it. Do you have another gun?'

He pulls away from her. 'No. And I wish everyone would stop asking me that.'

'Sorry,' Sarah says. 'I wish you did.'

He rewards her with a small smile.

They toss a coin and Diane wins. She and Pete get to keep the gun, while Sarah and Ethan head out empty-handed.

'Honestly, it would probably just get in the way,' Ethan says as they head out the door. 'We'll need to keep our eyes peeled though. We have to look out for each other, okay?'

Sarah nods.

'Did you check Asha's cottage?' he asks.

'Not yet.'

'Okay, well we'll stop there first.'

Oystercatcher cottage is much the same as Red-throated Diver. The living room is in the same place, and there are four bedrooms, though Asha and Gordon used only one.

Under different circumstances, Sarah might find it funny that Asha's cottage is as untidy as her bedroom used to be. The sheets are half on, half off the bed as if she couldn't decide what to do with them. Her duvet is on the floor, and her make-up clutters the sink, little jars of cream, mascara and eyelash curlers scattered all over the place. One of her wedding dresses hangs in the wardrobe, but there is no sign of the other, and as she walks into the kitchen, she notices an electric toothbrush plugged into the wall.

Ethan draws a breath. 'This confirms it. She never left.'

'But why would the boat leave without her and Gordon? It was their wedding. They were literally the most important guests.'

'Maybe they failed to turn up and the crew didn't have time to wait. They might have other commitments.'

'But no one even asked us if we'd seen them. It's so strange.'

'Has it occurred to you that Asha might have shot Gordon?' Ethan says. 'If she did, then she could have gone down to the boat and told them not to wait for her and Gordon.'

'Don't be ridiculous. Asha wouldn't shoot Gordon.'

'You saw her. She's a terrible shot. Perhaps she and Gordon borrowed a gun to practise with and then she shot him by accident. Of course she wouldn't come clean. Not perfect Asha.'

'Come off it! Why would they be hunting on their wedding night?'

'They had had a lot to drink. It might have seemed like a good idea.'

'So what, you think no one would notice if she caught the boat off the island without him?'

'Or she might still be here, hiding out.'

'Just no. This is Asha we're talking about.'

They check the cottages where the other guests stayed, but they are all empty. The beds have been stripped, and the bedding lies in neat piles on the mattresses.

'I think we can safely assume everyone else left,' Sarah says.

'We don't know for sure, though, do we? It could be one of them. Gordon's mad uncle, perhaps?'

'He didn't strike me as the least bit mad,' Sarah says. 'And a lot of people are a bit odd or eccentric. It doesn't make them killers.'

'Right, enough yakking. We've got to get going,' Ethan says. 'Grab anything that looks like it might be useful.'

'Like what?'

'I don't know. Any kind of weapon. I already grabbed a kitchen knife.'

Sarah finds a lighter and a bottle of water in the last cottage. She shows them to Ethan.

'Yeah, really useful,' he says.

She can't tell if he's being serious or sarcastic.

'Right, we'd better get a move on. I'll go in front, you can walk behind. Keep your eyes open at all times. Remember, the killer could be literally anyone. Until we know for sure, assume everyone's a suspect.'

Any of us, you mean, she thinks. They're the only ones on the island, aren't they?

'I went up to the lighthouse earlier, and I saw someone in the sea. I thought they were swimming but now I'm not so sure. They might have been... floating.'

He looks startled. 'You think it was Asha?'

'I really don't know. Can we... can we just walk together?'

'It's better to go single file at this point.'

As they approach the caretakers' cottage, Ethan finally agrees that they can walk side by side, like normal human beings. And when he does, he looks at her and says: 'I don't know if you know this, but Diane's... well, she's vulnerable at the moment.'

'Why?'

'There's some stuff going on at home.'

'Oh.' Sarah raises an eyebrow, but Ethan doesn't elaborate any further. Sarah is beginning to wonder if she knows Diane at all. First, Pete with his insights into her childhood and now Ethan.

'If you know anything...' she says.

'It's between her and Cameron,' he says simply.

She nods and they continue. Still, it's frustrating. Why is everyone being so coy? They all used to be such gossips. Perhaps he's afraid of what Diane would say if she found out he'd been talking about her behind her back.

TWENTY-TWO

Some might think this all started with the posting of the invitations, but when I think back, the events of this week began many years ago. When we all moved into that house together. There were never five people so poorly suited to living together. Alone, we might have been diluted by other, normal people. But together, we brought out the worst in each other. We urged each other on, encouraging each other in our deepest, darkest thoughts. One bad deed inevitably led to another. It's been a chain reaction through the years. We've pushed and pulled against each other, stuck together like a box of magnets.

We're attracted to each other. Attracted to trouble.

And now, here we all are, trapped together on Haarlorn.

Nobody's leaving until we settle this once and for all.

We can't all be alphas.

Some have to follow.

And this island isn't big enough for the five of us.

TWENTY-THREE
SARAH

Three Months Earlier, Glasgow

Sarah looks at the red-brick building. It has a large cheery sign that reads: *Brighter Tomorrow Counselling*. It feels absurdly optimistic given the circumstances.

'We're here,' she says, keeping her voice steady.

Pete doesn't move. He stares straight ahead, jaw tight, hands clamped around his knees like he's bracing for an invisible blow.

She turns to face him. 'Do you want me to come in with you?'

Silence.

'You said you'd give it a try. Just one session.'

His gaze shifts to her for a moment, then flickers back to the windscreen.

'If you won't do it for yourself, then do it for me.'

'What's the point?' he mutters, his voice so low it nearly vanishes into the hum of distant traffic.

She closes her eyes and counts to three. When she speaks, her voice is deliberate and measured. 'The point is you need help. You haven't left the house in weeks. It's not healthy. You need to get back out into the real world.'

'I talk to you,' he says flatly.

'But I'm not a counsellor. You need someone trained to help you.'

'I can't.'

'You *can*.' The words come out sharper than she intends, but she doesn't backpedal. She softens her tone, trying to coax him. 'You just have to open the door and go in. That's it.'

'I can't,' he says again, his voice cracking.

'Fine,' she says, throwing her hands up. 'I'm going to talk to them. If you've got any guts left, you'll come with me.'

She shoves the door open, stepping out into the cold. The slam echoes in the quiet street as she stands there, arms crossed, glaring at the building.

Pete doesn't follow.

She goes inside and explains to the receptionist what has happened. She doesn't seem remotely surprised. Her calm tone is infuriating.

'You could try again next week,' she suggests.

Sarah doesn't want to try again next week.

'Can't someone come out and talk to him?'

'It's important we respect his boundaries,' she says with a patronising smile. 'You can't counsel someone who doesn't trust you.'

'You can't counsel him at all if he doesn't get out of the bloody car!'

The receptionist shakes her head. 'Why don't you come in and sit? Take a few minutes to collect yourself before you get back behind the wheel.'

'I'm all right, thanks.'

Sarah already knows they won't be coming back here next week. She's way too angry.

. . .

The drive back is silent, the weight of it all settling heavily between them. Sarah's thoughts race. She has half a mind to turn Pete out and tell him to find somewhere else to stay, but she's not a monster. She knows it's not his fault. It's just... so infuriating.

She throws the car haphazardly into a space on the road outside her flat. The silence is oppressive as they climb out of the car. The tension follows them as she unlocks the front door and steps inside the flat.

There's a purple envelope on the mat. The handwriting is neat and flowery and it's addressed to both of them, as though they're a couple. She picks it up and tears into it, while Pete marches straight to the kitchen to flick on the kettle.

'It's from Asha,' she tells him, scanning the card.

'How is she? I haven't spoken to her in ages.'

'She's fine. More than fine... It's a wedding invitation.'

He looks over at her, a flicker of interest in his eyes.

'She's getting married in Orkney.'

For the first time in days, he actually looks animated, his face softening, his eyes bright.

Sarah tilts her head, watching him.

'If I buy you a ticket, will you come?'

He nods and breaks into a smile. 'I'd love to.'

She smiles back. It's the first real smile she's managed all afternoon. It feels like a small victory. She is finally making a breakthrough.

Thank you, Asha, she thinks.

She has no idea what to expect from a week away with her old housemates, but if it means getting Pete back into the world again, then it will be worth it.

TWENTY-FOUR
SARAH

When Sarah and Ethan arrive at Judith's, her car is still not there.

'Something's wrong,' Sarah says. 'She can't have been feeding the sheep all this time.'

'No, I'm beginning to get a bad feeling about this,' Ethan agrees. 'Either something has happened to her, or she's the shooter.'

Sarah shakes her head. 'She's not the shooter.'

'Why not? She's a crack shot with a gun.'

'Because I've watched enough true crime programmes to know women rarely kill, and older ladies even less so.'

'She is quite an odd one though, isn't she? Living out here on this desolate island.'

'What were we just saying? Being odd doesn't make a person a criminal.'

Ethan walks across the garden, and it takes Sarah a minute to realise what he's doing. He's heading towards the gun locker. He stops in front of it and tries the door. It's locked. Sarah is glad. The last thing they need is a free-for-all.

'Come on, let's go,' she says. She feels uncomfortable

being here, in this garden. It's too out in the open. A row of sparrows line the fence. They watch with dark, unblinking eyes.

'Wait a minute,' Ethan says. He punches in a four-digit combination.

'What the hell?'

'I was paying attention when Broderick took us hunting: 1468. That's the combination.'

She swallows hard as the door swings open. If he knows the combination, then he could have taken the gun that killed Gordon. But if he took it, wouldn't he hide this from her? He's being so bold about it. So typically Ethan that she has no idea what to think.

They both stare at the great armoury of guns. There are at least a dozen, and spaces for four more. Sarah hopes there aren't that many missing.

Ethan takes out two rifles. 'Just in case,' he says.

He hands one to her. She looks at it uncertainly, while he fills his pockets with ammunition.

'Where shall we go next?' she asks.

'If you can bear it, I think we should go back to where you found Gordon. Asha's most likely hiding somewhere near there. She wouldn't want to leave him, would she?'

'Okay,' she agrees, but she's not looking forward to the prospect of seeing Gordon's corpse again. 'It's not a pretty sight, I warn you.'

'I'll try not to look.'

They walk down to the beach. They don't get too close to the body, but the smell wafts towards them, and Sarah swats away the flies.

'Where would you go, if you were Asha?'

'I'd be hiding behind the rocks,' Ethan says. 'Think about it. They're walking along all lovey-dovey when someone starts shooting. Gordon gets shot. And she's... what? In shock, I suppose? But why didn't she come to us? That's what I don't understand.'

'She could be injured. Or maybe she doesn't know who to trust.'

'So you think it was one of us?'

'I'm not ruling anything out.'

They walk a long way, climbing from rock to rock. The boulders are so smooth, it's almost as if they were built for this exact purpose. They travel as far as the tide allows, then they have to turn back. There is a series of boulders that lead up onto the coast path. Ethan is already scrambling up them. Sarah struggles to keep up. Her foot slips and she makes the mistake of glancing down. It seems like a big drop. She sucks in a breath and finds a new foothold. She has to keep going.

For Asha.

Ethan is already striding ahead as she reaches the top. As she drags herself to her feet, she sees something glinting between the rocks. She pulls it out and finds a small silver compact. She pops it open. There is a little sand inside and the mirror has a crack in it, but it's the kind of thing Asha would like and she has an overwhelming sense that it belongs to her.

And it gives her hope that Asha is still alive, Asha has been up here. Hiding. Frightened.

She catches up with Ethan.

'Look what I found. Do you think it could be Asha's?'

He scarcely even looks at it.

'It could belong to anyone. It might have just washed up on the beach.'

She feels a twinge of annoyance. It belongs to Asha, she knows it does.

They keep on walking, staying on the coast path as they

make their way around to the other side of the island. After a mile or so, Sarah gets a stitch in her side.

'I really need a break,' she gasps, stopping to catch her breath. She rests with her hands on her knees and lets the salty air fill her lungs.

Ethan glances over his shoulder. 'I'm not sure this is the best place to stop. It's a bit out in the open.'

Sarah glances around, looking at the steep cliffs on one side and the endless expanse of the North Sea on the other. She really does need to rest, and it has been so quiet the whole time they've been out here. A part of her wonders if the shooter might have left the island, but she doesn't voice this to Ethan. She's sick of him disagreeing with everything she says.

Once she's got her breath back they continue on. She feels nervous as they approach the bothy. She hangs back as Ethan strides ahead and sticks his head inside.

'No one here,' he calls.

She follows him inside.

The hearth is cool and everything is just as she and Diane left it. The blanket and the baked bean can. It reminds her of a still-life class she took once, with ordinary items placed around a room for her to draw.

'Try to imagine the person these things belong to,' the teacher had said, as they began to sketch. 'Try to imagine what he or she was thinking as they used these objects, what kind of person they are.'

Sarah takes a closer look, trying to spot something she might have missed last time. She lifts the blanket and finds the wood beneath rotten and damp. Something flutters to the floor. She bends down to pick it up. It is a pair of knickers. They look like the same ones Ethan threw at Gordon at the wedding. For some reason, she doesn't say anything to Ethan. She puts the blanket back as she found it and stuffs the knickers underneath.

He turns and looks at her. 'The intruder might come back

here. If we sit here nice and quiet, we could find out who they are.'

Sarah swallows hard. Sweat pools at the back of her neck.

'I don't think I want to do that.'

She has to get out.

She bursts out into the light, her heart pumping as she leans against the bothy wall.

'Are you all right?' Ethan asks, stepping out after her.

'Shh!'

She freezes in place. Something is amiss. They both listen. There is a rustling in the bushes.

'It's just a bird.'

He's right. A pair of chaffinches take flight, their wings beating against the air in a fast rhythm. Everything is still again. Everything but Sarah's heart. She isn't built for this. She can't bear it.

They keep on walking, Ethan leading the way, until they come to a place where the coast road stops abruptly. They find themselves at the top of the cliffs, where the waves slam into the rocks below with a relentless, bone-rattling force, the impact sending up a froth of white spray. The roar is deafening, a constant assault of water against stone, as if the sea is trying to tear the land apart. The wind whips at them, carrying the salty sting of the surf, making the edge feel closer, the drop more treacherous.

'We must have taken a wrong turn somewhere,' Sarah shouts, because the coast road is supposed to take them all around the island, and this is clearly a dead end.

'I don't think so,' Ethan yells back, pushing out his chin.

That's right, Ethan hates to be corrected.

'Well, there's no more path this way,' she says in a more conciliatory manner.

'There should be a gun emplacement, left from the Second World War.'

'What's a gun emplacement?'

He shoots her a look. 'You know, a big reinforced concrete structure built into the ground for coastal defence. There's supposed to be one at the end of this path.'

'How do you know that?'

'I saw it on the map.'

'There's a map?' This is the first Sarah has heard of it.

He seems irritated by her question.

'I found one online before we set off. But the gun emplacement is supposed to be up here, looking down at the sea. I was just thinking it would make a great place to hide out. More hidden than the bothy.'

He takes another look around. 'Maybe it is here, and we can't see it because it's completely overgrown.'

Sarah doesn't like that thought at all. If he is right, then the shooter, whoever they are, could be pointing a gun at them right now.

'I don't feel safe here, I want to get going.'

'Just a minute. I want to see if we can locate it.'

Sarah bites back her anger. Typical Ethan. He doesn't care what she thinks at all.

'Did you go out again after we got back from the wedding?' she asks.

He squints at her. 'What do you mean?'

'I mean, did you go and see Asha? Maybe you popped next door to say good night to them or something?'

'Why would I do that, on their wedding night?'

She swallows. 'Well this morning, you were wearing Asha's veil. Where did you find it?'

His brow furrows, and he looks down at the sharp drop into the sea below.

'I honestly have no idea.'

'Well, what's the last thing you remember?'

'After we sorted out your bed for you, Diane and I had one more nightcap.'

'It looked like a hell of a lot more than one.'

He shakes his head. 'It probably was, but I don't remember.'

They both stare down at the sea for a moment, and then Sarah becomes aware of a distant alarm noise.

'Can you hear that?' she asks.

Ethan nods.

They turn and hurry across the muddy grass, until they find themselves back on the main road. Sarah looks around, trying to locate the source of the noise. And there it is.

Judith's car.

It is parked at a strange angle, the front end sticking out of the bushes.

They venture closer. Judith is slumped over the steering wheel, and there is a bullet hole through the front windscreen.

TWENTY-FIVE
SARAH

Sarah's hands tremble as she grasps the door handle and pulls. For a moment, the door sticks, and then Judith's lifeless body slumps towards her, knocking into her thighs. She stumbles back, heart hammering as Judith pitches sideways, her head lolling unnaturally against the seat. Strands of tangled hair cling to her face. Her seatbelt dangles loose at her side. There is a faint purplish bruise across her cheek. Sarah presses two fingers to her neck, searching for a pulse. For a moment, she almost convinces herself there's something there, a slight flutter, a trace. But no. She's mistaken.

She takes her wrist, tries again just to be sure. Her skin is cool, and she holds her breath as she waits, but there is definitely no pulse. She holds Judith's wrist a moment longer, wishing there were something she could do. Judith is wearing a delicate gold bracelet. It's odd to find it on such a stern, practical woman. It looks like real gold too. Perhaps that was why she had it on her. To safeguard it from whoever did this.

She breathes heavily, waiting for her slight dizziness to pass. She feels her own pulse thundering in her ears. If only she could have found her sooner, maybe Judith could have told her who did this. All day she's been one step behind and it's terrifying. Her brain scrambles to make sense of it. She doesn't know how long Judith has been here, but she guesses it's only been an hour or two. Maybe even less.

She swallows hard, trying to take in the details. The passenger seat contains a carrier bag of mushy apples. A few have rolled onto the floor. She glances at the back seat but it appears empty. Her mind is spinning. She so wanted to believe that Gordon's killer had fled the island, and yet here's another body. Whoever did this must still be here. She flicks through the possibilities. Maybe Broderick has returned. Could he have done this? He didn't seem to like any of them very much. But Judith, why would he kill her? Unless she saw something she shouldn't have. Or could it have been the intruder? The person in the bothy? The swimmer in the sea. Asha. Pete. Diane. Ethan.

What is Ethan doing?

She leaves Judith and walks around the side of the car to see what he's up to. He's popped the boot open and he's peering inside, having a good rummage around in there.

'What are you looking for?'

He jumps at her words and hits his head on the lid of the boot.

He glares at her, like it's her fault.

'Just taking a look.'

She regards him coolly and wonders what he could be searching for. A first aid kit, perhaps? A flare to alert passing ships? Or something more nefarious. A knife, maybe? More weapons?

Ethan runs his hand through his hair. His face is red and, all at once, he looks like a teenager again. Defensive, embarrassed. Not wanting to admit what he's feeling. His hands are empty as far as she can tell, and it occurs to her that he just wanted to avoid looking at the body. She wouldn't blame him if that's the case. It is pretty grisly.

She gets a proper look in the boot. All she sees are fishing supplies and animal feed, but no gun, and Sarah is fairly certain that under the same circumstances, she would be armed.

Ethan shuts the boot and looks at her.

'Right. We'll have to move her.'

'What?'

'The car's no good to her now, is it? We might as well take it.'

Sarah hesitates. And here she was, thinking he was squeamish.

'Do we have to? It seems so... disrespectful.'

'We need to find Asha,' he reminds her. 'She could be lying by the side of the road somewhere, bleeding out.'

She closes her eyes for a moment.

'All right.' She walks back round to the front and takes a deep breath, then grabs hold of Judith's shoulders. Ethan walks around to the passenger side and climbs across the seat to get hold of her legs.

Between the two of them, they manage to pull her all the way out. They lie her down on the ground and stare at her for a moment.

'Are you all right?' Ethan asks, his voice a little wobbly.

'Yeah, you?'

'Not really.'

He takes one last look and climbs into the car, settling himself behind the wheel. The keys are still in the ignition.

'Have you ever driven one of these things before?' Sarah asks.

'Nope.'

She sits patiently beside him while he gets used to the controls, but once he gets going, he puts his foot down. He speeds down the road, taking the corner a little too wide.

Sarah looks at him with alarm.

'You're driving too fast. We need to look for Asha.'

He slows a little, and they make a loop all the way around the island. Sarah searches the road with her eyes but there is no sign of anyone.

Asha is nowhere to be seen.

When they arrive back at the holiday cottage, Pete and Diane are at the window.

'Why are you driving Judith's car?' Diane shouts.

Ethan avoids her gaze, his shoulders slumping slightly as he lets out a slow breath. 'Judith is dead,' he says. 'We thought we might as well.'

'Shit!'

Diane lets them inside, and Pete pours them all a drink. Sarah has no idea what it is, but she doesn't ask. She takes a gulp and relishes the feeling of the alcohol burning her throat. She doesn't normally drink anything stronger than wine but today is different. Today she needs it.

Diane watches her closely. 'Do you want another?'

'No thanks. I'm going to take a shower.'

'Good idea, you look exhausted.'

Sarah nods. All at once, she can't bear the thought that she has touched a dead body. She imagines all the germs, all the flies and maggots, and feels desperate to scrub it off her skin. She fears all that death is catching.

The shower is a weak, dribbly affair. She has to hold it at a certain angle to get even a trickle of water. She smothers shampoo into her scalp and tries not to see the faces of Gordon and Judith when she closes her eyes.

Is it bad she didn't like Judith? She's still upset that she's dead. No one's life should end like that. It seems so violent and dramatic. So unnecessary. What could anyone possibly gain from it?

The water comes on in a big spurt and she washes the shampoo out vigorously. It returns to a trickle and she waits impatiently for more. She is so tired and confused. She just can't get her head around it all.

The shower slows to a mere drip and she groans in exasperation, then reaches for a towel. The one next to hers has a smudge of blood on it. It's probably Diane's. She has that wound on her hand. Or she could be on her period. But what if it's not hers?

What if it's Ethan's?

TWENTY-SIX
SARAH

Two Weeks Earlier, Glasgow

Sarah struggles with the driver's side door of her car, jiggling the key and pushing hard to get it to lock. After a few minutes, she gives up with a huff of frustration. Glancing up and down the street, she checks if anyone's watching. It's a quiet neighbourhood, but she imagines thieves eyeing her every move. She leaves the car unlocked and walks towards her flat. She'll ask Pete to look at it. He'll know what to do.

As she walks up the path to her door, she hears the creak of the gate and soft footsteps close behind, matching her rhythm. Her back stiffens, and she turns to see who it is. Relief washes over her when she spots a young woman, maybe ten years younger than herself. With her long black hair and full lips, she reminds her of someone.

'Sarah! Sarah, isn't it?'

'Yes. Do I know you?'

'I'm Charmaine Wallington.'

Sarah arches an eyebrow. 'Ethan's girlfriend, right?'

Charmaine licks her lips nervously. 'Listen, this is a bit awkward, but can I come in for a minute?'

Sarah notices Charmaine's hands are shaking. 'Of course. You look like you could use a cup of tea.'

'Thank you so much.' Charmaine wipes a tear from her eyes and follows Sarah inside.

'Pete, we've got a visitor,' Sarah calls out as she enters the flat. She is relieved to see Pete fully dressed and presentable. Some days when she gets home, he's still in his dressing gown, and he can go days without washing or changing. His beard is starting to grow out again, as if he's slipping back into his homeless persona.

'This is Ethan's girlfriend, Charmaine,' she says to Pete, then turns to Charmaine. 'Pete's another former housemate.'

'So, you know Ethan too?' Charmaine asks.

Pete nods. 'I'll put the kettle on, shall I?'

'Thanks,' Sarah says.

She leads Charmaine into the living room and moves a pile of laundry off the sofa so they can sit down.

Charmaine takes a seat, wringing her hands like she's about to break bad news. Sarah racks her brain, trying to figure out what she could possibly want. If Ethan were ill, wouldn't she go to his mum? Or maybe it's something else. Maybe Ethan's asked her to come here for a favour. But what could he possibly need? She hopes to God it isn't money, or a kidney.

'So, what's this about? Is Ethan... okay?' Sarah asks.

Charmaine rests her head in her hands. 'This is so awkward. I hope you don't mind me turning up like this, but I knew you lived nearby, and I thought maybe—'

Pete walks in with the tea tray and sets it on the table. There's a lull in the conversation as he places steaming mugs in front of them and opens a pack of teacakes.

'You were saying?' Sarah prompts gently.

'I think... it's easiest if I show you.' Charmaine swallows

hard and undoes the top three buttons of her cardigan, revealing ugly yellow bruising on her collarbone. Sarah exchanges a glance with Pete. His face tightens, his gaze darting to the untouched tea tray before settling back on Charmaine.

'Are you saying Ethan did that?'

Charmaine nods. 'He's... never done anything like that before, but what I want to know is, what was he like when you lived with him? Was he, you know, stable? Or did he throw his weight around?'

Sarah bites her lip, leaning back in her chair, searching for the safest answer. 'I mean, he can be a bit hot-headed, but I never had any... serious concerns about him.'

Pete coughs. 'What about that time he put his fist through the garden shed?'

'Oh no, he was just larking about, wasn't he?' Sarah says.

'I'm not so sure. It was right after an argument with Diane. He doesn't like losing, and she kept winding him up. Next thing we knew, he had his fist stuck in the shed.'

'He laughed about it,' Sarah points out. 'He saw the funny side.'

'So you didn't have any problems with him yourself, Pete?' Charmaine asks.

'Me?' Pete sits up straighter. 'No, never.' He waves his hand in the air, dismissing the idea.

His foot jigs against the table. Sarah shifts in her chair.

'What about that Belgian exchange student he went out with?' Charmaine says.

'She went back to Belgium.'

'She went back early. He never said why.'

Sarah shakes her head. 'I really don't remember.'

Pete sighs and looks at Charmaine. 'I'm sorry, I'm not sure we're going to be of much help to you.'

The tea sits on the tray, getting colder by the minute, but no one so much as glances at it.

Charmaine draws a breath. 'I heard there was an... incident with one of his housemates? Perhaps it was the other one, what's her name, Asha?'

Asha! That's who she reminds her of. Or a young Asha, at least. The way she looked back at uni. All long glossy hair and dewy cheeks.

Pete shakes his head. 'I don't think she'll have anything to add.'

'But if I can just speak to her?'

'She'll just say the same as us. Ethan's our friend.'

Charmaine looks at her sharply. 'That's not what I heard.'

Pete shakes his head. 'Look, I don't know where you're getting your facts from, but Asha's getting married soon. I hardly think she'd invite Ethan to the wedding if she was scared of him.'

'But...'

Sarah looks down at her hands. 'Why are you asking this, Charmaine? If you're having trouble with him, then really, you're better off talking to him, rather than digging around in his past.'

'I've left him,' Charmaine says. 'I'm staying with a friend now, but she made me go to the police. They arrested him.'

'They did?' Sarah is shocked to hear this. Surely, smooth-talking Ethan could talk his way out of anything.

'They think I might have a court case, but it would really help if I had a bit more evidence. Like a witness statement from his old housemates, explaining what he can be like. I'm not asking any of you to lie. I just want to get to the truth.'

Sarah works her jaw. All at once, she wants to get Charmaine out of there.

'Do you really want to put yourself through that? You've already left him. Why don't you get on with your life?'

'Because I need to know he's going to leave me alone, and

besides, there could be others. Men like Ethan think the world owes them. They never learn.'

'He's our friend,' Sarah says firmly. 'I'm really sorry you've had a bad time, but I really think this is a one-off. If I were you, I would try to move on.'

Charmaine rises to her feet and takes out a piece of paper. She scribbles something down and hands it to Sarah. 'This is my number. Maybe you want to have a think about it, both of you.'

Sarah takes the piece of paper and ushers Charmaine to the door. She watches as she walks up the path and thinks about calling her back, but she knows she'd only make things worse. Charmaine is better off out of it, out of all their lives. She doesn't need the drama, and God knows Pete doesn't. What's in the past is in the past.

She looks down at the piece of paper. Charmaine has such beautiful handwriting. She sighs and balls it up in her fist.

'It's a bit chilly in here,' she says to Pete, when she heads back inside, 'maybe you could start a fire?'

TWENTY-SEVEN

I'm in the bothy when Judith's car approaches. I thought she might work out something was sus when I told Broderick the honeymooners would be staying on instead of getting the boat with the others. He accepted the change of plans without a word, but I imagine she would have had questions. She's not stupid. And of course she has an escape route. You'd have to when you share a confined space with a bunch of strangers. People can be so unpredictable. You think you know them, and then, out of nowhere – bang! They do something that makes your head explode.

Judith is fiercely independent. She's not the least bit interested in anything anyone has to say. She might not have been worried when she heard someone had been using the bothy, but Gordon's body is another story. It's got her running scared.

I know exactly where she's going, too. There's a little dinghy hidden just below the rocks. And she'll know an easy path down the cliff. She's probably planning to head across to the mainland. And she'll almost certainly tell the police.

Honestly, I have no real beef with the woman. But she's got

this way of looking at me, like she's peeling back the layers of my skin and seeing all the ugly secrets underneath.

And I can't let that stand.

I make my way down to the shore and release the dinghy. I give it a wave as it rides off into the waves. It's impressive how quickly it moves, as if it can't get away fast enough. Once I'm sure it's gone, I walk back up the beach and return to the bothy to dry off. I'm just about to leave when I hear the sound of her car.

I rush outside, armed with the gun I stole from her. I flash her a smile and I bet her pathetic life flashes before her eyes as I squeeze the trigger.

Her car swerves. The tyres screech as she veers off the road, slamming into a hedge with a bone-jarring crunch.

And now she's just another casualty, another name in the island's long, bitter history of those who couldn't escape.

TWENTY-EIGHT
SARAH

When Sarah emerges from the shower, there is food on the table – chips, peas and fishfingers. She has given up fish, but her vegetarianism doesn't seem important right now. She is just grateful to whoever threw all this together. She didn't even know she was hungry, but now she eats ravenously.

Ethan and Pete both have guns next to them on the table, a constant reminder of the danger they all face. Sarah is sick of the sight of the guns. There is too much scope for accidents, especially now that everyone is drinking again.

She studies Ethan from across the table, looking for the little sparks of temper as he spars with Diane. She notes every twitch of his brow, and the way the muscles tighten in his jaw. She remembers now, how she used to make herself scarce whenever it started, like a child shielding herself from her parents' rows.

Diane is still a little pale. She hasn't got over the shock of seeing Gordon. That doesn't stop her arguing though. She and Ethan debate what they should do tonight. Clearly they can't all go to sleep with a killer on the loose.

'It makes sense for us to sleep two at a time,' Diane says.

Two people to watch each other, Sarah thinks.

Ethan shakes his head. 'We only need one person to keep watch. The killer will have to sleep too, remember.'

Sarah tilts her head. What if the one person to stay awake is the killer? What then?

'Better still, we could go out looking for them in the dark,' he is saying. 'They'll have to sleep somewhere. We could go and check out the bothy, and if they aren't there, we could try to find the gun emplacement.'

'We shouldn't go out in the dark,' Sarah says.

Ethan looks at her like she's an insect under his foot. 'It won't be that dark.'

'I don't think we should go looking for trouble,' Pete says. Sarah glances over at him. It's rare for him to get involved. 'And I thought we were only trying to find Asha?'

Ethan shoots a glance at him, then continues looking at Diane, as if they are the only two in this conversation.

'If I was the killer, I would take over Judith's place,' Diane says. 'Or one of the cottages. Why rough it outside when you can sleep in style?'

'Yes, we should check the cottages again,' Sarah says. She hates the thought that the killer could be so close.

Ethan turns and looks at her. His expression pierces right through her skull.

'Do you want to do that, Sarah? Or do you want one of us to do it?'

It's not pleasant, the way he says this. It's accusatory. He's saying that she's a coward, willing to sacrifice her friends to save herself.

'I'll do it,' Diane says. 'Sarah's already done enough for one day.'

Sarah nods gratefully. 'Take a gun with you,' she advises.

'Right, and while you're doing that I'm going to go and get firewood,' Ethan says.

Sarah lets out a breath. Ethan is no longer looking at her,

but she is hyperaware of his presence. He's scary, the way he can turn on you in an instant, then return to his charming self the very next moment.

She should have done more to help Charmaine, she thinks. She thought she was protecting a friend, but what kind of a friend needs protecting from domestic abuse allegations? She wonders if Charmaine tracked down Asha. And if so, did Asha agree to help her? That would give him a motive, wouldn't it? Maybe he tried to shoot her but Gordon got in the way.

Ethan is so sure of himself, even under the current circumstances. Where does all that confidence come from? Was he born with it, or did it grow inside him? At the same time the nagging doubts were growing inside her, pulling her down from within.

Everyone thinks Pete is the weird one, but Pete she understands. Ethan's the one who confuses her. Diane used to call him the wild card. Sarah should have thought about it more deeply, but it was so much more convenient to ignore it. Who'd want to rattle that cage?

Pete returns to the back door, supposedly looking out for the shooter, but she rather wonders if he's just looking out. It's quite a view from there. They are so close to the cliffs. A few more years and this whole cottage will go over and crumble into the sea.

There is a peace about him this week, since all the chaos started. He must be afraid; they all are. And yet she knows a part of him would welcome death. If he were to get hit right now, she wouldn't be surprised if he had a smile on his face. He'd be glad it was finally over.

She wants to hug him, but she's afraid he'd take it the wrong way. She really does care about him, deep down. Not in a romantic sense, but more like a brother.

She goes to him now. 'Pete?' she says in a low voice.
'Yeah?'

'Do you think Ethan could be the shooter?'

'What?'

'He memorised the combination to the gun locker. Why would he do that?'

Pete darts a glance at her. 'Why would he shoot Judith?'

'I don't know. Maybe he finally snapped.'

Pete is silent. Sarah can almost see what's going on inside his head. He's running through reasons it can't be Ethan.

'He wouldn't do that.'

'He's got that court case coming up. He might feel he has nothing to lose.'

'Nah, he'll get off with a slap on the wrist. Men like Ethan always do. Besides, if he was going to kill anyone, it would be Charmaine. He wouldn't just... go on a rampage.'

'How can you be so sure?'

She swallows. Out of the five of them, she is the keeper of secrets. She has dirt on each one of her former housemates. If the killer is one of them, then they should be coming after her.

'Ethan is hot-headed,' Pete says. 'But taking the gun shows planning. Gordon's death was premeditated. And the boat left without him. Someone was calm enough to head down there and tell them to leave. Otherwise, people would have been looking for him.'

Sarah nods slowly. But if not Ethan, then who?

TWENTY-NINE

SARAH

2013, Aberdeen

'I hate Valentine's Day,' Asha says. 'It's nothing but a cruel reminder of my eternal solitude.'

'Oh, shut up,' Diane replies. 'I seem to remember last year you got three bunches of roses, and a box of chocolates.'

Asha's face lights up a little, then falls again. 'But none of them were from men I fancied. Two of them were total creeps on my course. It was so bloody awkward taking lectures with them afterwards.'

'My heart bleeds,' Diane says. 'But yeah, I think we can all agree Valentine's Day sucks.'

'We can stay in and drink,' Sarah suggests. 'Pete too if he wants.'

Asha laughs. 'No, he'll be out clubbing, dancing on his own.'

Because that's exactly what Pete does. For all his impressive dance moves, he never seems to meet anyone when he goes out. He's too wrapped up in the music. He doesn't even make eye contact half the time. He enjoys it, though. Perhaps that's all that matters.

'I keep telling him, he should go on *Britain's Got Talent*,' Sarah says.

Diane's eyes light up. 'Great idea. We could go and watch. It would be a laugh.'

Asha warms to the idea. 'We might get to meet some celebrities.'

'He could become famous,' Sarah says. 'Then he could get us into VIP parties.'

'We might get photographed with him.' Asha's eyes are sparkling.

'You might,' Sarah says drolly. She can imagine it too, Asha getting in on the act. She's no dancer, but people are always fawning over her. She has that star appeal.

Asha heads to her room, and Diane leans towards Sarah.

'Do we really want to spend Valentine's with Asha? That's even more depressing than having no love life.'

Sarah shrugs. 'She lives here too.'

'Yeah, and she never lets us forget it.' Diane waves her arm around. There's evidence of Asha everywhere. Her pink jacket is slung over the back of a chair, her nail varnishes sit on the table, and her shoes are piled up along the wall.

'I bet she's going to get more flowers,' Diane says.

'She probably sends them to herself. I wouldn't put it past her,' Sarah replies, but she also sees the way men look at Asha. They fall for her, hook, line and sinker. It's perfectly plausible that there really are that many men lusting after her.

'What if we started a rumour,' Diane says.

'What sort of rumour?'

'We could say she has an STI.'

Sarah gasps. 'God, Di. Remind me never to get on the wrong side of you.'

Diane laughs. 'You can be so gullible! I was just joking, obviously. But I do like the idea of an anti-Valentine night. It'll be fun.'

'Is it too early to open the wine?'

'It's never too early.'

Diane gets up and starts rooting around for wine glasses, while Sarah sits at the table, wondering if Diane was in fact joking, because the truth is you never can tell with her.

On Valentine's Day, Ethan brings his new girlfriend, Celeste, back to the house after taking her out for a fancy dinner at a French restaurant. The date is going well. Celeste is smiling and relaxed, clearly having a good time. As for Ethan, he looks a bit too pleased with himself.

Sarah, Diane and Asha are all at home as predicted, and it's late, but no one wants to go to bed. They've been drinking, and they're all a bit morose, but then Pete comes back from the club, all pumped up.

Sarah puts on some music. Pete's body begins to move and contort in ways that seem impossible. They all watch. Celeste looks like she's been hypnotised. She can't take her eyes off him.

'Hey, why don't we go to my room?' Ethan murmurs in her ear.

'In a bit,' she says, still watching Pete.

After a few minutes, Ethan moves closer to Pete and waits for the perfect moment, then sticks out his leg. Pete crashes to the ground with a sickening thud. He screams in pain.

'Come on, get up!' Ethan says.

Pete writhes in agony.

Sarah rushes over to him. 'Where does it hurt?'

'My back.'

'Stop making such a fuss,' Ethan hisses.

Asha's eyes blaze with anger as she points accusingly at him.

'You can shut up, Ethan. This is all your fault. I saw what you did.'

'I didn't do anything!' Ethan rages. 'It's not my fault if he's a clumsy bugger.'

'I saw you,' Asha repeats.

Pete reaches for Sarah and holds her hand so tight she winces.

'You'll be okay, we're going to get you to the hospital,' she says.

No one notices until later that Celeste has scuttled off into the night.

There's a long, tense wait for the ambulance, during which Ethan glares at Asha in such a way that makes everyone nervous.

By the time the ambulance comes, Sarah has dosed Pete with painkillers but he's still in agony. They stand on the steps and watch as he's whisked off to hospital.

'He should sue you,' Asha tells Ethan as the ambulance heads off into the night.

'Come here and say that,' he challenges.

She squares up to him, but Ethan is taller. They stand chin to chin, glaring at each other, until Ethan leans forward and kisses her on the lips.

Asha pulls away and slaps him across the cheek. Diane steps in between them.

'Now, ladies. One at a time,' Ethan says. Then he slips away from them and goes to call Celeste.

'Pete should sue him,' Asha says, but they all know he won't, not if he wants to go on living with them. After all, Ethan is their landlord.

THIRTY
DIANE

Diane heads outside and takes a quick look around, to check there's no one in the bushes, before she ducks into Oystercatcher. Asha's perfume lingers in the living room, and as she walks through to the kitchen, she can imagine Asha sitting in here, cradling a glass of Baileys.

She glances around, her eyes sweeping every surface. There is a *plink* as a single drop of water drips from the tap and splashes into the sink. The kitchen has the most amazing view, even better than the one in their cottage. It is so close to the edge of the cliff that she gets the feeling that she is staring down into the abyss.

She shakes herself into action. After all, she hasn't come here to stare out the window. She swings around and opens the fridge door. The fridge is empty aside from a tiny bottle of medicated eye drops – Gordon's, according to the label – and a carton of milk.

Shutting the fridge door, she takes a step towards the bedrooms. Then stops short. The electric toothbrush is missing from its cradle. Sarah had said it was plugged in when she searched earlier with Ethan.

'Asha?' she calls softly.

There is no reply. She creeps into Asha's bedroom, checks the wardrobe and behind the curtains. She's not sure how she knows, but she's certain Asha has been here recently.

She checks the other rooms but the cottage appears to be empty.

And still it nags at her, the sense that she has only just missed her.

Next, she tries Skylark, then Hen Harrier, Hawk and Arctic Tern but all four cottages feel cold and soulless. She spots movement outside in the garden. It's Ethan. His back looks tense as he swings something large and heavy. She moves towards the window for a closer look. It's a large axe, and its blade glints in the light. She stays well back as he lifts it and hacks a branch off a tree for firewood. It seems cruel when Orkney has so few trees.

All at once, something Cameron said floats back into her mind.

'Ethan has a fake smile, have you noticed?'

She remembers laughing. 'What on earth do you mean by that?'

Cameron had grimaced.

'He could be the devil himself, and none of you would notice. No matter how bad his behaviour, how snide he gets, you all just let him get away with it. If Pete was to come out with any of the things he says, you'd put him back in his place, but with Ethan, you all just take it.'

Diane had objected to this. 'I stand up to him every time! I don't let him get away with squat.'

Cameron's intense, judgemental gaze had pierced her defences. 'But you're still friends with him, darling.'

'That's what friendship is, when you can show your worst side to someone and they still love you anyway.'

'No, friendship is having the guts to call each other out when your behaviour is so out of line that it's unacceptable. You argue with him because you love a good battle. You might get a kick out of it, but nothing ever changes. No one ever wins.'

She had thought Cameron was so wise then. She had believed he was such a good man. How wrong she was.

She helps Ethan carry the logs back inside and they set them down by the hearth. He gets the fire going and then Pete comes over. All three of them stare into the flames.

'There's some of Asha's wedding cake in the fridge, if anyone wants it,' Pete says.

'How did that get there?' Ethan asks.

Pete shrugs. 'Damned if I know.'

He goes and gets it out, cuts it up into little chunks and puts them on a plate.

Diane takes one, but her stomach reacts the way it always does lately. She runs to the bathroom to throw up. It's embarrassing how her body is letting her down. After a few minutes, Sarah knocks on the door.

'Are you okay?' she calls.

'I'm fine,' Diane says, wiping her mouth.

She stands up and flushes the toilet.

'You're not pregnant, are you?' Sarah says in a whisper.

'Nope, definitely not.'

'Good,' Sarah says. 'I mean, if you want that to be good?'

'I do.'

The truth is, Diane had always assumed they would have kids, one day. A little boy with Cameron's eyes. A little girl with her smile. She swallows down a sob, and Sarah pats her back in her usual motherly way. Diane shakes her off and goes to the sink.

'Sorry, I just don't feel like company right now,' she says.

'Of course.' Sarah backs away.

Diane looks in the mirror. She doesn't recognise the woman staring back at her, with bloodshot eyes and a runny nose, the very same woman who walked out on Cameron three days ago. She's nothing like the person she used to be. That Diane is never coming back.

The others have set up camp in the living room. Sarah is looking out the window, watching with unfocused eyes. Pete keeps an eye on the back door, in case anyone comes round the side. Ethan keeps the fire stoked. Diane is still in pieces. She feels her heart speeding up and slowing down. She wonders again where Asha is and how she's feeling. She has always loved being the centre of attention, but she won't be loving it now.

She drifts over to the fireplace and sits down beside Ethan.

'You okay?' he asks.

She nods. 'Yeah, I was just thinking about Asha.'

'Me too. Look' – he glances around, making sure no one is listening – 'what state was Cameron in when you left him?'

The hairs on her spine prickle.

'What... what do you mean?'

'I mean,' he lowers his voice, 'did he look like he accepted you were leaving, or did you get the feeling he was going to come after you?'

She leans back. 'Cameron would never...'

Ethan is frowning, gazing out the window.

'Think about it. He knows exactly where you are. Do you think he could have followed you here? I mean, he does have a kayak, does he not?'

'It's too far.'

'But not impossible? If he was angry enough?'

He stands and paces back and forth.

Diane shakes her head. 'If Cameron was that angry, he would come after *me*. Not Gordon or Judith.'

'He might still be after you,' Ethan says grimly. 'Perhaps they just got in the way.'

THIRTY-ONE
DIANE

2014, Aberdeen

'Do you want to go down the pub?' Ethan's voice breaks the stillness of the kitchen. The table is scattered with textbooks and a long-forgotten cup of tea.

Diane looks up from her notes, momentarily distracted by the clatter of a spoon hitting the floor. 'I've still got a fair bit to get through.'

He leans against the sink, his voice is smooth and coaxing.

'Come on, take a break. It would be nice to get a drink, don't you think? Just the two of us?'

Diane glances at him, her nerves tingling.

'I could come out for one,' she says, clambering to her feet. 'Just give me a minute to freshen up.'

He grins. 'Don't keep me waiting.'

Diane rushes to her room, scanning for something that sends the right message. She settles on a denim skirt and a casual shirt. She quickly wraps a scarf around her neck, adds some mascara and lip gloss. She looks sexy, she thinks, feeling a slight flutter in her chest. There was undeniable chemistry between her and Ethan when they first met, but she feels as though it fizzled out with Asha's introduction to the house. Maybe he's rethinking things now that they've got to know each other better. Maybe he's realised she's a lot more fun than Asha. There's certainly a lot more fire in their dynamic. She's good at conversation, much more so than Asha. She allows herself a smile as she hunts for her boots. She's not sure where the night will take her, but she's willing to find out.

They head to the only pub on campus. There are a fair few other students in there. It seems they aren't the only ones taking a break from their studies. Ethan heads to the bar.

'What do you want?' he asks.

'I'll have a pint, thanks,' she says, knowing it won't cost him too much.

He buys one for each of them and sits down at the table. Diane gazes at him, trying to decide whether she still finds him attractive. He is nice to look at, but it's his personality that really intrigues her. He can definitely be a bit arrogant, but he's intelligent too. There's nothing worse than men who constantly agree with her.

She starts telling him about a new film she's heard about. She's wondering if the two of them might like to go together, without Pete, Asha, or Sarah. Ethan nods and seems like he might be interested, but he keeps looking around the pub.

She finishes her drink and sets her glass down on the table.

'Do you want another?' she asks.

'Not yet,' he says. 'See those two girls over there? I want you to go and chat to them. See if you can get them to come and sit with us.'

'Why?'

His smile grows salacious. It's obvious why. She can't believe she's been so stupid. This is no date. He wants her there as his wingman. To make women feel comfortable so they'll come over and talk to him. That's what this is really all about.

Pete isn't much fun since he hurt his back, so he needs another partner in crime. She feels all the air puff out from her cheeks. She wants to pick up his drink and tip it over his head, but it's almost empty.

'Won't they think we're a couple?'

'I have thought about that. We'll need to drop subtle clues that we're not. You can mention your boyfriend.'

'I don't have a boyfriend.'

'You do now. Tell them his name is Pete.'

'Ugh. No way.'

'Yeah, you're really hot for Pete. Quick, before they finish choosing songs.'

She gets up as he asked and heads to the jukebox.

'You see that guy over there?' she says, glancing his way. 'He's really creepy. Whatever you do, do not go and sit with him.'

The girls nod and smile.

'Thanks.' They move on quickly, heading to a different part of the pub.

Diane returns to the table, cool as a cucumber.

'What did they say?' Ethan asks.

'They're not into men.'

'Oh. Well, OK. Can't win them all, I suppose.' He casts his eyes around the bar again.

'There's a hot bird standing at the bar. Go and talk to her.'

Diane wants to kick him, but she can't let him know she's annoyed.

In the end, she manages to get the girl to come over to their table. They chat for a while, but before Ethan can get anywhere, her boyfriend shows up and whisks her away.

Ethan sits there glowering. 'What on earth do they see in those goth blokes? They look like the undead.'

Diane looks over at him objectively. 'They've got cool clothes.'

'No, they haven't. They look ridiculous. That one looks like a woman.'

Diane rolls her eyes. 'Get with the times. Men can wear make-up.'

'Not real men.'

'Oh, gross. Just stop talking with your "real men" nonsense. Where do you get this bollocks?'

Pete comes in and sits down next to Diane.

'Didn't know you two were out tonight.' He looks from Diane to Ethan. 'I'm not interrupting anything, am I?'

'Get a life,' Diane says, flinging a beermat at him.

'Just asking!'

Ethan glowers at him. 'It's not a date.'

'You don't mind if I hang around then?'

'No,' Diane says.

A group of exchange students walk in, mostly girls. Ethan's eyes light up. 'Now she's just my type,' he says, pointing to one with long dark hair.

'She looks like Asha,' Pete says.

'She does not!'

'She totally does. Same nose and everything.'

Ethan looks at him with fury, then seems to shake himself. 'Right, I'm going to the bar.'

'Pint of lager, please,' Diane says.

'Get it yourself.'

THIRTY-TWO
DIANE

Diane pores over Sarah's hand-drawn map. It's crude, to say the least, uneven lines to mark the footpaths, labels scrawled in Sarah's curly handwriting. Nothing is to scale, and some areas are little more than vague blobs, but for now, it's the best they've got. She leans closer, her brow furrowed in concentration as she squints at the little red crosses Sarah has drawn to mark the places they've searched so far.

'You followed this path all the way to the end?' she asks, tapping her finger on a cross near the edge of the page.

'Yeah,' Sarah says, sounding a little impatient. 'There wasn't much there, just a lot of brambles and a couple of rabbit holes.'

Diane nods, her gaze drifting to another area of the map. 'And this one?'

Sarah hesitates. 'No, we didn't go that way.'

Diane presses her lips together. Her finger traces the lines, stopping at an empty spot just past the stone circle. 'What's this bit?'

'That's all overgrown. I thought we'd leave it for last.'

Diane straightens. 'Maybe we should check there next. If it's overgrown, you might have missed something.'

'You can if you want. I'm done in.'

Diane nods and tucks the map into her jacket pocket.

'Well. No time like the present.'

Sarah looks alarmed. 'You're going out on your own?'

They both look around, but Ethan has already slunk off to his room and Pete has flopped out on the sofa, eyes closed.

Sarah presses her lips together. 'I don't know, Di. Why don't you wait a bit and take someone with you?'

Diane looks at her with impatience. 'I'll be fine. Don't worry about me. I need to find Asha.'

A sad look crosses Sarah's face. 'Are you expecting to find her dead or alive?'

Diane exhales. 'Either way, I've got to know.'

'Just watch yourself, okay?'

She nods, her mind already on the route she plans to take. 'I'll be fine.'

She reaches for Ethan's gun and slides the magazine out. She checks the bullets lined up inside. Ready. Loaded. She puts on her jacket and braces herself, because Sarah's right. She needs to watch her back.

It's creepy, heading out on her own. Every shadow seems to move, every sound makes her stomach clench. But there's something liberating about it too. No one to answer to. No one to slow her down.

She follows the route she discussed with Sarah, but the brambles are a mess of thorny tentacles. No way anyone is hiding there. She shifts the rifle from one hand to the other and her tongue flicks against the dryness of her mouth. She wishes she'd thought to bring some water.

With a sigh, she looks around, trying to work out where the highest point is on the whole island. The answer is obvious.

The lighthouse.

She sees it rising up into the sky, its whitewashed walls standing out against the muted greens and browns. The wind whooshes past her, carrying the sharp scent of salt and decay. She shudders as she recalls the state of Gordon's body and picks up her pace.

The earth shifts with the wind, every blade of grass bending, every branch trembling. The air itself feels alive, charged with an energy that thrums just beneath the surface. The land is too volatile, too violent, as though the island resents the intrusion of those who dare tread upon it. Her boots scuff the ground as she approaches the lighthouse.

She hears a faint crunch behind her. Her breath catches in her throat. The wind tugs at her jacket, and a gull screeches overhead. She gets a cold sensation all down her back, like her time is running out.

She turns, scanning wildly.

All she sees is the grass, swaying in the wind and the endless expanse of the sky.

She keeps walking, her steps faster now, her ears straining for the slightest sound. The gulls shriek again. One of them zooms right by her face.

Instinctively, she raises the rifle.

The shot rings out, the recoil slamming back harder than she expects. She stumbles, her boot catching on uneven ground. The gull wheels away, surfing on the wind as it vanishes into the mist.

She lowers the barrel. Her hands shake and her shoulder throbs. Her ears ring with the echo of the shot.

It was just a bird.

The rifle shifts in her grasp and she adjusts her hold. She scans the horizon again, her eyes darting to every shadow, every dip in the ground. Her skin prickles as she takes another step forward. She hesitates. Everything seems to close in around her, her sense of safety evaporating. She's not sure, but she thinks she sees movement in the bushes. Abruptly, she turns and jogs back the same way she came. The sound of her own footsteps echoes through the air, the wind tearing at her clothes, the cool air slapping her face. She keeps going, pushing through the pain in her side.

She slows as the holiday cottages come into sight. She glances back over her shoulder one last time. Nothing moves now but her cheeks feel warm and her hand trembles as she reaches for the door. She slips inside, closing it firmly behind her and leans against the wood, her breath uneven. She smooths her hair and sheds her jacket and boots.

Sarah is sitting by the window. Pete by the kitchen door.

'How did you get on?' Sarah asks as she hands over the rifle.

Diane shakes her head. 'I felt like someone was watching me.'

Sarah looks towards the window. 'Do you think they followed you back?'

Diane lowers her voice. 'I can't even tell what's real anymore, I'm getting so bloody paranoid.'

Sarah nods. 'I know it's just the wind or whatever, but sometimes it feels like the island itself is breathing down my neck. I cannot wait to get out of here.'

Diane stretches her arms above her head, then heads over to Pete.

He eyes her curiously. 'That didn't take long.'

'No, I think I creeped myself out.'

'Really? You're one of the bravest people I know.'

'Maybe I used to be. I'm not firing on all cylinders these days.'

'Oh?'

'And I can't help but notice you're a lot more... vigilant. Is that why you took Broderick's gun?'

He looks at her. 'I didn't.'

'Is that right?' She arches an eyebrow.

He crosses his arms over his chest. 'Why would I?'

'Occam's razor; the most obvious explanation is usually the right one.'

'I don't know about anyone's razor,' Pete mutters, 'but I'm hardly going to want to get in trouble with the law now, am I?'

'Why's that?'

'Cos I'm a law-abiding citizen,' he says, sticking his chin out.

'So, it wouldn't have anything to do with having to share a house with Ethan again? Come on. It's no skin off my nose. I'm just curious, that's all.'

He looks at her, unflinching. 'Do *you* feel you need a gun to share a house with Ethan?'

'Of course not.'

He shakes his head. 'There's something off with you, Di. I can't quite put my finger on it, but you've changed. You're not the same girl I used to know.'

'I'm not a girl at all. I'm a grown woman.'

'That's just semantics.'

'No, it's not, Pete. Words mean something.'

'All right but did something happen to you?'

She tilts her head. 'Did something happen to you?'

'You know it did.'

There's something in the way he says it, like it's her fault. How could it possibly be her fault?

He looks across the room, and she realises it's not her he's directing his ire at, it's Ethan.

Ethan doesn't notice. He flicks through the DVDs and pulls out a copy of Monty Python and slides it into the player. They sit quietly for the first ten minutes or so, then people keep talking over it. He switches it off without a word and sits there with his arms crossed. Diane notices the red tinge creeping up his neck and imagines steam coming out of his ears.

'I was watching that,' Pete objects.

Ethan gives him a look, and he falls silent. This is the way it always was, Ethan lording it over them all, the self-appointed father of the house. Sometimes, Sarah used to try and soothe him, but not today. She stares out the window, shoulders rigid. Now, in these quieter moments, the burden of finding those bodies haunts her. Diane sees it in her eyes.

Pete is tapping his feet, which is really annoying, and more than once, someone pulls out their phone then remembers the absence of Wi-Fi. It is an unfamiliar feeling, this sort of pensive energy. As if they have been thrown back into a simpler time.

She yawns widely and makes herself a strong cup of coffee.

'How long till the ferry comes back for us?' Sarah asks.

'Five more days.'

'Do you think we're going to make it that long?'

Their eyes meet. 'Of course we are.'

'What about Asha?'

'I can't promise anything about Asha,' Diane says, staring into the fire. 'We did what we could. Tomorrow, we'll search again.'

Sarah glances over at Ethan and lowers her voice. 'There is another option.'

Diane raises an eyebrow.

Sarah leans forward, her voice barely above a whisper. 'I saw a rowing boat down by the pier. It's old, but I think it'll float. We could use it to get off the island.'

Diane takes a sip of her coffee, the bitter liquid settling heavily in her stomach. 'Are you serious?'

'We only need to get to the next island. It can't be that far.'

Sarah's fingers fidget with the hem of her jumper, twisting the fabric into a ball.

Diane sets her cup down on the coffee table.

'You make it sound so easy,' she says, meeting Sarah's gaze. 'But do you know how many people drown each day at sea?'

'It's safer than staying here,' Sarah argues, her voice rising slightly.

Pete's eyes flick in their direction, but he doesn't say anything.

Diane leans back, her arms crossing over her chest. 'Safe? You think rowing out into open water with no experience, no navigation, and no way of knowing the weather is safe? We'd end up capsized or stranded, or worse.'

Sarah's frustration is obvious, her cheeks flushed. 'There's a killer on this island. I just want a fighting chance.'

Diane exhales. 'And you think they'd let us paddle away without noticing? We'd be a slow-moving target.'

'So, what's your plan? Sit here until they come for us? Because that seems like a fantastic way to stay alive.'

'I'm not saying we do nothing,' Diane replies coolly. 'But rowing away isn't the answer.'

Sarah huffs. Diane watches her flick the kettle on for yet another cup of tea.

Pete clears his throat, breaking the tension that lingers in the air. 'Anyone for cards?' he calls out, holding up the deck.

Diane doesn't answer. She flops down in the armchair and stares down into the dark liquid. She doesn't know how much longer she can stay awake, but she's far too wired for sleep.

Pete abandons the cards and seeks out Sarah. Diane listens as they talk together in low voices.

'Tomorrow,' he's saying. 'High tide, around noon, or later, depending on the wind...'

He's actually going along with her crazy plan.

She stares into the fire, watching as the flames consume the logs, their edges blackening and curling in on themselves.

They'll get themselves killed.

The fools.

THIRTY-THREE
SARAH

The waves crash against the shore, spraying saltwater onto Sarah's legs as she and Pete drag the boat into the sea. It's heavier than it looks and the wood groans with each pull. Diane stands a few steps back, arms crossed, her face twisted with that maddening mix of scepticism and scorn.

'You're both mad,' she yells, her voice cutting through the hiss of the surf.

'We can't stay here,' Sarah yells back, more for Pete's benefit than Diane's. 'I'm not waiting around to get shot.'

None of them slept much and it shows. They all have dark circles around their eyes, and their movements are uneven and jittery.

Pete turns to Sarah. 'Are you sure about this?'

She casts a glance back at Ethan and Diane. 'Absolutely.'

Pete rubs the back of his neck, avoiding her eyes. For a moment, it looks like he might back out, but then he concedes. 'Let's get a wriggle on before the wind picks up again.'

He climbs into the boat and she follows, settling in as the wood creaks under their weight. She stashes the bags of food and drink under the seat. Pete pats his pocket, and she glimpses a hip flask as he reaches for the oars.

As they push off, Diane's voice carries over the waves.

'What's the name of the boat again? *Titanic*?'

Sarah tells herself that her derision is merely concern in disguise. That's how Diane operates.

'I give them five minutes,' Ethan says. 'The tide will wash them back in.'

She darts a glance at him. He's still holding his gun. 'For security,' he said.

But whose security? His or theirs?

The chill worms its way into Sarah's bones. Her nose is already numb and her ears smoulder with invisible flames. Pete rows steadily, his jaw set with concentration. He fights the tide, rowing away from the beach, out towards the open sea.

'Do you have any idea where we're going?' she asks, scanning the horizon.

He squints at the sky. 'South.'

She raises an eyebrow. 'How can you tell?'

'Position of the sun.'

'Well, that's something,' she says, trying to inject some optimism. 'Do you want me to help row?'

'Not yet. I want to get us clear of the island first.'

She glances back. Diane and Ethan are still standing there. Watching.

The boat creaks and sways with every stroke of the oars. The dark water stretches out in every direction, swallowing sound and light. Sarah huddles on the bench opposite him. She sees the strain in his shoulders, the way his jaw clenches with effort.

'Sarah,' he says, his voice little more than a rasp. 'There's something I need to tell you.'

She lifts her head, startled by the tone of his voice.

'What is it?'

He doesn't answer right away. His gaze stays locked on the water, his arms moving mechanically as he rows. 'I wasn't in the army.'

She frowns. 'What do you mean?'

'I know I let you think I was. But I wasn't. I was in prison.'

'Prison?' The word hangs in the air, raw and incredulous. 'Why would you let me think—'

'I didn't mean to,' he cuts in. 'It's hard to talk about it. It's hard enough to carry on existing, some days.'

She stares at him, her heart pounding. Pete doesn't stop rowing, but his movements are jerky now, the rhythm broken.

'I was done for drink driving. I'd had a few but I thought I was fine.' His breath hitches, but he doesn't stop. 'My stepdad was in the car with me. I lost control, and... he didn't make it. I killed him, Sarah. I killed him.'

The words drop like stones into the water. Sarah's hands tighten on the edge of the boat. Her breath catches in her throat. She tries to speak, but nothing comes out.

He shakes his head. 'I've told myself a million times I didn't mean to do it, but it doesn't matter. He's gone because of me. And prison' – he swallows hard, his voice breaking – 'it was hell. I deserved it, every second of it. But, oh God...' His voice catches, and he takes a shuddering breath. 'You don't come out of a place like that the same person. Not after what they did to me in there.'

'Pete.' Her voice is soft, unsure. She doesn't know what to say.

He laughs, but there's no humour in it. 'You think you know who you are, you know? And then you're in there, and you find out how small you really are. How little you matter.' His voice grows quieter, almost a whisper. 'I don't even know if I'm still me. The person I was before... I don't know if he survived.'

Her eyes burn, and she presses a hand to her mouth, trying to hold back tears. She wants to comfort him, to tell him it wasn't his fault, that he's more than his mistakes, but she knows it isn't that simple.

'You didn't have to tell me,' she says finally, her voice thick. 'But I'm glad you did.'

He glances at her then, his face raw with emotion, eyes glistening. 'You don't get it,' he says. 'I didn't want you to know. But if something happens out here, I couldn't leave it like this. You deserve the truth.'

Her chest aches, a knot of sorrow and something she can't quite name. She wants to put her arms around him and tell him he's not alone, but he's still rowing, the oars moving again with a steady rhythm she doesn't want to break.

'I'm sorry,' she says softly.

'Don't be sorry for me. Be sorry for him. For what I did to him. And to my mum. She loved him so much. I'll never forgive myself. Ever.'

The boat rocks gently, the water lapping against the sides. Sarah wipes her eyes. She wishes she knew which words would make it all better.

The boat creaks and she feels a little uneasy. Cold water laps at her boots, and she realises it's pooling at the bottom of the boat.

'Pete, stop!'

He slows, but keeps hold of the oars. 'What's up?'

She points at the water rising around her feet.

He curses under his breath. She leans down and traces her hands over the wood until they find the edges of a hole. Then another.

'Bloody hell! It's like a colander down here. Were these holes here before?'

'The sand must have been covering them.'

She swallows hard and stares at him for a moment, considering their options. 'The holes are small. Perhaps we could plug them with chewing gum?'

Pete shakes his head. 'I'm really sorry, Sarah. But I think we'll have to turn back.'

'No!'

Tears prick her eyes. She can see the edge of an island on the horizon. She has no idea how far it is, or how long it would take to get there. But it's not Haarlorn.

'We could just keep going.'

He follows her gaze. 'We don't even know if that island's inhabited. We could get stuck there, if we even make it that far. We'll have to turn back.'

Her stomach plummets as he turns the boat around.

THIRTY-FOUR
SARAH

Sarah's heart sinks as they head back towards Haarlorn. Pete is rowing with everything he has. The waves are higher now, crashing against the boat with a ferocity that sends sprays of icy water over the sides. They have drifted significantly and instead of returning to the beach, they now face cliffs and sea stacks as high as a fortress.

He rows with strained uneven strokes, his focus sharp as he battles the current. He doesn't speak, but the tension in his face tells her he's worried.

'It's like we're not getting anywhere,' she says, glancing nervously at the cliffs.

The waves bounce them back every time they get close.

Pete keeps his eyes on the water. 'We'll find a way.'

The towering walls of rock stretch endlessly above them, stark against the churning sea. She shivers as icy water seeps into her boots and trousers. It's pooling around her ankles now, creeping higher with every wave that sloshes over the side.

Her heart pounds as she cups her hands and starts baling the water out, throwing it back into the sea with little splashes. It feels hopeless, but she can't just sit there and do nothing.

'We're taking on too much water,' she tells him.

Pete doesn't reply immediately. His gaze is fixed on the cliffs as he rows. His face is pale, the strain of the effort showing. He looks at her, then at the oars.

'You want to have a go?'

'Yeah. Switch.'

She takes the oars, adjusting her hold before pulling them through the water. It's harder than it looks. The boat feels impossibly heavy, the waves pushing back with every stroke. Her arms burn after just a few minutes, and her rhythm falters.

She gasps for breath.

'Keep going. You're doing fine.'

She grits her teeth and pushes through, rowing with every ounce of strength she has. But it's no use. The waves are too strong, and the water inside the boat sloshes higher with each passing second.

'I can't,' she says. She lets go of the oars and slumps back, panting.

Pete begins rowing again, though his strokes are slower now. She watches him for a moment.

'I think we might have to swim back.'

'No. It's too rough.' He rows with renewed vigour. 'We're closer now. Look, I can see the beach.'

'Give me one of the oars.'

He hands her the right one, and they row together, the boat jerking awkwardly as they try to coordinate. They head out to sea a little, away from the cliffs, and round the island. She can see the beach properly now. She rows harder.

When the boat scrapes against the shore, she stumbles out, her legs almost giving way beneath her. Pete follows, dragging the boat further up the sand. The wood is swollen and waterlogged.

'Help me drag it to higher ground,' he says. 'We might still be able to use it, once I've fixed the holes.'

She looks at him with hope. 'Do you think?'

'I'm not promising anything, but I'll have a go.'

She hugs him, and despite the freezing cold, she's glad it's just the two of them. No Diane and Ethan to witness their epic fail.

They trudge back to the cottage, cold and shivering. Her boots squelch with every step and her trousers cling to her legs like icy chains. The cottage door swings open, revealing Diane and Ethan at the table. Diane looks up first, her face flickering between surprise and something softer before settling into its usual guarded expression. Ethan grins broadly, his chair tilting precariously on two legs.

'Back already?' he says, his tone dripping with amusement. 'Guess the great escape didn't go as planned?'

Sarah glances at Pete, but he's already dropped into a chair, and is unscrewing the cap on his flask. She straightens, ignoring the cold clinging to her, and squares her shoulders.

'It's not over,' she says, trying to keep her voice steady. 'The boat needs repairs, but we'll go again.'

Ethan lets out a bark of laughter, slamming his chair back onto all four legs. 'You're kidding, right? Have you got a death wish?'

Diane shakes her head, her lips tightening into a thin line. 'Sarah, be serious. Just be thankful you made it back safely.'

'We just need to fix the holes. It's worth a shot.'

Ethan shakes his head. 'Face it, Sarah, you're not exactly Ellen MacArthur.'

Diane sighs, leaning back in her chair. 'Look, I get it. You're scared. We all are. But trying again, in that boat? It's suicidal.' She pauses, glancing at Pete. 'You're not really going to let her talk you into this, are you?'

Pete concentrates on his flask. 'We'll see.'

Sarah's hands ball into fists, heat rising to her face despite the chill. 'I'm not giving up,' she snaps, glaring at Diane and Ethan. 'If you two are too scared to leave, fine. But I'm not just going to sit here and wait to be shot.' She stops herself, swallowing hard.

The room falls silent. She turns on her heel and storms to the bathroom, slamming the door behind her.

Inside, she leans against the sink, her breath shaky. She peels off her damp clothes and steps into the shower, cranking the water as hot as she can stand. It scalds her skin, but she welcomes the pain. It drowns out Ethan's smug grin and Diane's dismissive tone. It even dulls the gnawing doubt in the back of her mind.

Maybe they're right. Maybe she is crazy for trying.

When she emerges, wrapped in a towel, the room feels colder than before. Pete is slouched in the chair, flask still in hand. Diane watches her for a moment, then glances away.

'I'm glad you made it back,' Diane says softly.

Her eyes flick to the window. 'We've only got four more days until the ferry comes back for us. Don't you think it's safer to wait it out?'

Sarah doesn't respond. She sits on the edge of the sofa and stares at the floor.

She isn't ready to give up yet. Not on the boat, and not on herself.

THIRTY-FIVE
SARAH

2017, Aberdeen

'I want a picture with my uni friends,' Diane shouts, pulling her long wedding dress up so as not to trip over it. She doesn't really look like Diane, Sarah thinks. She's grown her short hair down to her shoulders, and her skin has a sparkly sheen that makes her look like a mannequin. She had a few drinks before the ceremony, and the alcohol has really calmed her nerves. She's a lot more smiley than usual, and there's a reddish bloom to her cheeks.

Her voice is the same though, clear and confident. Wedding guests laugh as she tugs off her heels and replaces them with comfortable trainers.

'Uni friends!' Cameron repeats.

Obligingly, everyone moves to one side, and it's just them: Asha, Ethan, Pete and Sarah. Somehow, Asha manages to be in the middle.

'Let Diane and Cameron go in the middle,' Sarah murmurs.

Asha looks surprised, but she moves over.

'Say cheese!' the photographer says.

'Cheese!' they chorus. The camera flashes and they hold the pose.

Satisfied, the photographer releases them, and they head towards the car park.

'Does everyone know where we're going?' Cameron yells. 'It's the hotel across the street from the Maritime Museum.'

Sarah and Pete follow Ethan to his brand-new Honda.

'You get a company car?' Sarah says envy creeping in.

'I've got a company car too,' Asha says like it's no big deal.

Sarah shakes her head at Pete. How the other half lives.

The hotel lobby is filled with laughter. Someone passes Sarah a glass of champagne, and she sips it slowly. There are a lot of people; Cameron's friends as well as Diane's.

Conversations hum with talk of graduate programmes and business trips to cities Sarah has only seen in films. She feels a pang, a sense of being left behind, like she's watching a club she's not part of. The corporate world was never her calling, but she's never felt it as starkly as she does now.

She follows the crowd through to the function room. There's a live band, which Pete is excited about. There's lots of dancing, lots of food. It's a great wedding by anyone's standard.

'When I get married, I'm going to have a band,' Asha says.

'Are you seeing anyone?' Sarah asks.

'No, but I'm sure Mr Right is out there somewhere. I just have to find him.'

Sarah smiles weakly. There are almost certainly a number of Mr Rights queuing up to meet Asha, but no such luck for her. She only ever seems to attract dull, needy men. Her last boyfriend actually told her she reminded him of his mum, as if this was the greatest compliment he could bestow.

'I still can't believe Diane's actually married,' Asha says, watching as Diane does the rounds, stopping at each table to speak to her guests.

Sarah nods. But she knows exactly what Asha really means: 'I can't believe Diane got married before me.'

Diane comes over to their table and flops down in an empty chair.

'Man, this wedding stuff is exhausting!' she says.

'Looks it,' Asha says without sympathy.

'The choir was good, wasn't it? I wasn't sure we needed them, but Cameron insisted. He said we had to drown out his Auntie Fran because she's got a really shrill voice.'

Sarah smirks. 'So has Pete.'

A waiter walks by with a tray of champagne glasses. Diane swipes one and takes a large gulp. 'I'm so thirsty.'

She holds out her glass, and Sarah clinks it. Asha raises hers.

'Best friends forever!'

Diane sets down her glass. She has a sentimental smile on her face. 'Thank you so much for all your help,' she tells them. 'Asha, I really appreciate you sorting out the hen night for me. And Sarah, I really appreciate you doing the invites. I don't know what I would have done without you. I love you both so much.'

Sarah and Asha grin at each other, enjoying this incredibly rare show of affection. They all hug, and for Sarah, this is the very best part of the wedding. The bit that makes it all worth it.

When they all sit back again, Diane's eyes are glassy, mascara smudged down her cheeks.

'One minute.'

Asha grabs a wipe from her handbag and fixes Diane's make-up. 'There. Better.'

'You look beautiful,' Sarah tells her.

'If a little drunk,' Asha says with a smile.

'I'm just really happy,' Diane says.

'You're allowed to be,' Asha says.

Sarah nods. 'Cam's a great guy.'

Diane's eyes skid from Sarah to Asha, as if she's waiting for a punchline. Sarah doesn't blame her. They take the piss out of each other with such alarming frequency that it's hard to know when someone's being genuine.

Diane turns and spots Pete.

'Pete!' She leaps up from her chair and throws her arms around him.

Pete laughs and helps steady her, then she spins off towards Cameron.

'Is Pete seeing anyone?' Asha asks.

Sarah watches her. 'Why? Are you interested?'

'Me? No, he's not my type.'

They both watch him for a moment. 'I bet he's good in bed though,' Asha says.

'Remember how he used to dance? He was so... bendy.'

They both giggle. 'Anyway, I think he likes you,' Asha says.

'Me?' Sarah bursts out laughing. 'I don't think so.'

He isn't her type either, physically. Too thin and geeky. She loves him as a friend, but she wants more from a relationship. She hasn't stayed single all these years just to settle for her old housemate. She wants excitement, romance. Someone who gives her butterflies. It's been a long time since she's experienced that.

Asha changes the subject and starts talking about her job in PR. It all sounds very glamorous. Very Asha.

Ethan has a great career too. He's living in Glasgow like Sarah, but they've only met up a couple of times. He always seems busy. When he isn't working, he's entertaining clients or jetting off somewhere, whereas the only people Sarah hangs out with are her parents. Perhaps he senses what a loser she is, because he never suggests getting together.

'How about you?' Asha asks. 'Where are you working?'

'I'm doing a temporary contract at the moment,' Sarah says, unwillingly. The last thing she wants to do is talk about herself.

'Well that doesn't tell me much,' Asha says. 'What company are you working for?'

'It's er... the council.'

'Right, so it's a consulting role?'

Sarah swallows. 'More of an admin thing. Excuse me, I need to go to the ladies.'

Asha stands up to follow her, but then some bloke wanders over and starts chatting her up. Men are always drawn to Asha. Maybe because she has an open, friendly face. The kind of face that makes them think they stand a chance, despite her being way out of their league.

Sarah walks out of the stuffy function room and stands in the empty lobby for a moment. The loos are on the right, but she walks right past them, pushing open the glass doors that lead outside, where she stands on the steps and breathes in the cool air.

What am I even doing here? she wonders. Hanging out with these people who are no longer in her life. She can't believe she's letting them get to her. It's ridiculous. Who cares if they're doing better than her? They're a bunch of self-centred weirdos and egomaniacs. They're only in her life because they happened to go to uni together. They aren't really her kind of people at all. She doesn't know why it's taken her so long to see it.

'You okay?' She turns and sees Cameron. His arctic blue eyes are even more intense than usual, thanks to the blue of his kilt.

'I'm fine,' she says with a smile.

'I'm supposed to have given these up,' he says, pulling out a pack of cigarettes. 'And I will. Just as soon as I'm done with this pack. I needed something to soothe my nerves this morning.'

'Oh. You were... nervous?'

'Well, they say it's the bride's day, and all the attention is on her, but I had to do my bit too, and I have a habit of overthinking things. Like, what if I lose the rings? What if she stands me up? What if I messed up the honeymoon reservation?'

'Then I'm sure she would have forgiven you, and anyway, Diane would never stand you up.'

He grins. 'Well anyway, I'm feeling a lot calmer now it's all done with.'

'Now you can enjoy yourself.'

'Exactly.'

He offers her a cigarette and she takes one. He lights hers first, then his, and they both look out as people walk up and down the road with their shopping.

'It all feels very surreal,' he says. 'This morning I was just me and now I've got a wife.'

'How do you know?' she asks. 'That you want to spend the rest of your life with someone?'

He shrugs. 'It's a practical decision as much as an emotional one. I mean, we were already living in each other's pockets, staying over a couple of nights a week and all that, so I thought we might as well make it official.'

Sarah puffs out a ring of smoke. 'Just for the record, I don't really smoke either. It's just everyone's here, going on about how great their lives are, and I've just moved back with my parents. It makes me feel a bit shit, you know?'

He touches her shoulder. 'Life's not a competition, Sarah.'

'I know.'

'And if it was, lord only knows what the rules would be. I think you'd have to get a tick in each column. I bet you're doing better in some areas. I mean, you can drive, can't you? Whereas I've failed my driving test three times so far.'

She bursts out laughing. 'Are you serious?'

'Deadly. Can't parallel park to save my life.'

'For some reason, that does make me feel a bit better.'

. . .

The reception is still in full swing when she heads back inside. The ceilidh band launches into a rousing rendition of the 'Gay Gordons'. Asha glides effortlessly through the steps, her movements graceful and precise as she spins and pivots with practised ease. Ethan struggles to keep up, his feet shuffling awkwardly. They look mismatched, like they're dancing two different reels.

'All right, Sarah?'

She turns as Pete lowers himself gingerly into the chair beside her. He winces as he settles.

'Is your back playing up again?' she asks.

He nods, grimacing. 'Yep. No dancing for me.' He glances towards the floor, his expression sour. 'Not that I'd want to join that circus, anyway.'

Sarah follows his gaze. Asha is twirling Ethan in a wide circle, her laughter ringing out over the lively strains of the fiddle and accordion. Ethan stumbles and loses his grip, but Asha catches him and spins them both into the next move with a flourish.

'What do you think she said to get him up there?' Sarah asks, raising an eyebrow.

'Probably told him he'd look pathetic if he didn't.'

'He looks pathetic anyway.'

They both laugh.

'I'm going to get a drink. Can I get you something?' she asks, balancing her handbag on her shoulder.

'A beer, thanks,' he says with a smile.

She nods and heads towards the bar. The queue is slow-moving, so she watches the dance floor. Diane is laughing, cheeks flushed as Cameron spins her around. They look good together. Diane has lost her usual inhibitions. She's too busy having fun.

Sarah flirts a little with the barman while he pours the drinks. He gives her a free shot and she necks it. The sweet liquid sears a path to her stomach.

'Any chance I could have your number?' he says.

She raises a brow. He probably uses the same line all night, but he has a great mouth so she agrees. He pulls out his phone and they exchange numbers. She smiles to herself. Maybe it hasn't been such a bad night after all.

When she returns to their table, Pete is not there.

She spots Diane on the edge of the dance floor, glugging champagne, and goes over to join her.

'Have you seen Pete?'

Diane turns, her smile faltering slightly as she shakes her head.

Cameron walks over to join them.

'You're looking for Pete? He just left. With Asha.'

'What?' Sarah's brow knits in confusion. 'But we were going to share a taxi to the station!'

Diane's lips part slightly, a faint frown forming. 'They didn't even say goodbye!'

Cameron shrugs, leaning against the nearby table. 'Asha was going on about how she's destined to die single or something like that. I think she'd had enough.' He picks up his champagne flute and swirls the liquid absently.

Diane tilts her head. 'You don't think... Pete and Asha.'

They all look at each other. Sarah snorts. 'Nah. Asha's way too picky.'

Cameron's smile flickers. 'You never know. Weddings do funny things to people.'

THIRTY-SIX
DIANE

'Why don't you go and get some sleep?' Diane says.

'I'm fine for now,' Sarah replies, her eyes fixed on the table, fingers tracing an invisible pattern in the wood. Dull grey clouds smother the horizon, making the sea indistinguishable from the clouds. The rain has been relentless, sweeping across the island in heavy, slanting sheets. It rattles against the windows, trying to find a way in. Diane finds the sound oddly comforting. It has stalled Sarah's ill-conceived plans, at least for now, and for that she is grateful.

Despite her words, Sarah's head starts to loll. She melts into her chair and gets the familiar long-eyed stare that Diane remembers so well. The room around them grows quiet, even Pete stops his infernal tapping. They watch the window, the way they would usually watch the television, as the sky moves in slow motion. Patches of pink peek out from the clouds, but it never goes entirely dark.

Nature is a splendid thing, but Diane knows it is not just a love of the wild that has them all watching. Every twitch of a bird, every owl call, every scamper of an Orkney vole sets their nerves on edge.

There is a sudden movement at the window.

'What was that?' Sarah asks.

'Hares,' Ethan says. 'I just saw three of them hop past.'

A smile forms on her lips. 'Really? How cute.'

She gets up and goes to the window. 'I can't see anything,' she says, sounding disappointed. She yawns and stretches. 'I suppose I should go to bed. You can wake me later, when you want me to take my shift.'

'Okay.' Ethan nods at her, still thinking he's in charge.

Pete takes up his position at the back door. He's chain drinking, but he seems content to sit there by himself.

'Has it occurred to you that Sarah could be the killer?' Diane says a moment later.

Ethan smiles. 'Go on then, convince me.'

'I don't think anyone was paying attention, but she was a pretty good shot when we had a go at the range. That's a bit odd, don't you think? I mean Sarah? I would expect her to be as useless as Asha.'

'No, I didn't notice,' he admits. 'I was watching you.'

She flashes him a smile. 'Seriously, though. I reckon she's been practising. Probably got Pete to give her some pointers.'

'You think they've been shooting together?'

'Well how else did she get so good?'

'If Sarah hit the target then it was probably just dumb luck.'

'She's got good hand–eye coordination.'

He waves her away. 'Trust me, Sarah is not the shooter. She's just a sad old cat lady. Except, instead of a cat, she has Pete.'

Diane laughs. Pete glances over at them. She'd forgotten he was there. She quickly busies herself, pouring another drink.

'Sarah didn't like Asha getting married before her. That makes her the old maid of the group, doesn't it?'

Ethan snorts. 'It's 2025, not 1925.'

'Believe me, she cares about this stuff, as much as Asha does.

Even in this day and age, she takes a lot of flak from her parents for being in her thirties and unmarried. Not only that,' she lowers her voice, 'I don't know if you noticed but Gordon was really triggering Pete.'

'Yeah, he reminds him of the bloke who abused him in prison.'

'But what if he doesn't just look like him? What if he is that bloke? Sarah's so maternal, she's practically leaking milk. If she thought Gordon was that guy...'

Ethan stretches his arms up over his head. 'It's more likely it was Broderick. Think about it. He's been stuck on this island for months on end. Just him and the missus. It's got to do a number on his head. And he's a crack shot with the gun.'

'But someone stole one.'

'That could just be a cover story. You've seen the way he looked at us. He resented us being here, encroaching on his territory, making them run around after us, cooking, cleaning. He didn't even like us using his guns. He was practically snarling when we went on our hunting trip.'

'But Broderick left. His boat is gone.'

'He could have hidden it. Or maybe he did leave – after he killed Gordon and Judith.'

'Why the hell would he do that?'

'I don't know. He really freaked out when that gun went missing. I think it was getting to him, having people on his island. Sarah told me he and Judith argued just before he left.'

'Yeah, but why stop there? Why not kill all of us?'

'Maybe he's going to pick us off one by one. The ultimate hunt.'

Ethan is grinning as he says this. He doesn't look the least bit scared. Diane grins too, a little more uneasily. She watches as Ethan stokes the fire. The adrenaline is starting to fade. She can't believe they still haven't found Asha.

'Maybe we should go to bed too,' he says. 'I don't think anyone is coming.'

Diane eyes him curiously. 'What makes you so sure?'

'I don't know. Just a feeling. Everything seems quiet. Settled. Back to the way it should be, I suppose.'

His hand wanders up her sleeve. She doesn't shake him off. It feels comforting, the warmth of his fingers on her skin. She feels her heart rate accelerating, and before she knows what she's doing, her lips are on his.

'Diane,' he whispers. 'I've wanted this for so long.'

She doesn't reply. He was always in love with Asha, not her. He pulls her closer, and she feels the warmth of his body. Before she knows it, she's tugging at his buttons, releasing his belt. She doesn't know where this is coming from, because she's hardly given a thought to Ethan or his body. She's been so consumed with everything else that is going on. But now it seems only natural that they should seek solace in each other. She has had such a bad run that she feels she is owed this little bit of pleasure.

She takes his hand and they both stand up.

Pete coughs and meets her eye briefly. He gives her a little nod and a smile, silently signalling that he will stay here and keep watch. Ethan turns and makes some kind of gesture too, and then they stumble towards the bedrooms. They pause on the threshold, silently debating which room to choose. She is the one to make the decision, pulling him into his.

He dominates the space, taking control with a primal hunger. He throws her onto the bed, and his teeth graze her skin as he tugs at her clothes. There is a delicious urgency in his actions. She wraps her legs around him and whispers her darkest desires in his ear. Then she closes her eyes and now it is Cameron who makes love to her. She lets the fantasy take over, the taste of him, the smell, until her mind is spiralling away, back to the life she left behind. She clings on tight, murmuring deep into his chest as she hears his heart beat against hers.

'I've missed you so much.'

'I've missed you too.'

The voice is all wrong. Her eyes fly open and she finds herself looking at Ethan. Her friend. Her housemate.

He shudders against her and then they both lie back, sweating and panting. Diane reaches for her clothes and slithers back into them, cold and unsatisfied.

She dresses quickly and returns to the living room where Pete is stoking the fire. The gun lies in his lap.

He arches an eyebrow. 'So. You and Ethan, eh?'

She puts a finger to her lips. She knows she can trust him to be discreet.

Ethan comes out a little later, unable to hide his smile. He takes the poker from Pete and resumes his position in front of the fire.

Outside, a twig snaps.

'What was that?'

Ethan's gaze flicks towards the window, then to the gun on the table. They wait a moment, two. But nothing happens. His hand shifts to the back of his neck. He rubs it absently and gives a careless shrug. 'It's probably nothing.'

THIRTY-SEVEN
SARAH

Eight Months Earlier, Glasgow

Sarah is on autopilot as she heads outside for lunch. The sandwich shop is busy today, just the last few sandwiches and rolls on display in the window. The door swings open letting out bursts of conversation. She ducks inside and asks for the same lunch she always buys. Egg mayo on granary bread.

'You're lucky, it's the last one,' the elderly shopkeeper tells her with a smile.

'Thank you. Can I also have a—'

He gives her a toothless grin. 'Bottle of ginger beer, got it right here, love.'

She cringes, embarrassed at being so predictable. She supposes it's nice, in a way. But how sad is it that the person who knows her best is a man old enough to be her grandfather?

As she steps outside, she glances at the space between the overflowing bins. She ignores the stench of rotting fast food and moves a little closer. In the exact spot where she found Pete, sits another homeless man, his shoulders hunched against the chill. As she watches, he shifts, trying to get comfortable in his makeshift bed. His face is worn and wrinkled, evidence of a hard life lived on the streets. His eyes look weary but vigilant as he scans the constant flow of people walking by.

Sarah, wrapped in her favourite red coat, stops in front of him, the wind tugging at the edges of her scarf. Office workers stream past her, holding their bagels and sandwiches. She clutches her own lunch, glancing down at it before taking a step closer.

'Hi, how are you doing?' she asks.

He looks up, his eyes squinting in the pale light. 'Not the best day,' he replies. 'But I've had worse.'

She glances at the sandwich in her hand, then back at him. The city sounds seem to fade for a moment, the distant rumble of a bus, the footsteps of passers-by, the faint rustle of leaves in the gutter. She holds out the sandwich, her hand tingling in the cold air.

'Here,' she says gently, 'have this.'

He accepts it with a nod, his fingers brushing hers briefly as he grabs hold.

'Thank you.'

As she straightens up and moves back into the flow of people, she casts a glance back, watching as he unwraps the sandwich with careful hands, as if it were something far more precious.

'Sarah? I thought it was you!'

She turns and sees glacial blue eyes.

'Cameron!'

He looks a little red in the face, but his smile is so infectious that she finds herself smiling too. It's very distinctive, his smile. One corner of his mouth lifts slightly higher than the other.

'Hey, it's Cameron!' calls out the homeless man.

Cameron gives him a wave.

'What are you doing here?' she asks.

'I'm here for an engineering conference.'

'Sounds exciting!'

It's good to hear his laugh, loud and booming. 'And what are you up to on this fine day?'

'I'm just on my lunch break,' she says. 'I work in the council offices, just over there.'

'Is that as exciting as it sounds?'

'Well, let's see. I've just finished a three-hour meeting on an update to planning regulations.'

'Wow. My conference suddenly seems a whole lot better.'

'I'm sure it is.'

His eyes dart from her to the sandwich shop.

'I was just going to grab a bite for lunch,' he says, 'but looking at the selection, I might have better luck elsewhere. What would you recommend?'

'There's a half decent pizza place up the road.'

'Pizza sounds good.'

'You have to go up the hill, and then it's through a little alley. I can show you if you like.'

They walk through the damp streets, rain pitter-pattering gently off their shoulders. The air vibrates with the deep, droning hum of bagpipes. She feels the steady beat of the piper's foot tapping against the ground and is lifted by the soulful melody. The music pulses through the city, echoing against the stone walls of nearby buildings. It follows them up the street, mingling with the murmur of the crowds and the rumble of the traffic. She steals a glance at Cameron, and he smiles back at her. Then a man creeps up behind him. She thinks for a minute that he's going to try and snatch his wallet, but then he presses something into Cameron's hand and melts into the crowd.

'What the...'

Cameron looks down at his hand. It's a rose.

'I guess this is for you,' he says. They both turn and look, and there's the guy, effortlessly slipping another rose into the hand of another man walking with a woman. This man takes the rose and slickly presents it to his girlfriend, as if he'd planned it all along.

'Must be some kind of hidden camera thing,' she says. 'They'll do anything for clicks.'

Cameron shrugs. 'Well, you got a rose out of it.'

She stops. They are already outside the pizza place.

'No queue,' she says triumphantly.

'Hey, I don't suppose you want to join me? I hate eating lunch alone.'

'Me too. I...'

She does have another meeting at two, but if she eats quickly, she ought to be able to manage it.

'Yeah, why not?'

The waiter guides them to a cosy table overlooking the Clyde.

'This is pretty nice,' Cameron says. He loosens his tie and lets out a sigh as he sits back and reaches for the menu.

'I'm going to be naughty and have a glass of wine.' He shoots her a look. 'Are you going to be naughty, Sarah?'

A blush creeps up her neck and she finds herself giggling. 'Yeah. Why not?'

They both peruse the menu for a few minutes.

He glances at her and she catches him looking. She makes herself look down at the menu.

The waiter comes back to take their order, and the bottle of chilled white wine arrives in an ice bucket. She waits eagerly while he pours. She glances out the window as raindrops streak down the glass, and feels lucky to be here, out of the rain.

She takes a sip of her wine. It's cool and delicious.

'I've never been in here at lunchtime,' she confesses. 'This is pretty nice.'

The conversation flows easily. She's never spent much time with him, one to one like this. But he's like an old friend. Understandable, since they've known each other for years. She knows things about him most people don't, like the fact that he was brought up by his fisherman father after his mother died. Like the fact he loves storms but hates driving.

There's only one subject they don't touch on: Diane. It's as if they are in some parallel universe where she never existed.

Service is slow, so they drink most of the wine before the food comes, by which time Sarah has almost forgotten the pizza altogether. It finally arrives at their table along with a flurry of apologies and they exchange gooey slices topped with tangy goats' cheese and salty Parma ham.

Sarah's eyes flick to her watch and she realises she is already late for her next meeting, but she can't bring herself to interrupt Cameron's story. He leans in, his voice low as he tells her about his time working on the oil rigs. She hangs on every word, captivated by the life he has lived, which is so much more fascinating, more adventurous than anything she has ever done.

She has played it safe all her life, she realises with sudden clarity. She's always been the good girl. Always done what others expect of her. She needs to break out of her comfort zone and live a little.

Cameron's phone beeps and his gaze drops to the screen. His expression shifts from animated to worried.

'I hadn't realised the time. I'd better get going,' he says with regret, signalling to the waiter. 'Can I have the bill please? I'll get this,' he offers.

'That's okay, I prefer to pay my own way.'

He nods, consulting his phone for a moment. 'I'll be finished around seven. If you're free then, why don't you come over to my hotel for dinner? It's this one.' He opens his wallet and pulls out a card.

Sarah takes it, a shiver running down her spine as their fingers touch.

'Great, I'll—'

'Bring Pete too if he wants.'

'Oh. Of... of course. I'll see what he's up to.'

She swallows hard and smiles. But she has no intention of inviting Pete. She deserves a night out of the house, away from his suffocating company. Away from the overwhelming irritation of him following her from room to room like a dog. When she wants a drink, he's in the kitchen, when she wants to relax, he's in the living room.

Pete is harmless, but it doesn't feel like her own home any more.

She doesn't blame him, she blames herself.

It's all down to her own foolish drunken mistake. If she hadn't slept with him, things would still be normal. She wouldn't feel so guilty every time she checks the council's listings to see if there are any new live-in opportunities for single, vulnerable men. She wouldn't find herself constantly censoring herself, apologising whenever she snaps at him, making it up to him by bringing home ice cream and wine.

But deep down, she understands what has happened to the pair of them. Instead of helping Pete, she has let him bring her down to his level.

THIRTY-EIGHT
DIANE

'Di? Diane, wake up. Seriously, I just went into the living room and Pete and Ethan are on their last legs. We need to give them a break.'

It takes Diane a moment to understand what Sarah is talking about. She yawns and stretches, then scrambles out of bed to find that she has slept in her clothes, and she sees no point in changing. Following Sarah into the living room, she finds Ethan half asleep in front of the cold fire, a gun in his lap, while Pete leans against the kitchen counter.

He is nodding off, leaning further and further to his right like a human Tower of Pisa.

Diane claps her hands. 'Right, boys, off to bed. Our turn.'

Neither of them argue. They are both way past it. They stagger off to their rooms like zombies, leaving Sarah to make tea and toast while Diane patrols.

Diane briefly considers telling Sarah about her and Ethan, but what would be the point? She's not in love with Ethan. He is just a substitute. She's sure, deep down, he doesn't love her either. They are just making the best of things, marooned on this island with no other release.

Ethan is probably desperate to get out of here, but fraught as it has been, Diane isn't so sure there's anything else out there for her. Life as she knew it is pretty much over.

Sarah makes the tea too weak but Diane drinks it anyway. The milk has an unpleasant tang to it, but she drains every last drop, polishes off her plate of food and then gets up to make another round. It seems her appetite has finally returned. She probably has Ethan to thank for that.

'Who do you think will be next to die?' she asks Sarah as she waits for the toast to pop.

She enjoys the shocked expression on her friend's face. Sarah can be so vanilla at times, clutching her pearls and claiming to never have a dark thought in her head. But Diane saw the way she looked at Asha in her wedding dress. She has always, always been jealous of her.

'Probably Ethan,' Sarah says. 'He's annoyed the most people.'

Diane studies her carefully. 'Not me?'

'No! Why would you say that?' Sarah's response is quick, almost defensive.

Diane shrugs. 'I've ruffled a few feathers.'

'Sure, but...' Sarah can't even finish the sentence. She shifts, glancing towards the window. 'Do you think Asha's still out there?'

'I don't know. It's been two days.'

'Is that all? It feels like a lifetime.'

'Three more days and the ferry will come back for us.'

'If it's not too late by then.'

Sarah meets Diane's eye, then looks away.

Hours later, Ethan emerges from his room. He drags Pete out with him.

'You could have let him sleep a bit longer,' Diane says. 'We don't all need to be up.'

'It's best we keep to a routine,' Ethan says.

Diane purses her lips. She's getting a little sick of the way Ethan throws his weight about.

Sarah makes Pete a cup of tea. She doesn't make Ethan one.

Ethan is a little twitchy. He sidles over to Diane and tries to hold her hand but she pushes him away.

'Not in front of everyone.'

'Pete already knows.'

'Sarah doesn't. I'd rather keep it that way.'

His eyebrows narrow. She's not sure if it's the rejection that bothers him, or the fact she's disagreed with him. Their arguments always brought the heat to their friendship. But now that they've slept together, Diane doesn't feel the urge any more. It's as if someone's poured a bucket of cold water over her.

'Last night,' he says, lowering his voice, 'I wasn't just taking advantage. I've liked you for a long time, but you never wanted to know.'

'That's not true, you were always after Asha. All of you.'

Pete appears right next to her. 'No, I always liked Sarah.'

Ethan and Diane both stare at him, confused at his sudden intrusion in their conversation.

Diane glances at Sarah, who is in the kitchen. Either she hasn't heard, or she is pretending she hasn't. Diane doesn't blame her for not wanting to open this particular can of worms.

Ethan goes back to building up the fire, while Pete heads to the kitchen and begins pulling things out of the drawers. He piles up tape, gum and glue on the counter. He and Sarah talk in low voices, but she can hear them, talking about the boat again. She'd hoped they'd given up.

She shoots Ethan a look. 'They're going to get themselves killed.'

A moment later, Sarah and Pete come out to the living room and start pulling their boots on.

'You're wasting your time,' Ethan tells them. His voice is edged with irritation.

Sarah glances back at him, but doesn't reply.

'I think I'll head over to Judith's again,' Diane says. 'I'll have another go on the radio. And there might be a flare or something. I'm sure Judith and Broderick must have something useful.'

'You can feed the chickens while you're there,' Ethan says. 'And bring back some eggs.'

Sarah turns and looks at him. 'Why don't you help her? There are sheep to feed too.'

He cuts her down with his glare. 'Thanks, but I have more pressing things to see to.'

'Like what?'

'I'm going to make a massive bonfire. Big enough that planes will see it.'

'They'll just think we're having a bonfire.'

'Not if I write "help" in really big letters in the sand.'

Sarah pulls a face. It's clear she doesn't think much of his plan. Diane doubts it will have much effect either, but Ethan needs to keep busy. He'll drive himself nuts if he's not doing something. He's like a caged bird trying to fight his way out.

'Come on, let's get going,' Pete says. He seems keen to pull her away.

'Good luck,' Diane calls after them. 'Be careful, out there, okay?'

'It's you two who should be careful,' Sarah says. Probably, she's thinking about how few days are left. Someone on this island is a murderer. If they want to kill again, they will have to strike in the next couple of days. Before the ferry returns.

THIRTY-NINE
SARAH

'I can't believe we still haven't found Asha,' Sarah says as she and Pete walk down to the pier. 'It really is starting to look like she left without Gordon, but that doesn't make any sense.'

Pete shakes his head. 'No way. She wouldn't leave him. I hate to say it, but I think she's in the sea.'

'Oh God.'

She remembers now, seeing someone in the water when she looked out from the lighthouse. She'd assumed someone was swimming. But what if they were actually drowning?

A sour taste rises in her throat. Her breakfast feels like it's climbing back up, stronger, sharper now. More acidic. She looks around at the scenery and tries to think of something else.

'But maybe I'm wrong,' Pete says. 'There's still a chance she's hiding somewhere.'

Sarah swallows hard, her throat burning. 'Asha must know who the killer is. If we can just find her, she can tell us everything.'

She knows how desperate she sounds, but she can't stop. The thought of finding another body is unbearable.

The sound of the waves grows louder as they reach the pier.

The sand shifts slightly beneath their feet, cool and damp from the tide.

A faint droning cuts through the air. Sarah looks up as a small plane appears in the sky, its white body and tartan tail standing out against the blue.

They jump up and down, shouting and waving their arms. Pete stomps on the sand, his voice cracking as he yells, 'Help!'

Sarah throws her arms wide, waving frantically, her gaze fixed on the plane.

'That'll be an inter-island plane,' Pete shouts as it fades out of view. 'Like the one that flies from Westray to Papa Westray.'

Sarah doesn't answer. She's too busy staring, willing the plane to turn, to dip its wings, to do *something*. But it doesn't. Its path stays straight, the tartan tail disappearing against the horizon.

Her arms drop to her sides, her chest rising and falling with shallow breaths. Of course it hasn't seen them. She exhales sharply.

'Maybe Ethan's ideas weren't so stupid after all.'

'Today is clear,' Pete points out. 'But a lot of the time, this place is too misty for a plane to see anything.'

She looks around for the boat. She could have sworn they left it right here, but there's no sign of it. She looks at Pete, who is scanning the empty beach, as if expecting to find something she's missed.

He crouches down and brushes his fingers over some grooves in the sand. 'The tide couldn't have reached this far,' he says. 'Not unless there was a storm.'

She follows the trail. The grooves lead all the way down to the water. Her breath feels shallow as the realisation takes shape. 'Then someone took it,' she says, her voice trembling. She turns to him, her hands curling at her sides.

She stares at the shoreline, her stomach tightening. The

grooves in the sand seem sharper now, leading her thoughts in a direction she doesn't want to go.

'Do you think it was the killer?'

He doesn't answer. They both stand in silence, listening to the sounds of the waves.

Now there really is no way off the island.

FORTY

SARAH

Eight Months Earlier, Glasgow

'What are you getting dressed up for?' Pete asks as Sarah steps out of her bedroom, wearing her little black dress.

She looks at him and swallows.

'I've got a work thing. Dinner and drinks.'

He eyes her with suspicion. 'You never said. I've already made us a veggie sausage casserole.'

'Great, well save me some in case I'm hungry when I get in. You know what these things are like – embarrassingly small canapés, little picky bits. I'll probably be ravenous.'

He looks at her with his large watery eyes, and she feels bad for judging him. Pete is still going through a lot. He still gets the tremors, especially late at night. He doesn't like being left alone. It frightens him. But Cameron is only here for one night and she needs this.

She catches the bus into town. Cameron's hotel is a fancy one, down by the water. The sun glistens off the sleek modern exterior, but that doesn't stop the seagulls nesting on the roof.

Stepping inside, it feels as though she has entered an art gallery. The walls are adorned with vibrant, abstract pieces, and the carpet is woven with swirling patterns that seem to come alive under her feet.

She spots Cameron right away, leaning against a polished mahogany bar, his sleeves rolled up to reveal muscular forearms. He's ditched the tie and is now wearing a crisp black shirt, with the top buttons undone. She catches a whiff of his musky cologne as she walks towards him.

'Hope I'm not late?'

'Sarah!'

She feels a jolt of electricity as he kisses her on the cheek.

'No Pete?' he asks, looking behind her.

'No, he couldn't make it. He had a er... another commitment.'

She flushes and hopes he can't tell she's lying.

Pete never goes anywhere. He doesn't even like to walk down to Morrisons. The last time he went out, he got really paranoid. He said he felt like every single person on the street was looking at him, and he ended up hiding under a bridge for half a day.

'Shame,' Cameron says, sitting back down on his bar stool. 'I know we probably shouldn't, but I thought we might start with a cocktail?'

She smiles and takes the menu. The old Sarah would be sensible and stick to something safe and familiar. But she doesn't get out much, so today, she's going to make the most of it.

'I'll have a banana mai tai,' she says.

'And I'll have a dirty Martini.'

They watch as the barman pours, mixes, and garnishes their drinks – hers with a bright yellow wedge of pineapple and

Cameron's with three plump green olives speared on a toothpick.

'Do you eat the olives?' she asks.

'Oh yes, they're amazing.'

Her breath catches in her throat as he leans over and places one between her lips. She closes her eyes, savouring the flavour as she chews and swallows. When she opens them, he is grinning widely.

'Well?'

'Not bad,' she admits. She still finds the texture odd, but infused with alcohol, it no longer tastes like an olive. It's more like some kind of fruit.

He reaches for another and rolls it over her lips before popping it into her mouth. He watches intently as she chews, not taking his eyes of her until it's all gone. She reaches for her mai tai and takes a long swig.

Somehow, they have shuffled closer together so that their thighs are almost pressed against each other. He must feel it too. He rests his hand in the space between them, his fingers brushing the hem of her dress, raising it slightly. A shiver runs through her, but she doesn't correct it. A little later, his hand returns to the same spot. This time he is definitely doing it, inching up her dress to expose her thigh. Her cheeks flame with heat. She should stop him, but she is too turned on.

They order more cocktails, and now he is openly touching her, running his hand up and down her leg, caressing and squeezing. He's not even trying to be discreet.

She removes his hand firmly.

'People can see us,' she tells him.

'Maybe we should go somewhere they can't,' he says, holding up his room key.

She meets his eye, and a tingle of electricity shoots through her body.

'I think I'm going to sit here and finish my drink,' she says.

To her relief, Cameron removes his hand and picks up the drinks menu. 'What about a strawberry woo woo?'

She should excuse herself and leave. But it's just a drink, she tells herself, so she nods and waits impatiently while he gets the attention of the barman. He keeps his hand on the counter, and it drives her crazy. Even worse than when he was running it up and down her thigh. He has nice hands, with long pianist's fingers. His gold wedding band gleams under the lights but he makes no attempt to hide it. She finds this reassuring. If he were in the habit of fooling around, he'd take it off, wouldn't he?

She drains the remainder of her drink a little too fast, and the barman replaces it with the new one.

Cameron clinks her glass.

She thinks for a moment. 'To... old friends.'

His eyes glint with amusement. They both take a sip. He smiles at her. She smiles back. He has his room key on the counter in front of him now. She can't stop looking at it.

Was he serious about going upstairs? She never took him to be that sort of man. He always seemed so quiet and serious.

'So do you plan on staying here, in Glasgow?' he asks.

Sarah shakes her head. 'I've never given it much thought.'

'It's just, I remember you talking about going travelling. Didn't you want to go to Cairo at one point?'

Her eyes widen. 'That was years ago. You remember that?'

'Of course. I remember everything about you.'

She swallows hard. She's so used to always being the one to listen to other people's thoughts and opinions. Other people's problems, if she's honest. She's not used to anyone treating her like what she says matters. Not even Pete.

Her eyes go to the keys again.

She wants to go with him so much. She wants to know what it would be like to kiss him, to feel his body pressed against hers. They have a connection, she is sure of it. It's not just physical, this feeling that's building up inside her. She wants him. She wants all of him. Body and soul. But then she gets a flicker of Diane in her wedding dress. She was so happy, her face shining with excitement. And Sarah was her bridesmaid for Christ's sake.

'I can't do this.'

She wants him so much. She craves it with all her body. But she snatches up her bag and gets down off her bar stool, her legs a little wobbly.

He looks shocked. 'Wait! You don't have to go.'

She meets his eyes one last time. Those glacial blue eyes.

'Oh, I do,' she tells him.

Because there is no way she can stay a moment longer in his company without doing as he suggests and going with him, up to his room.

No, she is better than this.

'At least let me call you a taxi?'

'Thanks, but no thanks.'

She stumbles out of the hotel, her vision blurred from all the alcohol she has consumed.

A frigid gust of wind rips through her, sending a shiver down her spine as she leans against the railing. Her bleary eyes follow the gulls as they dart and swoop, their cries piercing the air like an alarm. And without even turning round, she knows he is still at the window.

Watching.

FORTY-ONE
DIANE

Everyone is back at the cottage when Diane steps through the door, bags of eggs and potatoes swinging from her hand. The smell of damp wood and wet clothing hangs in the air, and she shakes off the light drizzle clinging to her coat.

'How did you get on?' she asks, scanning the room. Pete is slumped in a chair, his arms crossed. He grunts in response, barely looking up. Sarah sits at the table, her face tight with tension.

'I built the bonfire,' Ethan says. 'But then it started pissing down.'

For a moment, the sound of rain pattering against the window is the only response. Then, out of nowhere, Pete's shoulders start to shake. He covers his mouth with his hand.

Ethan glares at him. 'What's so funny?'

Pete waves a hand, unable to stop himself. His laughter fills the room. Diane looks at Sarah, who shrugs.

'Well, I'm glad someone finds it funny,' Diane says.

'I'm sorry,' Pete says. 'It's not funny. But if you don't laugh, you cry.'

Sarah looks at Diane. 'How did you get on?'

'I went on the radio and repeated my message over and over but I don't know if anyone heard me.'

'But they might have?' Sarah says.

'We can only hope.'

Diane flops down on the sofa. 'And still no sign of Asha, I take it?'

Everyone shakes their heads.

'I can't understand why she invited any of us to her wedding in the first place,' Sarah says.

Diane looks up. 'We're her friends. The only ones she has, apparently.'

Sarah shakes her head. 'We were all so awful to her. Do you remember her twenty-first, when we pretended we were going to throw her a party, but we didn't? We left her all sorts of hints and talked about it when we knew she could hear us.'

Ethan shakes his head. 'I thought we were really arranging a surprise party.'

Sarah's eyes widen. 'It was your bloody idea!'

His face goes tomato red. 'It was not!'

Sarah shoots Diane a bemused look.

'It was your idea,' Diane confirms. 'You said we should take her down a notch or two.'

They all look at Pete.

'I threw her a little surprise party of my own,' he says. 'I took her to Pizza Express. It would have been nice, but the waiter seated us at one of those big round tables and the whole time we were there, she kept looking around, as if she was expecting more guests. And then they brought her out a cake and the whole restaurant sang "Happy Birthday" to her.'

'Oh, dear lord, we were awful.'

'Everyone does bad things when they're young,' Diane says.

Sarah grimaces. 'We were really bad,' she says in a small voice. 'What about all those times we went for a night out and left without her?'

'Why would you do that?' Pete asks.

Sarah shrugs, but Diane doesn't mind admitting it.

'She was such an attention whore. Whenever we went out, she was more interested in talking to strangers than hanging out with us. It got really annoying, so we figured she could get one of her randoms to walk her home. But in essence, we just left her with a bunch of creeps.'

She looks around at each of them. 'You know what? We deserve this.'

'We do,' Sarah agrees.

'Asha said you'd been getting crank phone calls. How long has that been going on for?'

Sarah looks at Pete. 'I don't know. A few months now.'

Diane keeps looking at her. 'You don't think...?'

'What? Asha? You've got to be kidding me.'

'Why not? She's into drama, isn't she?'

'All the same. It's a bit... weird.'

Ethan shakes his head. 'Now you're being ridiculous. There's no way Asha would do that. She doesn't have it in her.'

'But she might have,' Sarah says.

He folds his arms. 'No. I refuse to believe it. It's not her. End of.'

Diane tilts her head. 'Just because you don't think so doesn't mean we should rule it out.'

Ethan turns to meet her gaze, and Diane doesn't know why, but she feels an all-consuming urge to get a rise out of him.

'Hey, does everyone remember the time Ethan lost his mind and punched a hole through the shed?'

Sarah starts laughing, and Pete joins in, but Ethan stands completely rigid, his fists clenched so tight they might break. Diane leans in way too close.

'You need therapy.'

He opens his mouth to say something, but she's not interested. She storms out of the cottage, leaving the door wide open behind her. She strides across the garden, waiting for the adrenaline to leave her body.

The wind is picking up and she hears the rush of the waves. She sees a flash of colour in the bushes, and feels the sensation of something whizzing past her, once, twice. She turns to run back into the cottage.

That's when she feels her shoulder explode.

FORTY-TWO
SARAH

The door flies open and Diane stumbles inside, blood pouring from her right shoulder.

'I've been shot!' she screams, gasping for air.

Pete rushes to the door and shoots off a warning shot.

Sarah sees someone fleeing through the bushes, and her blood runs cold.

'Stop shooting! It's Asha!'

Asha crashes through the foliage, her dark hair streaming behind her, legs moving with desperate, unrelenting speed. A moment later, she is gone, swallowed by the mist.

'Never mind her, help Diane,' Pete says. He shuts the door but keeps it open a crack, watching with his gun.

Diane collapses onto the floor. She lies there convulsing, holding her shoulder.

Sarah rushes over and kneels down on the floor beside her.

'Let me see!'

The wind howls, biting into Sarah's skin as she examines the damage. Diane's T-shirt glistens with blood. Thinking fast, Sarah pulls a sanitary pad from her handbag and presses it to the wound.

Ethan takes a look. He gets the kitchen scissors and cuts away at the fabric so they can see the wound clearly.

'The bullet's still in there. We have to get it out. Sarah, get me the first aid kit and your make-up bag. Diane's too.'

Sarah runs into her room. As she grabs her make-up bag, she sees her phone on the floor between the bed and the nightstand. She freezes for a moment, confused. How the hell did it get there?

This is not the time. She grabs her bag and runs out to Ethan with it. Then goes back for Diane's. Ethan rummages through them, pulling out a pair of tweezers and some cotton wool. Then he grabs a bottle of whisky and hands it to Diane.

'Drink, it will numb the pain.'

Diane takes a swig directly from the bottle. Her hand shakes badly as she tries to hand it back to him.

'Have some more,' he says. 'Believe me, you'll need it.'

Diane takes another gulp, then lies back, groaning in pain.

Pete is still at the door. 'I think she's gone,' he calls.

'Thank fuck for that,' Diane calls back.

No one smiles. They all know they are in deep, deep shit.

'Sarah, can you bring me that lamp?' Ethan asks as he gets everything ready.

Sarah goes to the table and stretches it as far as the cable will allow.

The lamp casts shadows over their faces, and Sarah clearly sees the panic in his eyes.

All at once, it occurs to her that all Ethan's confidence, his bluster is just for show. Deep down, he's just a frightened little boy, who thinks he always has to be the best, and doesn't want anyone else to see his weakness.

He fumbles through the supplies.

'Do you have a sewing needle?'

'Asha has,' Diane says, her breath quickening. 'I saw it in her bedside drawer.'

A heavy silence lingers in the air as they all come to the same realisation. Asha might still be out there. But Diane is a shocking shade of white and Sarah has the feeling that if they don't get the bullet out of her soon, she's not going to make it. She looks at Ethan and he stares back at her. Neither of them blink.

'I'll go,' Pete says.

They all turn and look at him.

'Thank you,' Diane whispers. Her eyelids flutter shut.

'No, stay with us,' Ethan says, taking her hand. 'Don't you dare die on me,' he whispers fiercely.

Sarah turns away, watching with concern as Pete opens the door.

'Pete?'

'Yeah?'

'Be careful, okay?'

Pete glances back at her. 'I'll be as quick as I can.'

With Pete gone, someone needs to watch the window. Sarah picks up her gun and walks over to it, opening it just a crack, and sticks the gun out, ready. Pete runs past, and she watches the bushes, ready to react. A surge of adrenaline courses through her veins and she feels giddy. She has never felt so alive.

Pete's cheeks are flushed when he returns. He hands Ethan a miniature sewing kit, his breath visible in the cold air. Ethan rolls up his sleeves and heads to the sink to wash his hands. Sarah follows suit. Ethan fills a small bowl with whisky and dips a clean tea towel into it, using it to sanitise the tweezers.

They exchange glances. Diane doesn't look so good. Her eyes are bloodshot and she's getting the tremors.

'Keep drinking the whisky,' Ethan tells her. His hands shake in spite of his confident air.

'I don't know if this is going to work,' he whispers.

Sarah meets his eyes. 'We have to try.'

Gingerly, Ethan peels away the pad. The wound is ugly and raw, and the pad is soaked with blood. Sarah's eyes widen in horror as she sees the tip of the bullet, lodged just beneath the surface of the skin. The sight makes her stomach churn.

Ethan takes a breath and grits his teeth, then he pours whisky over the wound, though they all know it's a poor substitute for proper antiseptic. Diane writhes, shrieking and swearing. Her screams echo off the walls.

'It's all right,' Sarah says, trying to keep her own voice from shaking. 'Just hold still. It won't be long.'

'No,' she begs. 'I can't. Just leave me alone...'

Ethan raises his chin.

'You're going to have to hold her still,' he tells Sarah.

She swallows hard, her heart racing as she presses down on Diane's good shoulder. Diane continues to thrash about, her fingernails digging into Sarah's arm.

'Pete, come over here and help me!' Sarah yells.

Pete sets down his gun and moves towards them. He hugs Diane's middle, holding her in place. There is something so desperate in his expression, as if he can feel her pain.

'You can do this,' he says as Ethan holds the tweezers over the wound. His hand is shaking so much that he nearly loses them, but then he clenches his jaw and tries again.

Diane's body convulses wildly, and she lets out a guttural scream.

Ethan passes her a napkin. 'Here, put this in your mouth.'

Diane grips it between her teeth, champing down on it to stifle her screams. Ethan keeps going, digging into the wound with surgical precision.

Diane stops fighting it. Her body goes rigid as everyone around her falls into a tense silence. The only sounds are the crashing of the waves and the howling of the wind against the windows. Ethan's hand trembles as the tweezers grip the bullet. His forehead is slick with sweat as he begins to draw it out with agonising slowness. Diane's tears mix with the sweat on her face, eyes wide with pain and fear. Sarah feels every ounce of tension in her body, her muscles coiled tight like a spring ready to snap. And then, with a triumphant cry, Ethan pulls out the bullet.

'Got it!'

He holds it up for them all to see. It is amazing how such a tiny piece of metal can cause so much pain and turmoil. Relief washes over them all, and Sarah collapses back against the sofa.

They are not prepared for the gush of blood. Ethan tries frantically to staunch the flow.

'Sew her up!' Sarah shrieks.

There is so much blood, and Diane has become very calm. Her breaths come in shallow gasps as she drifts in and out of consciousness. Ethan hovers over her, his hands red and slick with blood, his own breathing ragged and panicked. He fumbles with the needle and shakes his head. He looks over at Sarah.

'You're better at sewing than me.'

Sarah takes the needle, and with it, the responsibility for saving her friend's life.

Her hands feel like sausages as she attempts to thread.

'Bring the lamp closer!'

Pete does as she asks, and she tries again, threading it through and then she looks down at Diane's wound, knowing she must act now but not wanting to touch her.

This is not like embroidering a napkin or stitching on a button. She pricks Diane's flesh with the sharp needle and feels the way the blood oozes around her hand. So much blood, she can scarcely see what she's doing. She perseveres, forcing the needle in and out of the broken flesh. It is so difficult to force the needle through, and yet Diane barely flinches. Sarah blocks out all that is going on around her, the wind and the rain, the ever-present danger that threatens them all. She becomes laser focused, drawing the needle in and out, in and out, until she has closed the wound.

Once she has finished, Ethan pours the last of the whisky over the jagged stitches.

'Hopefully that will keep it from getting infected,' he says.

Sarah crawls away, leaving a trail of bloody handprints on the floor. She can finally breathe again, but the weight of all that has happened settles heavily in her chest.

FORTY-THREE

SARAH

2018, Edinburgh

Sarah pushes open the theatre door and steps into the busy backstage area. She spots Asha straight away, admiring herself in front of the full-length mirror and adding the finishing touches to her already perfect make-up. She wears a deep burgundy gown with a fitted bodice that makes her narrow waist even more impossibly tiny. As Sarah takes in her long flowing skirt, delicate lace sleeves and sequined neckline, she feels a flash of envy. She swallows it down and remembers to smile as she walks towards her old friend.

'Look at you, Lady Macbeth!'

Asha breaks into a grin. 'Thanks! I can't believe the show's tonight. I'm not ready!'

Sarah looks around. 'When are your parents going to get here?'

'They can't make it. They're both needed at the restaurant. They're really slammed this week.'

'Oh, what a pity!'

'I know. It's a bummer. But never mind, I saved front-row seats for you lot!'

Sarah hesitates, guilt twisting in her stomach. 'Diane just rang. She and Cameron aren't going to be able to make it.'

'Oh no!' Asha looks gutted.

Sarah doesn't tell her what else she heard when Diane rang her. It sounded like she was in the middle of a slanging match with Cameron. She hopes she's okay.

Asha forces a smile. 'I've still got you and Pete and Ethan.'

Sarah raises a brow. 'Is Pete coming? I haven't heard from him in ages.'

'Well, he never got back to me, but I sent him an invite so, I'm hoping...'

'Oh, well then. We will just have to see. What about your friends from work?'

Asha's brows knit together and Sarah realises she's put her foot in it. She forces a smile on to her face. 'Anyway, I'm here, and I can't wait. You're going to be fabulous.'

Asha forces a big brave smile. 'Too right. Can't wait to get my hands bloody!'

'Oh, spoiler alert!'

Asha cracks up. 'Surely you already know the plot?'

'Not really.'

'Didn't you do it at school?'

'I skived a lot towards the end. I was seeing a very sexy boy from the college. We were at it like rabbits.'

'Right, well you're in for a treat then. It's one of my favourites.'

Sarah's phone beeps and her face falls.

'What's wrong?'

'Ethan can't make it. He's got a work thing.'

'Oh, for goodness' sake!'

Asha's face contorts in a momentary flash of anger. It's strange, but Sarah doesn't think she's ever seen her like that before. Asha is always so in control of her emotions. She watches curiously as her calm demeanour shatters. Her eyes blaze, her nostrils flare, and she releases a primal scream that reverberates throughout the room, causing the windows and doors to rattle in their frames.

Everyone around them freezes. Then, as if on cue, they break into thunderous applause.

'Bravo!' someone shouts.

Sarah shakes her head. She doesn't understand theatre people. Is she the only one who can see the raw emotion pulsating beneath Asha's skin?

She is sure Asha is just as stunned as she is, but the attention calms her down enough for her to take a bow.

'I'm sorry. I know you wanted us all here,' Sarah says softly.

Asha swallows hard, fighting for self-control. Her smile is brittle, her eyes shimmering with unshed tears.

'It's fine. Really. I'll be fine. I'd better finish getting ready.'

'Break a leg out there. You're going to be incredible,' Sarah says.

She hugs Asha carefully, mindful of her make-up. But as she turns to leave, she glances back one more time and sees her standing alone backstage, and it occurs to her how odd it is that Asha has always been the queen of her little circle, but she doesn't seem to have any other friends. It's as if she doesn't fit in anywhere else.

'I can do this,' she hears Asha say to herself as she walks away.

This is probably not the time to tell her that she has to leave early.

FORTY-FOUR
SARAH

Pete fetches more whisky and passes it to Ethan. They both drink as Diane did, straight out of the bottle. Ethan offers it to Sarah but she refuses. They need to be on high alert, not dull their senses. It's only a matter of time until Asha comes back.

She picks herself up off the floor and goes to the bathroom to wash her hands. The sink turns red with blood as she scrubs, and she pictures it gushing down the pipes and out into the sea.

Afterwards, she fetches Diane's duvet and pillow and brings them into the lounge. Diane appears to be sleeping, but it's hard to say. She vaguely responds as she covers her up. Sarah stands there for a moment, monitoring her breathing. Despite all their efforts, she isn't sure with any certainty that Diane will last the night.

Pete looks up as she walks into the room, but Ethan refuses to meet her eye. She looks at him with curiosity. His head is angled towards the window, but it's clear he isn't really seeing anything outside. His posture is stiff, his hands clasped in his lap.

She studies him more closely. His eyes are bloodshot, the

whites tinged with red and his nose looks pink and raw. If she didn't know better, she'd say he'd been crying.

She knows Ethan well enough not to push. If he wants to talk, he'll talk. For now, it's better to let the tension settle. The three of them sit in uneasy silence, adrenaline coursing through their veins, too wired to rest, too wary to relax.

Pete leans back in his chair, nursing a beer and keeping one eye on the door. Ethan sits near the window, a bottle of whisky cradled in his hand. He takes a long sip, staring out into the twilight.

She perches on the arm of the sofa, her gaze flicking between Diane's shallow breathing and the window. Outside, the wind continues to howl.

Pete has his head bowed. He's muttering to himself, over and over again. 'It doesn't make sense. Why would Asha shoot Diane? Asha is lovely.'

He looks up at her like a wounded dog.

Sarah exhales. Pete's the only one who would describe Asha in that way. He never found her annoying, as she and Diane have. And he's probably never been jealous of her, if she's brutally honest. Jealous of the way things always turn out for her. How she only has to smile and people fawn all over her. She glances at Diane. She's felt that jealousy, and she's sure Diane has too. But it's not enough to make you want to kill her. And it's certainly not enough to make someone go on a rampage.

So what the hell did happen?

She thinks of Asha – sad, lonely, misunderstood Asha. Gordon seemed like everything she ever wanted. Maybe not the pin-up husband Sarah would have imagined for her, but he seemed to check all the other boxes. There's no way Asha would kill him, is there? But then, up until a few hours ago, she didn't think Asha would shoot anyone.

It is hard to imagine what would have turned Asha from a blushing bride into a menace with a gun.

A stray tear runs down her cheek, and she wipes it away.

'She's always been the one to hold this group together. The one to arrange everything. Her life always seemed so perfect, I never understood why she did that. It's only now I realise she might have needed us, and we've all... well, what do we do when we get together?'

'We laugh at her,' Pete says.

'Exactly. So perhaps we've had this coming.'

Ethan puffs out a long breath. 'Why do people do anything?'

They all fall silent.

'Right, well I suppose I'll try and get some sleep,' Sarah says, getting to her feet. She looks at each of them in turn, trying to read what's going on in their minds. But it's impossible. They each look as dazed and exhausted as she feels. She heads to her bedroom and lies awake for the longest time.

Is this her fault?

She lets the tears slide down her face. An avalanche of memories runs through her mind. Diane mocking Asha, Ethan tripping Pete. Her and Pete being too wet to do anything. Always letting things slide because they're nervous or uncomfortable. She pulls the blankets right up over her head, but she can't make it all go away, all those years of toxic friendship.

She should have been a better friend, but she can't take it back.

She closes her eyes, but she's too tense to sleep.

She feels as though Asha is in the room with her, watching her. Twice, she has to get up and check the wardrobe. There is nothing in there but clothes, hanging limp and lifeless. And yet when she returns to bed, she still can't shake that feeling of being watched.

. . .

In the morning, she heads out to the living room to find Diane is sitting up in her armchair. She grabs onto Sarah's hand.

'I want to go outside,' she says. 'I want to breathe in the fresh sea air.'

Sarah glances at the gun Pete has just handed her.

'I'm not sure that's a good idea,' she says. 'Maybe you should wait until later when Pete and Ethan are up. Just in case...'

In case Asha comes back, is what she wants to say, but the words die in her throat.

Diane shakes her head. 'I want to see the sunrise.'

It's morbid, the way she says this, as though she doesn't expect to see many more. Sarah has no idea if she is right. The last thing she wants is to go outside, but how can she deny Diane what could be her final wish?

She gathers up their boots and coats and helps to get Diane ready. Then she opens the door and steps outside, supporting Diane with one arm, while holding the gun in the other.

Who is she kidding? As if she is really going to shoot Asha. She doesn't have it in her.

They walk, painfully slowly, round the back of the cottages until they reach exactly the right vantage point. The sun is large and bold, burning like fire on the horizon. It makes Sarah picture some Viking god, holding his torch aloft. Diane is unable to stand for long. Her legs are shaking badly.

'Wait there.'

Sarah leaves her for a moment and pops inside to get her a chair. She returns and Diane sinks gratefully into it.

Sarah stands beside her and they watch for a while as the sun bubbles over, spilling its light onto the horizon.

'You hear that?' Diane says.

Sarah tightens her hold on the gun, until she realises Diane is talking about the dawn chorus.

They listen together to the sound of the birds singing into the wind. The crex-crex of the corncrake, the drumming of the snipe. She doesn't know why they call it a dawn chorus. It's uncoordinated and chaotic and she's never understood the purpose of their song. She always thought the male birds were singing to attract attention, but today the sounds seem more fraught to her ears, and it occurs to her that they might be trying to defend their turf.

The bird world is often violent and dangerous. They look so peaceful and idyllic, fluttering about in the wind, but in reality, there's a life or death battle to be won.

It's a bird eat bird world out there, after all.

Sarah tilts her head. Since when did Diane become such a nature lover? Cameron's influence, she supposes. She could imagine him sitting out in the garden, watching the birds. A smile forms on her lips. If she makes it out of this nightmare, she is going to make more time for the good things in life, the quiet things.

'How are you feeling?' she asks. 'Are you in a lot of pain?'

'It's getting closer now, I can feel it,' Diane says.

'What is?'

'I feel this warmth washing over me. He's looking down on me. I know that I will be with him soon. All this will be over.'

She closes her eyes again. Her breathing is slower and more irregular. Her skin looks mottled, and when Sarah takes her hand, it feels ice cold.

She wonders if she should bring her back indoors but Diane seems so content out here, so instead, she fetches her duvet and makes her as comfortable as she can. If she does not survive this, at least she will have spent her last few hours in the best possible way.

Sarah swallows down a sob. She can't bear this, this waiting for it all to end, but at least Diane seems so much calmer, so much more at peace.

. . .

'What were you thinking?' Ethan demands, when he and Pete finally surface. 'Bringing her out here? It's completely out in the open.'

'It's what she wanted,' Sarah says, staring him down. 'We don't know how much longer she's got. There are two more days until the ferry comes back. She might not hold out that long. She wanted to see the sunrise, and to listen to the birds and do all the things she thought we were going to do when we came to Haarlorn.'

Ethan looks like he's going to argue, then, quite unexpectedly, he flops down on the floor. His shoulders shake and he holds his head in his hands. Sarah rubs his shoulder gently, unsure whether he wants her to comfort him or leave him to it.

Minutes pass, and when he looks up again, the steely look has returned to his gaze.

'I want to find the damned gun emplacement,' he says. 'If we can find that, we'll find Asha. That's got to be where she's hiding.'

'I'll come with you,' Pete says.

'No, I will,' Sarah says.

Not because she really wants to, but because she cannot be the one to be with Diane when she dies.

She just can't.

FORTY-FIVE
DIANE

2020, Inverness

Diane blows her fringe out of her face. She hears Cameron on the phone in the spare room. He's been in a meeting for over an hour and it shows no sign of ending. She glances down at the spreadsheet in front of her. The job she used to enjoy is starting to feel like a prison, tying her to this desk, forcing her to input numbers and answer emails. She is surprised how much she misses the company of other people. Some of her colleagues are actual donkeys; the boss who waffles on without purpose, the intern who asks the same stupid questions over and over, but now, two weeks into lockdown, she misses the buzz. So when a message pops up on her screen from Asha, instead of ignoring it as she usually would, she finds herself replying straight away:

Hey Asha, great to hear from you. Not up to much but it's bin day tomorrow, so there's that to look forward to.

She feels a little indignant when Asha does not reply straight away.

She goes back to her work and is about to start reading an incredibly boring report, when Asha calls on video.

She accepts and finds herself staring into Asha's rather perfect-looking flat. Everything is spick and span and Asha herself is dressed up as though she is going clubbing. Diane, meanwhile, is in her pyjamas. She usually slips a blazer over the top if she has an on-screen meeting. No one can tell.

'Hi, how's it going?' she asks.

'I swear if I spend another minute alone in my flat, I'm going to kill someone.'

'That bad?'

'Well, let's see. My downstairs neighbour just had a baby, so I have to listen to it wailing every couple of hours. Then my upstairs neighbour has decided this would be a good time to do some DIY, so there's constant drilling from his flat. I reported him to the council but they don't give a monkey's, as long as he stays home. How much longer is this bloody lockdown going to go on for?'

'Hopefully just a few weeks,' Diane says. 'They've got to get the number of cases down, haven't they?'

'If you mean cases of beer, I'm on it.'

Asha pans over to her sideboard which contains three crates of Corona.

'Those were all they had left at the supermarket. I've got wine too, but it feels kind of lame drinking by myself.'

Diane looks up as Cameron wanders out to the kitchen to get a biscuit.

'Don't mind me,' he says when he sees Asha on the screen.

'Cameron!' Asha waves her arms with excitement. 'It's so good to see you. I'm so starved of interaction, I've been sitting by the window all day, hoping to see the postman.'

Cameron nods. 'I know what you mean. I'm actually looking forward to heading down to Sainsbury's later. I've got a new silk mask to wear. So much nicer than those scratchy paper ones.'

Asha leans forward slightly, her eyes sparkling. 'Get you, you trendsetter.'

Cameron grins and glances briefly at Diane, but his gaze lingers on the screen.

'And what about the lack of cars on the road?' Asha says. 'That's the weirdest thing. At night, I can't hear anything. Where I live, there was always honking and car alarms going off. But now it's just the baby and the drill.'

Cameron raises his mug to toast Asha.

'To the baby with the drill!'

Asha's laugh pierces Diane's ears like a thousand needles and she quickly turns down the volume.

In the weeks that follow, there are more video chats. Asha gets Sarah to join. Ethan too, when he's not battling conspiracy theorists on Twitter. But no one seems to know what has happened to Pete. They set up a group WhatsApp. It becomes a daily occupation to update each other with all the ins and outs of their lives. Diane becomes a witness to Sarah's attempts at baking sourdough and Ethan's home workouts. But most of the time, it is Asha who dominates the conversation.

'So, anyway, I've been chatting with someone new. He's a mathematician. I was quite into him until I decided to stalk him a bit.'

'Let me guess, he's married?' Diane says.

'How did you know?'

'Lucky guess.'

Being beautiful does not protect Asha in the dating wars. In fact, it seems to go against her.

'Like I keep telling you, you should take a picture with a bucket over your head. That will weed out the creeps.'

Asha shakes her head, but Diane is serious. If Asha wants to meet a decent man, she's not going to find him through dating apps.

She is so glad she never had to resort to any of that nonsense herself. She met Cameron towards the end of university. Things were so much more simple back then. You met someone. You went out a few times and that was it. Insta love.

'He said he was going to take me to the Caribbean,' Asha says, flipping her hair over her shoulder. She looks fed up. 'But seriously, if I want to get married by my thirtieth birthday, I can't afford to waste time.'

'Is it really that important?' Diane asks. 'I mean, age is just a number.'

'Well, look at you, all settled down. I just want a little slice of that happiness.'

Diane laughs and thinks of her simple life in Inverness. She and Cameron spend most of their time at home. Even before lockdown, the biggest event on their social calendar was their weekly trip to the pub. Not very glamorous, compared to most of her friends, but Diane is fine with that. There's a certain contentment in settling down and not having to put yourself out there any more.

'Hey, do you remember that time I found a massive spider in my shoe?' Asha says.

Diane meets her eye. 'Ethan put that there.'

'What?' Asha looks shocked. 'That massive thing?'

'Yep, he found it in the shed and brought it in.'

'Why?'

'He thought it'd be funny.'

'Oh my god, I nearly had a heart attack when I saw it.'

'I know,' Diane says. 'It was funny, just not for you.'

Asha looks thoughtful. 'He pretended to be as scared as I was.'

'He just wanted you to owe him when he got rid of it for you.'

'Devious, wasn't he?'

'That's one way to describe him.'

'Do you remember the time he walked in on you in the shower?' Asha says.

'That wasn't his fault. Pete told him it was empty.'

'Surely he could hear the sound of running water?'

'Apparently not.'

Asha's always happy to rehash the past, retelling old stories, over and over again until Diane's sick of hearing about them. But she has very little to say about her current life, beyond her ongoing search for a partner. It's kind of sad, Diane thinks. To be so welded to the past.

'Hey, let's all get together, when all this is over? I could come to Inverness, or better still, we could go to Glasgow and see the others,' Asha says.

'Sounds good.'

There is a soft beep, and Ethan joins the call.

'What did I miss?'

Diane leans back in her chair. 'Oh, just Asha spilling about her tragic love life.'

'Thanks for that,' Asha says, rolling her eyes but grinning. 'But yeah, it's true. Apparently, I have a talent for finding the worst of the worst.'

Ethan's camera flickers on, revealing him with his usual mischievous expression. He leans forward, resting his chin on his hand. 'Worst of the worst, huh? So what's your plan? Just keep collecting horror stories until you're sixty?'

'Sounds about right,' Asha replies, her laugh light but self-deprecating.

Ethan's smirk widens. 'Nah, don't worry about it. If you're still single at thirty, I'll marry you myself. Problem solved.'

Asha snorts, shaking her head. 'Oh, brilliant. Can't wait to tell my parents.'

'You laugh now,' Ethan says, 'but you'll be begging to marry me in a few years.'

Asha's laugh sounds a little unnatural. Hysterical even, as if she can't imagine anything worse.

Ethan goes very quiet and Diane can't help but wonder if he actually meant it.

Asha stops laughing and changes the subject, launching into a story about her parents.

Diane goes back to her work and Sarah joins the call. Diane switches off her camera, but she keeps them on in the background, like a radio.

FORTY-SIX
SARAH

Sarah and Ethan take the car and drive back to where Ethan thinks the gun emplacement should be. It's easier searching by road. They can cover the ground so much quicker.

'We went that way last time,' Ethan says, pointing to an area off to the side. 'So I think we need to go this way.'

Sarah starts to nod, then she changes her mind. 'I think we should retrace our steps. We were tired last time. We might have missed something.'

His face hardens and she sees that she has misspoken. He doesn't like being called tired. He finds it patronising, and his male ego can't handle any kind of criticism, as Charmaine found to her cost.

'Just stop the car!'

He hits the brakes, and they both climb out. A thick mist is rolling in from the sea, clinging to the heather and swallowing the landscape in a blanket of cold, grey silence. She glances back at Ethan. He is furiously signalling her to follow him, but she has a hunch.

'I'm probably wrong, but I'll just take a look over here,' she says.

He grunts and they separate, setting off in different directions.

It's strange. He's the one with the gun, and yet she feels safer on her own. She walks for a couple of minutes, her boots crunching over the damp, uneven ground as she pushes through the gorse. It's a difficult path and the prickly branches claw at her jeans.

Her eyes scan the curve of the headland. The land slopes gently down towards the cliff edge, where the waves whisper below. Her pulse quickens and some instinct tells her that what they are looking for is close, hidden somewhere among these tangled weeds.

Ethan must have reached a dead end, because he backtracks and starts hurrying back towards her. She knows he will hate that she's now the one in front, the one leading the way.

Then, through a break in the mist, she sees a shadow, just a little darker than the gorse and bracken. She can make out the edge of a concrete structure, nearly consumed by time and nature, as it juts out from the cliffs. Its roof is thick with moss, and vines cling on all sides like hidden limbs.

She stops so abruptly, Ethan almost bumps into her.

'There,' she says, pointing.

He follows her gaze, squinting through the mist, and then he sees it too. A grin spreads across his face, but it fades quickly, replaced by a flicker of unease.

'You think she could be in there?'

Sarah scans the gap that must have once been an entrance. It's half-hidden behind a curtain of ivy and cobwebs. The mist coils around it, giving the opening a mysterious, hollow look. She crooks her head, listening for the sound of breathing, but she can hear nothing but the crash of the waves and the whirl of the wind.

Ethan slides his hand into his pocket and pulls out his phone, shining the light into the space.

They exchange a look and then they move forward in tandem.

Sarah crouches low, pulling hard on the ivy curtain. She is hit by the scent of damp earth and something metallic, like rusted iron. Ethan shines his phone further into the darkness, and the beam cuts through the shadows, revealing a cracked concrete floor strewn with junk and old leaves. The place seems empty, aside from the strange shadows that form around the window spaces, where men must once have stood and pointed their guns out to sea.

She takes a breath and straightens, glancing back at Ethan.

He nods, still holding the gun, and they edge closer, their footsteps muffled by the thick layer of moss on the old concrete stairs.

As they step over the threshold, the wind picks up, stirring the mist around them, letting it drift down to fill the empty space.

Sarah steels herself, listening, waiting, but it really is dead down there. They reach the bottom and look about, going from window to window to look out at the sea. On a clear day, this place would make an incredible lookout, but today, all they can see is the mist.

There's only so long Sarah can hang around in there. She feels a strong need to get out, to breathe in the fresh sea air.

'I'll wait for you outside,' she says, hoping he'll take the hint, but Ethan is nerding out, fascinated by their discovery, snapping selfies posed with his gun. She shuffles up the steps quickly, eager to get away. When she reaches the top, she stands there, catching her breath. She finds a better path back. One that doesn't require her to fight with the brambles. It is now so misty, she can only just make out the car. She shivers as she walks towards it and tries the handle. Ethan must have locked it, even though they are here, in the middle of the wilderness. She bites down a bolt of irritation.

How long does it take to examine an underground tomb, because that's what it felt like to her. An empty space where men once lived and fought for their lives, but now it belongs to no one but their ghosts.

A shadow emerges from the gorse.

'You've got the keys,' she says, sticking her hand out for them.

But it's not Ethan.

It's Asha.

FORTY-SEVEN
SARAH

Asha emerges from the mist, dishevelled and hollow-eyed. Dirt streaks her face, and her clothes hang in tatters. She looks desperate, her gaze darting around, wide and unsteady. Whatever she's been through has left her raw.

'It's okay, I'm not going to hurt you,' Sarah says, raising her hands to show she's unarmed.

Asha's eyes linger on Sarah's hands. For a moment, Sarah imagines her reaching for a hidden weapon, but something about her posture tells her she won't.

Slowly, Asha steps out from the shadows, her hands trembling, empty. The two women edge closer and something unspoken passes between them. Tears spill down Asha's cheeks, and Sarah feels a painful tightness in her chest.

'Asha, please! What happened?'

Then, the light shifts. The sun slips behind a cloud, and Asha goes stiff. Sarah follows her gaze and her stomach drops. Ethan has caught up with them. He has his gun raised, his face hard. He swings the barrel between the two of them. Sarah steps back and then he trains it on Asha, pointing it at her chest, at the very place Gordon was shot.

THE WEDDING PARTY

'Did you shoot Gordon?' he asks.

Asha meets his eyes. There is so much hate in that look, so much venom. 'If you have to ask me that, then you don't know me at all,' she spits.

'Do you know what happened to Judith?' Sarah asks more gently.

Asha's eyes flick to her for the briefest of moments, before returning to Ethan. She grabs the gun, pushing it downwards, away from her chest.

Ethan's face grows hotter as he swings it back up. It's now pointing directly at her face. 'If it wasn't you, then who?' There is sweat dripping down his brow.

'You can tell us,' Sarah says gently.

Asha looks at Ethan, at his finger twitching at the trigger. It is a look of pure hatred. The world seems to stop, Sarah is so tense she can barely breathe. Then, without warning, Asha spins on her heel and starts to run.

'No, wait!' Sarah yells. 'Ethan, put that thing down, for God's sake.'

Ethan's gaze is ice.

A shot splits the air. The bullet whistles past Asha's ear and buries itself in the dirt.

Asha flees into the mist, her footsteps swallowed by the fog.

Sarah whirls on Ethan, anger burning in her eyes. 'What are you doing? She wasn't armed. We could've taken her back with us. She's the only one who knows what's going on.'

His expression is hard, unyielding. 'I couldn't risk it. You saw what she did to Diane.'

'I could've talked her down,' she says, fists clenched.

'You should be thanking me,' he says, the gun still in his grip. 'I just saved your life.'

FORTY-EIGHT
SARAH

Four Months Earlier, Glasgow

'Hello?'

Sarah doesn't recognise the number, but she answers the phone without thinking, jamming it to her ear as she butters her toast.

All she can hear on the other end is the sound of heavy breathing. In. Out. In. Out.

She slams down the phone.

'It might be one of those marketing calls,' Pete says when she mentions it to him. 'You know, they call a lot of numbers automatically and wait for someone to pick up. Sometimes when someone answers, no one is ready.'

'Then why does it sound like a dog panting at me?' Sarah asks.

'That's probably your imagination going into overdrive. It could just be a machine.'

His words are comforting, but she decides not to answer any more withheld calls.

Unfortunately, it's not always as easy as that. For instance, the doctor's surgery withholds their number as standard. She doesn't want to miss calls about her medication.

And she misses a call from the garage because she doesn't want to answer a number she doesn't recognise. And that delays her from getting a slot she needs for her MOT.

It's so frustrating.

The more she doesn't pick up, the more the calls keep coming, until even Pete admits that someone has to be behind it.

The calls come in at all times of the day and night. She switches her phone to silent, but the missed calls still drive her crazy. She answers by accident once or twice, and each time she's met with the same disconcerting heavy breathing.

'You should take the phone into the toilet and have a noisy dump,' Pete says when she tells him.

Sarah rolls her eyes at him. 'Gross!'

She has a better idea.

She buys a horn and the next time she gets a call, she waits for the noisy breathing, then blares it.

'Hey!'

It's Asha.

'I can't hear a bloody thing now!' Asha sounds indignant.

'What... why were you breathing like that?' Sarah asks.

'I just... came back from the gym,' Asha gasps.

Sarah stays on the line while Asha gets her breath back. She's still suspicious. Why is Asha calling from this number?

'I'm at work,' Asha says. 'Left my phone at home this morning.'

'How did you get my number then?'

'Still got my address book. The one with the princess on it.'

Sarah bursts out laughing. 'Are you serious?'

She had been with Asha when she bought it in a gift shop in their first year at uni. Ethan made a point of calling Asha 'Princess' whenever she said something he didn't agree with. Instead of getting insulted, Asha played along. She took to wearing a tiara around the house and bought herself the sparkly address book.

'So you go to the gym in the middle of the day?' she says.

'We have one in the building. There's a pool too.'

'Of course there is.'

'So have you heard from Diane lately? She didn't answer my last couple of messages.'

'I expect she's just busy with work.'

She has no idea if Diane is actually busy. Diane goes through periods of not being bothered to answer Asha, who pesters like a small child at times. Asha also uses a lot of text speak, which is kind of wearing. She hates when people spell stuff like they're little kids and use words that should be reserved for teens. Asha probably wants to think of herself as young still, but the truth is, she's rapidly approaching thirty. Not that there's anything wrong with that, but she's always made such a song and dance about being married by the time she's thirty. She's even joked she'll marry Pete if she's still single in her thirties. She's gone very quiet on that idea lately. Obviously, she's not that desperate.

On Valentine's Day, someone drops a dozen red roses on Sarah's doorstep. She shivers in the cold air and looks around, but there's no sign of anyone.

She picks them up. The roses are a little wilted and look like they need water. She wonders how long they've been there. She looks for a note but finds none. Taking them inside, she hunts for a vase. She can't remember the last time anyone bought her flowers. Her ex, Todd, wasn't the most romantic. He used to say that people who bought their girlfriends presents on Valentine's Day were 'trying too hard'.

She gives up on the vase and settles for a pint glass, fills it with water, and unwraps the roses from their packaging.

She pricks her finger, and a drop of blood lands on the counter. She sucks off the blood and wipes the counter, then picks up the roses again, more carefully this time.

Pete walks into the room.

'Oh, roses!'

She thrusts the flowers into his arms. 'Someone left these. I think they're for you.'

There's a weird smile on his face as he accepts them.

She checks her phone. She recently changed her number. The silent calls have stopped. No more heavy breathing, but she's still on edge, constantly expecting the next call. And she can't help but worry that now she's cut off this avenue, the caller might try something else. Something more personal.

Apparently, Pete knows exactly where the vase is. She walks into the living room to see the roses positioned in a neat arrangement on the windowsill.

'Got any plans for tonight?' he asks, indicating the roses.

'No,' she says. 'I'm just going to stay in and watch TV.'

'You and me both.'

She wishes he didn't look so pleased about it.

She remembers their student days and the anti-Valentine's nights.

'Maybe I should call Ethan and see if he's around tonight. We haven't seen him in ages.'

The smile freezes on Pete's lips. 'There's a reason for that,' he says.

Sarah sighs. The truth is, Ethan only ever deigns to hang out with them when he doesn't have something better to do.

She and Pete settle down for an evening at home. She has little interest in the film he puts on, preferring to text on her phone for most of the evening. When the film ends, Pete stands up and stretches.

'Are you coming up?' he asks.

'No, not yet,' Sarah says, barely looking at him.

He nods and heads up the stairs.

She puts on another programme and continues to scroll. She knows she should probably go to bed too, but she's feeling down in the dumps. Diane is on Instagram, posting pictures of the wonderful night she's had. She and Cameron have been to the theatre, apparently. It sounds like they had a lot of fun.

Then she gets a photo from Asha. She's holding her hand up, revealing a huge diamond ring.

'Oh, for goodness' sake!'

She groans and gets up to pour herself a fresh glass of wine, but while she's in the kitchen, she hears a weird scratching sound at the window.

Someone's in the garden.

She goes to the door and checks it's locked, then picks up a paperweight and places it on the coffee table. Just in case.

A moment later, the doorbell rings. She goes to the peephole and looks out. It's Ethan, staggering about on the doorstep. She unlatches the door and lets him in.

'Bloody bitch,' he mutters.

'Sorry?'

'Charmaine,' he says, staggering into her kitchen. 'Got anything to drink?'

He's already had more than enough, but Sarah pours him a glass of wine anyway. A part of her is happy to see someone having a worse night than her.

'What happened?' she asks as they sit down at the table.

Ethan shakes his head. 'Just an argument, that's all.'

'Oh.' Sarah doesn't know what to say. 'Did you see Asha's post?'

'No.'

She shows him.

'She's a stupid bitch as well,' he says. 'Who's she engaged to, anyway?'

'Don't know much about him,' Sarah admits.

'I don't know why everyone makes such a big deal about Valentine's Day. It sucks,' Ethan says.

'Agreed.'

His eyes drift over her body. She's still dressed in her work clothes. A white shirt and plain black yoga leggings that look like smart trousers. She pretends not to notice. He lets out a loud sigh.

'Show me that picture of Asha again?'

She does. They both look at it, and Ethan shakes his head. 'How did she get the poor sucker to propose?'

'Men are always falling in love with Asha,' she tells him pointedly.

'Well sure, she's nice to look at. But to marry?' He pulls a face. 'I bet she's going to be a first-class nag.'

'I don't know. She sounds happy.'

'Yeah, well it won't last. She'll be on her own again soon enough.'

'Nothing wrong with being on your own,' she says.

He glances at her. 'I don't mean you. You've got Pete.'

'I'm still on my own,' she says emphatically. 'Pete's on his own too. We're just sharing a roof right now.'

'Yeah, well Pete was always going to be on his own. He's one of life's losers.'

She knows she ought to defend Pete, but she's too tired, so she reaches for the wine and pours them both a glass. It's only when she turns her head that she sees Pete standing on the stairs, watching them. She opens her mouth to say something, but he just shakes his head at her and heads back up the stairs.

FORTY-NINE

I work on controlling my facial muscles. My legs twitch and my jaw aches. I feel like I'm losing control of my body. It's such an effort to sit still and act normal. I nod at my friends, even smile at them if the occasion demands it, but inside I'm a simmering ball of rage.

Rage that so many days have passed and I still have not finished what I started.

Rage that I have to go through with this charade, when all I can think about is the final kill.

What am I even doing here, keeping up pretences? They'll all know it was me soon enough. I bet some of them already suspect it.

But they can't know for sure, so they don't dare say anything. Not in my hearing, anyway. I meet their eyes and point the finger of suspicion at everyone but myself.

I've learnt the hard way you've got to stand up for yourself, because no one is going to do it for you.

It's time to get a little justice.

It has to happen today.

And heaven help me, I'll kill anyone who gets in my way.

FIFTY
DIANE

Diane opens one eye. Her hand trembles as she presses it to her cheek. She feels the heat there, the proof that she's still alive, but the hand does not feel like hers. It feels foreign, like she's trapped inside someone else's skin. There is a low murmur around her. Sarah, Ethan and Pete are arguing about what to do next. Their voices buzz in and out of her ears, but she can't make out the words. She wishes she knew what they were planning. She can't trust them, she knows that much. They may have saved her life once, but one wrong move and she is dead.

The world feels unreal, as though it's being pulled apart at the seams. Her head swims, and she's not sure if she's awake or in a dream. Wasn't she just in a different place a moment ago? Wasn't there light and warmth? She blinks and everything shifts again, shadows dancing across the curtains, the cottage creaking in the wind.

Her body shakes. Her shoulder radiates with pain.

Pills. She needs pills. Sarah gave her some, but how long ago was that? She has no idea. All she knows is she needs more.

Sarah's voice cuts through the fog, but it's distorted, like a whisper on the wind. Diane tries to make eye contact, but her gaze is unfocused. She tries a smile, but no one seems to notice.

Help me! The voice inside her cries, but she can't find the words.

She slumps back against her seat exhausted.

She feels a hand on her forehead, and then again on her neck. What is Sarah doing, looking for a pulse? It feels invasive, ice-cold fingers against her skin. She feels a ripple down her spine. Is she checking to see if she is still alive?

Sarah lingers for a moment longer than necessary, and Diane can't help but wonder if she is waiting for something, some sign that she's still present in this decaying body. The thought stirs a knot of panic deep inside her. She doesn't want to be reduced to a fragile thing that others must monitor, to be poked and prodded like a broken doll. She wants to know what Sarah finds there. Is her pulse strong and hardy, or does it feel as though she's already slipping away?

The darkness inside her head grows deeper, and the cottage feels cold, even though the fire still burns in the hearth. Diane wraps her arms around herself, trying to hold onto something real, but she fears she's already slipping away.

FIFTY-ONE
SARAH

Three Months Earlier, Glasgow

Sarah finishes work late one night, as she often does these days. She walks quickly. The car park is almost empty. A nearby streetlight flickers on and off, casting long shadows across the cracked tarmac, and her footsteps echo in the silence as she walks towards her car. She pauses for a moment, listening to the night. It's too still, too empty. All her senses are on alert. She resumes walking, slower this time, but the unsettling feeling lingers, crawling under her skin like an itch she can't scratch. A hooded figure steps out of the darkness from right behind her car.

Her heart lurches in her chest, a sharp, visceral thud. She spins on her heel, panic surging through her veins, and flees back towards the building, her breath coming in short, ragged gasps, but when she reaches the door, she finds it locked.

She hammers on it with her fists. 'Let me in, let me in.' There's no sign of any security guards. How is it possible they've locked up in the few minutes it took her to get from the door to her car?

She turns quickly and feels for her keys in her pocket. She clutches them tightly as she hurries down the road and through a dark alley. She runs as fast as her heels allow her. Something cold and wet drips on her from above, but she keeps on going, running towards the light, until she bursts out into the shopping precinct. Here are people, late-night shoppers, couples holding hands, children skipping along beside them. She ducks into a shop doorway and stands there, getting her breath back. She waits for several minutes, but no one emerges from the alley.

And still, she doesn't dare go back down there. Someone was following her, she's sure of it. She can almost hear them breathing, panting like a dog, just as they did when they rang her and didn't answer.

She looks down at her hand and sees that she's trembling. Her stalker is messing with her head, and she doesn't know how to make them stop.

FIFTY-TWO
SARAH

Ethan drives too fast. He seems to have forgotten that Sarah is the one to have found the gun emplacement, and the way he tells it, you would think he deserves a medal. Sarah scarcely glances at him as she gets out of the car, her throat tightening with frustration she can't quite articulate.

Inside, she finds Diane exactly where she left her, fast asleep, her breathing soft and steady. Pete sits beside her, a bottle of something half empty in his hand. His alcohol fumes fill the air.

Sarah's shoulders sag, her frustration deepening. He's been drinking a lot this week, more than she's ever seen him do before. It's like all the work she's done with him has unravelled. She needs him to stay focused, to be someone she can rely on. But his glassy eyes and the slow, deliberate way he lifts the bottle to his lips say otherwise.

Ethan heads straight for the hearth. He adds more logs, building it up into a raging inferno. Sarah stands by the door until she's unable to hold it in any longer, then she storms over to him, her boots thudding across the floor.

'You think you can control everyone,' she says. 'But all you do is push people around. I could have got Asha talking. If you'd left it to me, she would be here with us now, telling us what really happened and we wouldn't be sitting around like lemmings, waiting to see who's next.'

His back remains rigid, the fire casting a glow over his face.

'I did what I thought was best. I was protecting you. I didn't want you to end up like Di.'

They both look over at Diane. Her breathing is shallow, her skin damp with a feverish sheen.

'It's not me you should be worried about,' she says, with more malice than she intends.

Sarah feels the ground beneath her shifting. There's no steady footing, no one she can trust completely. She rubs her temples, the weight of the past week pressing down on her. For a fleeting moment, she thinks about waking Diane, just to hear her voice, but the thought passes. Diane needs her rest. Sarah will just have to hold it together.

Ethan takes off his shirt and walks around bare-chested even though it's not that warm inside the cottage.

'He's gone full Rambo,' Pete murmurs to Sarah.

She smiles, but the way Ethan's swinging his gun around makes her sweat. She wishes he'd put the safety on, but she knows from experience you can't tell Ethan anything.

She looks at him with a steely gaze. 'Level with me. Did you take Broderick's gun? I don't care if you did. I just want to know.'

Ethan looks at her like she's just asked if the sky is green. 'Of course not. Why would you even ask me that? I didn't take any guns until I had reason to. After the murders.' There's a flicker of irritation in his eyes as he says this.

Sarah studies him carefully. 'Be honest with me, Ethan.'

He bangs his fist down on the table. 'I am being honest, damn it!'

'But if you didn't, who did?'

Pete shoots her a look and she moves back, towards him. They sit together, cold despite the fire Ethan's built. Her clothes feel damp. She's not sure if it's the cold or her own sweat. So much has happened and she just wants to get it all straight in her head. Why would any of them take the gun? Why would any of them kill Gordon and Judith? She still doesn't believe it was Asha.

Pete stares into the flickering light, the fire reflecting in his eyes. The hours drag. Outside, the sky begins to soften with the approach of evening, streaks of muted pink and gold threading through the persistent mist. Ethan's eyelids grow heavier until they finally close, his body slackening as sleep takes hold. He leans towards Diane, his face softening as he snores.

Sarah pulls a blanket around her shoulders. She should really go to bed, but someone needs to keep watch, and she's the only one still sober.

'I have another confession to make,' Pete says. He speaks so quietly, she almost doesn't catch it. She sits up, her senses prickling. It isn't like Pete to spill his guts, and yet she has a feeling he's about to. She's discovered more about him in the last few days than she ever learnt in the last year of living with him.

'Gordon,' he says.

'What about him?' she asks, searching his eyes for the truth.

'When I first saw him, I thought he looked like one of the guys I was in prison with...'

Sarah nods, but she is already searching the room with her eyes, checking the location of the nearest exit. Checking the location of the guns.

'He looked just like him, but with less hair. I knew him as Scrote, but obviously that was just a nickname. I watched him closely when we went out hunting, but he acted like he didn't know me. He was all smiley and talkative. Completely different to the scary, imposing man I remember. But that deep rumbling voice. That distinctive accent. I could never place it before but the more he talked, the more convinced I became that it really was him.'

Sarah frowns. 'So what did you do?'

Pete hangs his head. 'I'm not proud of this, but I remembered the code to the gun locker. It's 1468, the date Orkney and Shetland were transferred from Norway to Scotland. I had an Orcadian teacher at school who drummed it into us.'

Sarah stiffens. 'So you took a gun?'

'Yeah, I hid it under my bed.'

'What did you do with it?'

'Nothing, I swear. I just didn't feel safe knowing he was in the cottage next door, and I hated the thought that Asha was in there with him, thinking he's some wholesome gentle giant.'

'So?'

'So on the morning of the wedding, I went round there. I pretended I was after some milk, but I got Asha to step outside with me so I could warn her.'

'And what did she say?'

Pete swallows hard. 'She said I was mistaken. That Gordon was never in prison. She said if I couldn't accept that, I should go home.'

'And then what?'

'And then... nothing. I went and took my anger out on the scarecrows. Then I went to the wedding and kept my mouth shut. I figured I would let Asha have her big day. And then I would speak to her again when she came back from her honeymoon. She clearly didn't believe me, so I was going to get her some evidence, make her believe who he really is.'

'But the gun, Pete. What did you do with the gun?'

He shakes his head. 'I thought it was still under my bed. I

went to get it after Broderick came round, but it was gone. Someone else must have taken it.'

'But no one else knew it was there!'

'Well someone must have seen me with it. I thought I was careful, but clearly not careful enough.'

Diane stirs, her eyelids fluttering open.

'I want to go back outside,' she says as Sarah offers her some water. 'I want to watch the sunset.'

She looks so frail, her cheeks hollow, her lips dry, but Sarah sees the resolve in her tired eyes. So she forces a smile and helps her to her feet.

Ethan's eyes snap open.

'Are you both crazy?' he says, watching them. 'Asha is still out there, in case you haven't noticed.'

Sarah looks over at him. 'Why didn't you shoot her when you had the chance then?'

Everybody looks from her to Ethan.

'I-I just wanted to warn her away.'

'If you really thought she was going to shoot us, you would have shot her.'

'She shot Diane, didn't she?'

'What if that was an accident?'

'I was unarmed,' Diane points out.

'But we all know Asha's a terrible shot,' Sarah says.

'There's something wrong with her,' he says. 'She's sick or something.'

Sarah looks at Diane. 'What do you think?'

'Hey, I'm already shot,' she says weakly. 'I've got nothing left to lose.'

Sarah nods, but there's something in that phrase that bothers her. That's how Asha looked too. Like she had nothing left to lose.

. . .

When they come back inside, Ethan has thrown together a basic meal of pasta with tomato sauce. Diane manages a few bites, sitting in her chair. Sarah joins Pete and Ethan at the table.

Pete eats one-handed, twirling the pasta around with his fork. He gets sauce all down his chin.

'Clean yourself up, man, it's embarrassing,' Ethan says, tossing him a napkin.

Pete laughs in response. 'Who the hell cares what I look like right now?'

'I do,' Ethan says. 'You're putting me off my dinner.'

Pete hangs his head. 'It's funny. I used to think of you as a friend.'

Ethan blinks. 'What are you talking about? We are friends!'

'In that case, I'd hate to see how you treat your enemies.'

Ethan sighs. 'I tell you these things for your own good, mate. Do you think Sarah wants to look at you like that? You need a shave, too. You look like you're still homeless.'

Pete jerks up from the table. He reaches for his gun and points it at Ethan, who's left his own gun by the door.

'Whoa! What are you doing?'

'You never did apologise.'

'For what?'

'Ruining my life.'

'What are you on about? I think you did a pretty good job of that yourself, mate.'

'You know what I mean. If you hadn't tripped me, I would still be dancing. I might even have made it to *Britain's Got Talent*.'

'Like they'd have let you on! Anyway, you've only got yourself to blame. All those crazy dance moves you used to do – the bending and twisting and body popping. It's no wonder you screwed up your back.'

Pete's voice drops, becoming low and venomous: 'You think you're Teflon, don't you? Like nothing can stick to you. Well that's where you're wrong, Ethan. No one escapes forever. One day, you're going to get what's coming to you.'

'Oh yeah, and what's that?'

'Retribution.'

Ethan's laughter echoes through the room. Even now, when Pete is pointing a gun at him, he can't take him seriously.

'I don't think so, mate, that's just the natural order of things. I'm the alpha, you're the beta.'

Pete's hands shake. He wants to shoot him so badly, Sarah can see it.

But Ethan isn't even scared.

To her relief, Pete lowers the gun and goes to sit beside Diane. But then he positions the gun on the floor and gazes down into the barrel.

'Pete!' she calls out, but he ignores her. He sits there, toying with the trigger.

She looks at Ethan. 'Do you think we should take it off him?'

Ethan watches Pete for a moment. 'No, I think that would be more dangerous than what he's doing now.'

'Will you talk to him?'

'I don't think that will do any good.'

She feels a spark of anger igniting inside her. 'Could you at least try?'

He shakes his head. 'I'm not getting near him when he's in this mood.'

She looks at him closely. Has she misjudged him? Is he actually scared? Or is he really so callous that he doesn't give a damn?

Ethan prongs a piece of pasta and pushes it into his mouth, chewing slowly. It appears the conversation is over.

She pushes her plate away and stands up from the table. She can't stand to look at any of them, so she puts on her boots and heads for the back door. She knows Asha could be out there, but right now, it is not Asha who is freaking her out.

The cool air blows in and she gets a whiff of the sea. She steps outside, her boots sinking into the damp earth as the wind lashes against her. She moves slowly, measuring each step, until she's standing as close as she dares to the edge of the cliff. Her gaze is drawn downwards, and there, barely visible amidst the jagged rock face, she spots a nest, clinging perilously close to the sharp, wind-battered crags. The nest is fragile, woven from tangled seaweed and brittle twigs and it trembles with each breath of the wind. She watches, her heart in her mouth as it sways back and forth and she knows that at any moment, it will be torn away, spiralling into the black void below. The faint, mournful cries of the seabirds echo from somewhere high above, the sound almost lost by the crashing of the waves beneath, like ghosts in the gloom.

When she heads back inside, Ethan is on guard duty and she is relieved to see that Pete is no longer clutching his gun. She focuses on the washing-up. The repetitive nature of the chore is comforting, but she can't get Gordon's face out of her head. Or Judith's.

Is there some pill she can take, she wonders, that will eradicate these harrowing images, or will they continue to haunt her forever?

She thinks of Asha too, remembers the stricken expression on her face.

What the hell happened, Asha? What has become of you?

As the evening wears on, Pete drinks himself into a coma, while Ethan is on guard duty, standing by the window practising his poses. Diane nods on and off in her chair. She still finds that more comfortable than her bed, though Sarah can't imagine how she's getting any sleep sitting up like that. She has a feeling

Diane is afraid to go to sleep. Afraid to relive the whole terrifying incident. She can't imagine what that must be like.

Sarah is growing tired too. A yawn escapes her mouth, and Ethan notices.

'You and Pete go to bed. I'll sit up with Diane.'

Sarah wants to argue, but she really is knackered.

She wakes Pete, and nudges him towards his bedroom, then heads into her own.

She sets her alarm, so she can relieve Ethan in the morning. Then she brushes her teeth and climbs under the covers. She's about to go to sleep, when she notices her phone, sitting on the nightstand. With all that's happened, she hasn't got round to checking it. The battery is dead, so she plugs it into the wall and waits impatiently for it to charge.

She knows there is no coverage on the island, but what about before that? She's been waiting on a message that never arrived. Is there any chance it came through before she lost her connection? She waits a few minutes, and the phone blinks back to life. She reaches for it lovingly, like a new mother lifting her infant from the crib.

There are three new messages, one from her phone company, two from Asha:

Don't let anybody get me pissed. You know I'm a terrible drunk!

WTF is up with Diane and Cameron? I think it might be over! Tread carefully. You know what she can be like!

Sarah waits, but that's it. No more texts.

There's a beep, and she sees she has a voice message. She doesn't recognise the number, but she eagerly presses play.

Instantly, she hears heavy breathing, in and out, in and out. It would be almost comedic if it weren't so freaky. She forces herself to keep listening. The heavy breathing continues, for over a minute. Then it goes silent. Just before the recording cuts out, she hears another sound.

She plays it back, listening intently. The minute of heavy breathing. The moment's silence, and then, at the very end, a cough.

Pete's cough.

She inhales. She has shown Pete nothing but kindness. How dare he do this to her? How dare he terrorise her with these phone calls? They have actually been quite frightening. They've made her fearful, less willing to go out.

But that's exactly what he wants, isn't it? To keep her afraid, so she'll let him stay.

She can't believe what a fool she's been.

FIFTY-THREE
SARAH

Sarah lies awake, stewing for some time, trying to work out what she ever did to Pete to make him treat her this way. She is fuming with anger, but she's also deeply hurt. She opened her home to him. More than that, she trusted him. And now it turns out, her boss was right after all. She should never have let him in.

Despite her disturbed sleep, there is no need for her alarm in the morning. The longer she remains on this island, the more attuned she becomes to the rhythms of nature. She senses the position of the sun creeping above the horizon, and she hears the early calls of the birds stirring to life. The world outside is awakening, and for the first time, everything seems to make sense in a way it never has before. It's a strange comfort, the quiet promise of a new day and she feels ready for the challenge. She will find a way off this island. Even if she has to do it alone.

She slides out of bed and is just about to head to the bathroom when a loud crack tears through the cottage, freezing her mid-motion. Another follows, louder, closer. Her breath catches, and her chest tightens as panic surges through her.

Her eyes dart wildly around the room, seeking safety, but it feels like the walls are closing in. There's nowhere to hide. She won't fit in the small wardrobe, and there's not enough space under the bed. The sound echoes again in her head, impossibly loud, like it's right outside her door. Her heart pounds against her ribs, each beat sharp and frantic. Her breaths come in quick, shallow bursts as she darts to the window and fumbles with the latch. It doesn't open far enough for her to climb out. Panic surges through her and she staggers back, pressing herself against the cold wall. The chill seeps through her jumper, grounding her just enough to stay upright. She stands there, frozen, ears straining for the next sound. She hears two more shots: Bang! Bang!

She waits for the creak of footsteps.

Waits for the door to burst open.

Waits to die.

All is silent for a minute, and then another. The absence of sound is almost worse, pressing against her ears and amplifying the pounding of her heart. She doesn't know what to do. Should she stay alone in this room, or is it better to run? The question buzzes in her mind until her legs move of their own accord, propelling her out the door and across the hall.

Her feet slip on the smooth floor, but she doesn't stop. 'Pete!' she whispers. 'Pete!'

His door swings open. She stumbles, and he catches her arm, pulling her inside. His grip is firm, steady, and when the door closes behind them, it feels like a shield.

He pulls her closer, his body warm against her own, though her chest still heaves and her hands tremble uncontrollably. He's wearing nothing but a vest and boxers, his feet bare on the cold floor. And in his free hand, he holds a rifle, the metal dark and heavy.

His eyes meet hers. He's eerily calm, as if he's already

assessed the situation and made a plan. She grips his arm tighter, her breath catching.

'What... what do we do?'

'You wait here, I'll check it out.'

Sarah stares at him, her heart racing. 'No. I'm coming with you.'

He glances at her, his expression unreadable. 'Stay behind me. Don't get in the way.'

She swallows hard, her legs trembling as she follows him towards the door.

He opens it slowly, then stands there, listening for a beat. She listens too. Even the birds are silent.

He glances at her, then takes a few steps towards the living room. He stops in the doorway, blocking her view.

She stands on her tiptoes and peers over his shoulder.

At first glance, everything looks normal. She searches the space with her eyes, trying to spot Asha. Diane is in her armchair, head lolling to one side, while Ethan is splayed out on the sofa, his gun lying useless in his lap. For a moment, she thinks they're both asleep. But as she inches closer, a heavy metallic smell fills her nostrils. The pungent, coppery tang makes her wrinkle her nose and instinctively cover it with her hands.

'Don't look,' Pete warns. But she's already seen, and now she can't look away.

Rivulets of sweat trickle down her spine as she surveys the room, her heart racing in terror. She fixates on the bullet holes – one in the middle of the tablecloth, three in the wall, another on the ceiling. The last one must have caught the back of Ethan's skull. Blood cakes the wall, dotted with chunks of brain matter and fragments of tissue. Bile burns her throat and a gut-wrenching scream claws its way up from deep inside her. She gives in to it, screaming and screaming, unable to stop.

Diane opens her eyes. Then immediately winces in pain.

'What...?'

Sarah swivels round to look at her. 'Diane! You're still—'

Diane sees Ethan and then she's screaming too. Howling like a dog.

'No! Ethan! No!'

She struggles to get out of her chair. It's clear she wants to go to him, but her body won't cooperate. Sarah's legs have turned to mush. She flops down to the ground, rocking and crying and punching the floor.

Pete's expression shifts from confusion to something darker. Without a word, he approaches Ethan and reaches out to touch his skin. Even though there's zero chance of him still being alive, Pete's hand shakes as if his very touch might somehow bring him back to life. But of course, all that happens is that he feels his cold body and shakes his head in despair.

'Asha did this?'

Sarah hauls herself to her feet and heads towards the door, her hand trembling as it wraps around the doorknob.

'What are you doing?' Diane's voice is strained, edging into panic. 'You can't open that. She might still be out there.'

Sarah's resolve hardens. She tries the door and meets resistance. She pushes harder until the door flies open. Asha lies on the ground, her eyes wide open, staring lifelessly up at the sky. A single bullet hole mars her forehead, blood trickling down in a dark stream over her face. The sight makes Sarah catch her breath. She stumbles backwards, her pulse roaring in her ears. She remembers the last time she saw Asha – her desperate, frightened eyes, and she knows she could have talked her down. She could have found a way to save her if only Ethan hadn't been quite so stubborn.

Now, that chance is gone. They're both dead, and there's no way to bring them back. The weight of it crashes over her, the way the wild waves crash against the rocks. She stands there, paralysed, staring at Asha's vacant expression.

Despite the bullet wound, the wide eyes, and the blood, there is still something hauntingly beautiful about that face. Her features carry an eerie grace, as if caught in a final moment of serenity that belies the violence that took her. The sight sends a shiver through Sarah's spine, and her gut twists with regret and a lingering sense of loss.

Pete steps outside too, his eyes widening at the sight of Asha's body. He points out the gun. Sarah hadn't even noticed it before, lying almost a metre from the body, as if it flew out of her hand at the moment of impact. He turns abruptly, his shoulders stiff as he heads back into the house. A few moments later, the clinking of glass echoes from the kitchen.

Sarah lingers in the doorway, then moves back inside, her legs feeling like lead as she crosses the room to where Diane sits. She lowers herself down beside her.

'Asha's dead too,' she says quietly.

Diane's expression doesn't change immediately. She blinks, her breath coming out in a shaky exhale as she processes what Sarah has just said. Her eyes search the floor for a moment, as if she might find a different reality there.

Finally, she lifts her head. 'Who shot her?'

Sarah looks over at Ethan. His gun lies on the floor beside him. 'I'm guessing Asha shot at Ethan – badly – and he managed to exchange fire before he died. Didn't you hear the gunshots?'

'I was playing dead,' Diane admits. 'What else could I do?'

'I heard them too,' Sarah says. 'I didn't know what to do.'

'There's nothing you could do,' Diane tells her. 'If you'd come in a minute earlier, you and Pete could have got caught in the crossfire.'

All at once, Diane is crying, big ugly tears carving paths down her cheeks.

'I can't believe it. I feel like I'm in a nightmare.'

'We all are,' Sarah says.

Pete returns from the kitchen and sits down heavily beside them, and the three of them fall into a fragile silence, each lost in their own thoughts.

Diane is the first to speak. Her voice sounds cracked and small. 'Does this mean it's over?'

Sarah wants to reassure her, to offer some hope, but a chill runs down her spine as she remembers the voice message from the night before. Pete's message. She glances sideways at him, a knot forming in her stomach.

'I hope so,' she says softly, but the uncertainty lingers in the air between them, thick as the haar that is forming outside. He's not the man she thought he was. He's not her friend. She can only assume he was in his room when Asha and Ethan were shot. But she doesn't know for sure.

'Now what?' Diane says.

'Now I think I need some of that whisky,' Sarah says.

'That's a shame. I think we finished it all last night.'

Diane is right about the whisky. Sarah looks through all the cupboards, but there's nothing. She looks over at Pete, resenting him all the more.

'I bet there's more at Judith's,' he says.

Sarah jerks her head up. 'Are you seriously suggesting we raid her house for booze?'

'We have to go over there anyway to feed the animals.'

'How long till the boat comes?'

'We just have to make it until tomorrow.'

Pete's voice becomes gruff. 'I want to go home now.'

Sarah looks at him coldly. *You don't have a home,* she thinks. But she won't tell him just yet.

Not until they're safely off this godforsaken island.

FIFTY-FOUR

Five Days Earlier

I retrieve my gun from its hiding place and follow Asha and Gordon, planning to stalk them to their room. The fact that the cottage doors have no locks works in my favour.

They won't be expecting me.

They won't stand a chance.

But instead of heading back to their cottage, they walk all the way down to the beach.

They make no effort to be quiet, their voices echoing across the sand dunes.

They are talking about us, her old housemates. My ears burn and I quicken my step.

Asha stands on her tiptoes to kiss Gordon. They look so picture perfect.

I pull the hood up over my head, just in case they happen to turn round. It's not a disguise exactly but it makes it harder to see my face.

I reach for the gun I borrowed. I need to get this right.

I peer through the scope, the crosshairs aligning with my

target. I only planned to shoot Asha, but as I watch them, I am reminded of how ridiculously happy they are, how Asha seems to truly love him, and that's when I realise that shooting only Asha would be letting her off lightly. I want her to suffer, the way she has made me suffer.

I creep forward and crouch in the darkness. I squeeze the trigger. I am amazed and delighted when he goes down.

It's like felling a tree.

Asha looks at me in horror. I'm not sure if she sees my face, but I can't take any chances. I stand and walk towards her, firing as I go. Gordon draws his last breath as she runs and disappears into the shadows. I follow, searching every rock, but somehow she slips away, her good luck working in her favour one last time.

I walk back to Gordon, feeling cheated.

Still, she can't hide for ever. There are only so many places you can hide on this island.

Asha is as good as dead.

FIFTY-FIVE

SARAH

'If we leave her out there, she'll be eaten alive by wild animals,' Pete says, pacing around the kitchen.

'There aren't too many of those. Except the rats and rabbits,' Sarah says.

Pete pulls a face. 'Ugh, I hate rats.'

She wonders if he's speaking from experience. He must have seen a few in his time on the streets.

'We could move her into one of the cottages?'

He shakes his head. 'Shouldn't we just leave them both as they are so the forensics people can see what happened?'

'If they ever get here.'

Sarah is starting to lose hope that anyone is ever going to come.

Today feels different. It's not just all the senseless murders. It's the way the mists are descending on them. When she looks out the window now, she can't see anything but white, and she finds it suffocating, as though unseen hands are trying to smother her.

'Let's move to Judith's house. We could have another go at her radio, see if we can make contact with the mainland.'

'Sounds like a plan. What about Diane?'

'I can hear you,' Diane calls from the living room.

'Well, what do you think? Shall we move to Judith's?'

There is a slight pause.

'We're out of painkillers, so we'll have to go over there anyway,' Sarah says.

'All right then, whatever you think.'

Sarah almost falls over. She doesn't think the opinionated Diane has ever uttered such words in her life.

'Right then,' she says, looking around at all the mess they've created. 'No time like the present.'

Sarah packs up their bags and carries them out to the car while Diane sits with Ethan, or what's left of him. She can hear her, talking to him, telling him how much she will miss him, and she grits her teeth, because fond as she was of Ethan, it feels wrong to gloss over the truth and paint him in a light that doesn't acknowledge the shadow he cast. The side Charmaine warned her about. The side they all chose to ignore.

She wonders how Charmaine will feel when she hears he's dead. Will she be upset, or will she dance on his grave?

Pete goes round gathering up all the guns.

'What are you doing?' Sarah asks, appalled. After all, at least two of those guns are murder weapons.

'I want the guns where I can see them,' Pete says. 'Besides, they belong to Broderick. He's going to want them back.'

'If I were him, I wouldn't want to come back here. To the island, I mean,' Sarah says.

'Well, he might feel differently. After all, this is his home.'

They head outside, stopping to take one last look at Asha. Sarah wishes she could carry her down to the beach so she could lie beside Gordon, but there's no way she could manage that. And for all she knows, she's got it all wrong and Asha is the one who shot him. But she doesn't think so. Even now, Asha looks totally serene.

Diane doesn't look so good. It's clear that she's in pain. But she makes it out to the car and collapses onto the back seat. She lies there, writhing and whimpering at every bump in the road as Sarah drives slowly through the mist.

FIFTY-SIX
SARAH

Eight Months Earlier, Glasgow

Sarah feels as though she has sidestepped a hurricane. What on earth was she thinking? What was he thinking? To think she had come this close to sleeping with Cameron, Diane's Cameron. There is no way this could go anywhere but straight to hell.

She returns home to Pete. He makes her a cup of tea and quizzes her about her night. She tells him she is tired, but she sits beside him on the sofa, and they watch back to back episodes of *Shetland*.

Diane doesn't mention anything in their regular messages, so she guesses Cameron hasn't told her about their meeting. Probably just as well. It's easier to keep quiet if she just says nothing. That way, she won't have to lie.

She tries to forget about him and carries on with her mundane life, which still consists of travelling back and forth to work, and spending long dull evenings at home with Pete. She still wants rid of him, but he seems to be increasingly reliant on her, and she doesn't have the heart to turf him out.

Cameron remains constantly in her thoughts though. She replays the time they spent together over and over in her head, analysing every part of their conversation, reliving the excitement of his touch. And at night she dreams about him. Dreams she didn't do the right thing, and instead took his hand and let him lead her up to his hotel room. And every morning she wakes up, filled with a sense of longing and frustration. She knows without a doubt that if he weren't Diane's husband, he would be hers.

She begins to resent Diane. She rakes through their history, looking for a reason to justify her infatuation. Diane was always so blunt when they lived in their shared house. Often lacking in kindness and sympathy. Unlike the dramatic Asha, who wore her emotions on her sleeve.

It eats away at her, and a small, terrible part of her wishes something would happen to Diane. Some kind of illness or accident. Something that was nobody's fault, but would mean that Diane would be conveniently out of the way. And then, a little later, if it were revealed that Sarah and Cameron had formed a relationship, no one would blame them. They would think they were seeking comfort in each other. It would seem perfectly natural, and Sarah could enjoy her relationship without guilt.

But Diane continues to thrive. No fatal accident befalls her. No terrible diagnosis; in fact, it seems as if she's in the best shape of her life. She flaunts her perfect marriage to Sarah through constant messaging, bragging about their steamy sex life and how amazing Cameron is in bed. Each message is like a stab to Sarah's heart, twisting the knife of jealousy deeper until she can't bear it any longer.

Finally, after just two months, she cracks. She takes a couple of days' holiday from her job and tells Pete she's going to be away on a business trip. Straight away, he gets the look of a frightened dog about him.

'I don't like it when you're not here. It doesn't feel right.'

'Well, you'll just have to get used to it,' she tells him coldly, because who the hell is he to tell her how to run her life?

'Are you seeing someone?' he asks.

'Of course not,' she says. 'I don't want anyone either, I'm happy the way I am, carefree and single.'

She doesn't know why she says this, but she can't tell him about Cameron, and there is no way she's letting Pete get any ideas about the two of them. The sympathy she once had for him is wearing thinner by the day, like a big ball of string that is being stretched and stretched until it's just the thinnest fibres left.

She doesn't even tell Cameron she is coming. She arrives in Inverness and checks into a small seedy hotel on the edge of the city. She knows that he is used to luxury, but this is all she can afford. She lets herself into the room and sets down her suitcase, then puts on a skimpy new set of lingerie. It is nothing like the underwear she normally wears. There is so little fabric, she feels a little ridiculous, especially once she's slipped her feet into her favourite heels.

She crawls onto the bed. The sheets are cool against her skin, every nerve alive with the thrill of what she's about to do. She arranges herself in what she hopes is an alluring pose, her body stretched out on the bed, curves framed against the crisp white linen, and she snaps a selfie and sends it to Cameron, with nothing but the name of the hotel and the words, 'Room 267'.

It's the boldest thing she's ever done, and as she lies there, heart hammering, she knows he's done this to her. He makes her daring, reckless. He makes her want to shatter every pointless rule she's ever followed. The air conditioning is up too high and goosepimples prickle her skin, but that's nothing compared to the heat building inside her, the raw anticipation that beats in her chest.

She clutches the phone in her hand and stares longingly at

the screen. She sees that he has read her message. But he does not reply.

The seconds tick by. Her stomach twists and her cheeks burn with shame. Maybe he won't come. Maybe he'll see the photo and think she's pathetic and block her number. After all, she had her chance with him, and she blew it.

But she can't let go of the small, desperate hope that he wants this as much as she does. That he might still be thinking of her, even after all this time.

There is a sharp knock on the door. It could be room service, for all Sarah knows, but she keeps her nerve.

'Come in!'

The door swings open, and there he is, filling the doorway, looking at her like she's something he's been hunting for. He's even more devastatingly handsome than she remembers, his dark hair slicked back, the lines of his suit moulding perfectly to his frame. His face is flushed from sprinting up the stairs, and his eyes hold a dark, dangerous glimmer that sends a shiver through her entire body.

He lingers in the doorway, leaning nonchalantly against the frame, those glacial blue eyes sweeping slowly over her scantily covered body. It's a slow, deliberate inspection that makes her feel totally vulnerable and exposed. She can practically feel the heat scorching her skin. Her breath catches, and she squirms under his scrutiny.

His lips twitch, then stretch into a slow, lopsided grin that makes her heart race. He takes one step into the room, and then another, closing the door behind him with a soft click that echoes loudly in the tense silence between them. The air thickens with unspoken desire and anticipation as he kicks off his shoes.

FIFTY-SEVEN
DIANE

When they arrive at Judith's cottage, Pete checks the house is empty then he and Sarah help Diane inside. Her body trembles with pain and exhaustion as she collapses onto the sofa.

'Pills,' she reminds Sarah.

'Yes! Yes of course.'

Sarah jumps up and hurries off. Diane hears her in the kitchen, rummaging through the cupboards. She comes out, holding up a little pill box.

'These should work.'

Diane sucks down a double dose. Gradually, the pain subsides enough that she can drink the soup Sarah heats for her.

A fierce wind whips through the room. Despite their best efforts, they've failed to find any source of heat, aside from the ancient Aga, and no one wants to go outside and chop firewood. Better to huddle on the sofa under blankets and duvets. There are plenty of those, hot water bottles too.

Pete stomps around in the kitchen, slamming cabinet doors and rattling pots and pans around. But he isn't preparing a meal; instead, he's hunting through all the cupboards, pulling out every kind of alcohol he can find: dusty bottles of ale, gin, vodka and martini. He doesn't care about the age or quality of the drinks; he just needs something to numb the fear and despair that consumes him. He comes back out, clutching a pint glass containing a disgusting concoction of all the drinks he has found and sits in the corner, silently sipping it until it's all gone.

Diane dozes off and on. In between, she senses a strange, tense energy between Sarah and Pete. She is too tired to get to the bottom of it, and the searing pain from her bullet wound continues to gnaw at her as the painkillers wear off.

'Can you get me some more?' she asks Sarah.

'There's only a few left. Maybe you should save some for tomorrow?'

Diane gives her a dark look. 'I need them now.'

Sarah doesn't need to be told twice. She disappears into the kitchen and returns with the rest of the packet.

Diane swallows them all and lies back against the sofa cushions. She feels the pills coursing through her veins, numbing her mind and body until she is nothing but a hollow shell. Gradually, the pain loosens its grip and she is able to breathe once more.

As the day draws on, Pete and Sarah argue over who will sleep where. Judith and Broderick's bed is out of the question; the very thought makes everyone's skin crawl.

'Maybe we should go back to the holiday cottages, there are plenty of beds there,' Sarah says. 'We could pack up whatever we need and take it with us.'

Pete shakes his head.

'Asha's body will be lying outside, all rotten and disgusting. I can't see that again. I just can't.'

'I'm staying here,' Diane says. She doesn't have the energy to move.

So they all bed down as best they can in the living room. Diane takes the prime spot on the sofa, Sarah the armchair.

'I can sleep anywhere,' Pete insists, and he proves it by curling up on the floor. No one sleeps for long, even now Asha has been killed. They all suffer from frazzled nerves and look at each other with blank, haunted expressions.

When Diane closes her eyes, she sees the shadow of death hovering over her like a grey cloud. It's an icy, unnerving presence that seeps into her bones. At times, the pain is so relentless, she hears their voices – the dead ones – all shouting at once, making it impossible to pick out what any of them are saying. It's as if they're trapped in a never-ending loop, their voices echoing and overlapping. She tries to block them out, but their presence is impossible to ignore. Their spirits refuse to rest in peace.

'Diane?'

She blinks and sees it's just Sarah.

'I really think you should take Pete in, when this is all over.' She's not even subtle about how she says it this time. Pete is down on the floor, between them. He can hear every word.

'I don't think that's going to be possible,' Diane says.

'Just think about it. Please? He could help take care of you while you recover.'

Diane closes her eyes again so she doesn't have to deal with her. The voices retreat enough for her to sleep for a while, and when she wakes up, Pete and Sarah are sitting in front of a pathetic little fire that looks more like a bird's nest. She watches for a while, not bothering to let them know she's awake. It's interesting to watch the two of them, to observe their weird dynamic.

'Are you hungry?' Pete asks.

Sarah shrugs.

He jumps up and disappears into the kitchen for a moment,

returning with a jar of olives. He takes one and leans over to Sarah, pressing it against her lips.

'Eat it, Sarah. You know you like it.'

Sarah shoves him away so violently that he falls backwards, hitting his head on the coffee table. Blood drips down his face, but he staggers to his feet and faces her. Diane watches, half expecting him to take a swing at her, but instead, he bursts out laughing. He laughs and laughs and frankly, the sound is far more sinister than anything she's ever heard before.

FIFTY-EIGHT
SARAH

Sarah stares at Pete. She is shaking with rage, but also with horror. She never meant to hurt him, but she was so angry she couldn't help herself. She is aware of Diane, watching them both, and she is desperate to smooth things over again. If only she could rewind the past few minutes. Scratch that, she wishes she could rewind this entire week.

She draws a breath. 'I didn't mean to do that. That was very childish of me. I hope you can forgive me?'

Pete stops laughing and his mouth hangs open in confusion.

'Actually, Pete, can you help me a minute? I need some help outside... with the chickens.'

Pete's eyebrows hit his hairline but Diane doesn't seem to notice. She's too out of it to pay much attention. They head outside to the garden, but instead of walking down to the chicken coop, she stands on the lawn, her arms crossed.

'I know it was you,' she tells him.

Pete looks perplexed.

'Me what?'

'I know you're the heavy breather. You've been stalking me for months, scaring the life out of me.'

Pete shakes his head. 'How can you even say that?'

'How indeed!'

She pulls out her phone and plays him the message. She watches his face as the truth slowly dawns on him. There's no getting out of this one. She's caught him red-handed.

He looks at her with those puppy dog eyes he's grown so good at.

'I was desperate,' he admits. 'I knew I was losing you. I couldn't handle it. I'm in love with you, Sarah, have been since the day I met you.'

'Now you're being ridiculous.'

'Am I? Have you ever known me to chase after anyone else?'

Sarah casts her mind back. Now she thinks about it, Pete's love life has been impressively non-existent.

'I was in love with you for years. I never said anything because I didn't think you'd feel the same way. But then you took me off the streets and we spent time together, just the two of us. And I started to believe it might be fate.'

Sarah holds her head in her hands. 'I should never have slept with you,' she says with a sigh. 'I never meant to give you false hope. But Pete, why the hell did you do that stuff? You scared the life out of me.'

He shakes his head. 'I don't know. The first call wasn't me. It must have been a wrong number or something, like I said at the time. But you were so freaked out about it, you were really clingy and I liked that. I liked the idea that I could protect you and make you feel safe. After a while, you forgot about it, so I thought, what if you got another one of those calls? What if you got a few of them? Maybe then you wouldn't go out so much. Maybe you would stay home with me.'

Sarah folds her arms. 'Stop making excuses, Pete. It wasn't just the calls. You've been stalking me. I sensed it a couple of times, but I thought I was being paranoid. But you just did that thing with the olive, just like Cameron, and then I knew you must have been watching us that night. What a sad little man you are, what a filthy little perv.'

His face hardens, and he looks at her with an expression she's never seen before.

'Cameron is Diane's husband, not yours. I can't believe, that out of all the men in the world, you had to choose him. You've always been too picky, just like Asha. Well, you know what? The cat's out of the bag now and I won't keep your secrets for you any longer. It's about time Diane knew the truth.'

FIFTY-NINE
SARAH

Three Months Earlier, Glasgow

Sarah presses herself closer to Cameron, savouring the warmth of his body against hers. She knows they can't stay like this forever. Sooner or later, she has to return to her life, and he to his. But right now, she clings to the moment, letting it stretch out just a little longer.

Her thoughts turn to Diane, and the resentment burns hotter now that she knows this isn't just sex; it's something she never thought she'd find. She looks up at him, her heart in her throat.

'I think I'm falling for you,' he whispers, his fingers gently tracing patterns through her hair.

'I bloody hope so, because I don't think I can live without you.'

Their eyes meet, and an understanding passes between them, an acknowledgement that, in another life, they would belong to each other completely. It's a bittersweet recognition, one that makes her chest ache as they hold on to each other a little tighter.

But when they return to their separate lives, the feeling doesn't fade. If anything, the distance makes it sharper. Sarah wrestles with the guilt, but the taste of something better, a life she can almost imagine, clings to her like a shadow. She craves it. She just needs to get Diane and Pete out of the way.

The darkness of her own thoughts shocks her. She doesn't dare voice them to Cameron, but they linger, unwanted. She catches herself imagining ways, accidents that could remove the obstacles between them, but always pushes them aside. It isn't who she is. Not really.

Asha's wedding is only weeks away, and Sarah is already dreading it. Cameron has bowed out, knowing they can't risk being seen together. The idea gnaws at her, the thought of being alone on that isolated island with both Diane and Pete. What if something were to happen? How would anyone ever know it was her? But no, she tells herself, she could never do that.

Could she?

SIXTY
SARAH

One Month Earlier, Glasgow

Sarah and Cameron speak to each other whenever they are alone. For her, that means sitting in her car, just outside her flat, before she heads inside of an evening. It feels like a long time since they last snuck away together and she aches to hold him in her arms again.

Then, one day, in a fit of madness, she bares her heart to him over the phone:

'Move in with me?'

She expects him to refuse, to call her crazy, but instead, his reply takes her breath away.

'When?'

She struggles for words, excitement twisting in her chest. 'When Diane goes to Asha's wedding. You can move your things into my place. And while I'm there, I'll try to convince her to take Pete in.'

There's a pause. 'I don't even have to tell her we're together,' Cameron says. 'That'll make it easier on her. I'll just say I need space. She won't know I'm with you. She won't have a clue.

And if you can persuade her, she'll have Pete for company – they'll be there for each other. Diane's strong. She'll need a bit of time, but she'll move on. And when she does, we can tell her the truth, once it's not so raw.'

Sarah closes her eyes, wishing she could reach through the phone to touch him, to make the promise feel more real.

'I know it sucks, lying to everyone, but it'll be worth it in the end,' he says, his voice low and certain.

'I know it will. I love you, Cameron.'

'I love you too.'

SIXTY-ONE
DIANE

Pete and Sarah return from the garden. Pete still has blood pouring from his ear, but he doesn't seem to notice.

He sits down beside Diane and takes her hand in his.

'It's about time you knew the truth about your so-called friend Sarah.'

Sarah steps quickly in front of him.

'Pete, don't. Can't you see she's already been through enough?'

Pete shakes his head, his jaw tight. 'It's not right, Sarah. She deserves to know.'

Diane lifts her head, her eyes narrowing. 'What are you going on about now?'

He draws a breath. 'Sarah's been having an affair with Cameron.'

Sarah squeezes her eyes shut for a moment, then looks up at the ceiling as if searching for strength. Her face twists with a mix of guilt and relief, as if a weight has finally been lifted.

'I'm so sorry, Diane, but it's true,' she says in a low voice. 'I never meant for this to happen, but I've fallen in love with him and he feels the same way about me. He's moving his stuff out of your place right now, while we're here. He's coming to live with me in Glasgow. That's why I wanted you to take Pete in.'

She throws a look at Pete, her voice hardening. 'He's not staying with me when we get back. He'll need a place to live, and I thought maybe you could help each other.'

Diane's mouth falls open. At first, she can't speak. She can't say a word.

A strange numbness seeps in, like a creeping cold.

She looks down at her hands. 'Cameron is not leaving me,' she finally says. 'And in case you haven't noticed, I'm not going to make it out of here. So, save your confessions, Sarah. And as for Pete? He's going to have to find somewhere else to go.'

Without breaking eye contact, she begins to peel back the soggy bandage from her shoulder, revealing the wound beneath, a jagged seam of stitches that look like they were made by a shaky hand, uneven and pulled too tight. The skin around the wound is swollen and angry, a deep, mottled red that fades into purple bruising. Worse still, a foul, yellowish pus seeps from between the stitches, and the edges of the cut have turned black. The air fills with a sickly sour smell. Her shoulder twitches involuntarily, as if the underlying muscles themselves are recoiling from the damage.

Sarah stumbles back, a horrified gasp escaping her lips, while Pete blanches, his bravado evaporating in an instant.

Diane meets Sarah's eye. 'You wanted me out of the way? Well congratulations, you've succeeded.'

SIXTY-TWO

SARAH

Sarah slumps against the wall, her head in her hands. She's always thought of herself as a good person. A helpful person. That's been the narrative of her life. Even when she whispered with Diane about Asha behind her back. They were only joking, having a laugh. She didn't really mean it. That isn't who she is.

Pete is fussing over Diane. There are tears in his eyes as he returns from the kitchen with antiseptic and attempts to clean her infected wound. Diane is swearing at him, shrieking at him to leave her alone.

Sarah drifts back outside. It's almost morning, but all she can see is the haar. She stumbles across the garden to the chicken coop and fumbles with the latch on the door, her fingers clumsy and uncoordinated. The door swings open and she steps inside. The smell of hay and feathers fills her nostrils as she inexpertly scatters the feed, unsure how it's supposed to be done.

The chickens and ducks have been busy laying. There are eggs everywhere. Some of them have smashed on the floor while others are in neat little piles on the straw. She gathers up as many as she can and places them in a bowl. The birds watch her every move, their beady eyes trained on her with an unsettling intensity. They peck furiously at the ground, as if searching for something hidden beneath the dirt.

'Thank you,' she says, 'for the eggs.'

They stare back at her and it occurs to her that they are missing Judith. She's careful to close the door after her, not just to keep them in, but to make sure they don't follow her back into the house.

As she crosses the lawn, clutching the bowl of eggs, the haar swirls around her, thick and disorienting. A shadow shifts in the fog, and a figure lunges out of the mist. She flinches, the bowl slipping from her hands, eggs smashing on the wet grass.

It's Pete. His face is flushed, his breathing ragged, and he looks half mad with excitement.

'For goodness' sake, Pete! Now look what you've made me do!'

He isn't listening. He's jumping up and down with excitement, talking so fast, she can't understand what he's saying.

'I didn't catch a word of that.'

'Boats! There are boats on the horizon. Someone is coming!'

She rushes indoors and finds the binoculars. He's right. There are little lights out there. Boats heading their way. But will they be able to find the island in all this mist?

Her heart pumps fast. 'We've got to get to the lighthouse.'

She runs around, grabbing her phone and bag.

'Come on,' Pete says, hauling Diane to her feet.

'Where are we going?' Diane asks dreamily. She can scarcely stand.

Sarah rushes ahead of them and jumps into the car. She slides easily into the driver's seat, her fingers tapping the dashboard. It would be so easy to drive off right now. To leave them both behind. And yet something makes her wait as Pete and Diane emerge from the cottage, Pete supporting Diane as they walk out to the car. They are all in this, the three of them. They've been through hell together this week. It doesn't feel right to leave without them.

She watches Diane struggle to slide herself into the back. Her skin has taken on a sickly sheen, her movements sluggish, each step costing her more strength than the last. She gasps as she settles into her seat, wincing in pain.

Pete opens the passenger side door and slides in beside Sarah. She senses he's as determined as she is to be rescued. She starts the engine and keeps her eyes fixed on the road ahead. She drives as far as the narrow track allows, then pulls up abruptly. The rest of the journey must be made on foot. She turns and looks back at Diane. Her breathing is laboured and her face is clammy. Her usually sharp gaze is dulled, like she's drifting away.

'Why don't you both wait here?' she says. 'I'll run up to the lighthouse and switch on the lights.'

Pete is already climbing out of the car, and she sees with exasperation that he's grabbing a gun from the boot. What does he need that for?

She is about to say something when a missile shoots up into the air and crackles overhead. Pete stares at her for a moment.

'Go! I'll cover you. Just get to the lighthouse.'

She hesitates. How does she know she can trust him?

She searches his eyes for any sign of deception, then nods gravely.

Her heart is pounding in her chest. She runs faster than she's ever run before.

Sweat beads on her forehead and her muscles burn with exertion. She's scared the shooter will follow her inside. If they do, she has no way of defending herself. She has to rely on Pete to keep his word. She doesn't like it, but what choice does she have? She presses ahead, into the lighthouse and up the stairs, panting hard.

Her legs tremble beneath her as she reaches the lantern room. Faced with an array of unfamiliar switches and levers, she focuses on the most obvious one: a large switch in the centre. She flicks it on, and the light roars to life, a brilliant beam that slices through the dense mist. It sweeps out over the water, illuminating the sea and guiding the boats away from the rocks, towards the safety of the inlet. There are at least two of them out there. She assumes one is the ferry, but she's not sure about the other. It looks like the police. She thinks of all Diane's attempts with the radio. Was somebody listening after all? Is that why they've sent help?

She stands there in awe as she catches her breath, bathing in the glow. A surge of elation rushes through her. She wants to jump up and down. But she knows it's not over yet.

She strains her ears for any sign of danger. She can't hear anyone coming up the steps, but they might be sneaky. She makes her way to the window and looks out to sea. The boats are getting closer by the second. She hurries back down and finds Pete and Diane waiting for her. Pete high-fives her.

'Nice one!'

'Any sign of the shooter?' she asks.

'No, I think it might have been a flare.'

'A flare?'

She glances around. 'But who on earth would have set it off? There's no one else on the island.'

He shakes his head, unable to answer, and Diane leans heavily against him, a small smile forming on her lips.

'It's over,' she says softly. 'It's finally over.'

The boats pull into the inlet, their engines roaring as they approach. Sarah's heart races as she sees a team of heavily armed police officers disembark, accompanied by two large German shepherds.

'Hands up!' The command echoes through the air.

She and Pete lock eyes and raise their hands in surrender. The police approach, ready for any sign of resistance.

'Hands behind your heads! Drop to your knees!'

The orders are barked out with authority, sending a fresh surge of adrenaline through Sarah's veins. She can't shake the fear that lingers in the back of her mind. There is someone else on the island. And until they're caught, no one is truly safe.

'I'm injured,' she hears Diane say. 'Careful, I have a bullet wound in my shoulder.'

A policewoman glances at her, firm but cautious, and nods, loosening her grip as she reminds them of their rights. The words are almost unintelligible over the howling of the wind. Step by step, the police guide them down towards the first of the waiting boats, which sways back and forth in the dark waters.

Sarah is feeling emotional. She wants to squeeze her friends' hands, to celebrate the fact that they are safe. But since they are cuffed, she has to do as she is told.

They sit and wait while a police officer verifies their identities. She tries not to worry about the cuffs. She understands that they will need to unravel this whole mess and separate the victims from the shooters. All the same, the hard metal digs into her wrists, and there is a hardness in the police officer's tone that she doesn't like. She has been through hell, and she deserves a little more compassion.

'I suppose you think it's all over?' Diane murmurs as the police run their checks.

'I hope so,' Sarah says. She's still thinking about the flare, wondering who could have launched it. She remembers that someone was camping in the bothy. She thought it must have been Asha, but what if she was mistaken? What if there was someone else?

Well, it doesn't matter now. She's going home to her lovely, familiar flat. And Cameron. Cameron will be there, waiting for her. She hopes Pete's not going to make a scene. Perhaps the police will help him. They'll have to, won't they, if Diane isn't up to it. Someone has to take him, because after what she has discovered on the island, she is done with him.

'You really think you can be happy with Cameron?' Diane says, as if reading her thoughts.

Sarah presses her lips together.

'I really wish he could be anyone else,' she whispers. 'Anyone but your husband.'

Diane nods bitterly. 'So do I.'

SIXTY-THREE
DIANE

Diane shakes her head. Sarah doesn't understand. She has no idea what it's like to love Cameron. Oh, falling for him is easy; he knows all the right words, the right moves. But keeping him? That's a different game altogether, one that consumes you and drives you half insane.

Two police officers step forward.

'Diane Lomax?'

'Yes, that's me.'

'You are under arrest for the murder of your husband, Cameron Lomax. You do not have to say anything, but anything you do say will be noted and may be used in evidence.'

Sarah lets out a strangled cry, her knees giving way beneath her as she collapses against Pete. The words barely register – she's reeling, gasping, drowning in disbelief. But Diane? Diane doesn't flinch. She knows this script well. It isn't news to her.

The police officer continues. It's clear he's trying to keep the emotion from his voice, and he almost succeeds but that slight burr gives him away.

'We found Cameron unresponsive in your hallway. There was nothing we could do. He was too badly injured.'

Diane's silence is colder than the mist around them.

'Did you stab your husband, Diane? Did you leave him at the bottom of the stairs to bleed out?'

Diane glances at Sarah, the friend who never saw the shadows beneath her smile. A slow, deliberate grin creeps across her face, one that's more defiance than remorse.

'Yes,' she says, her voice cutting through the fog. 'Yes, I did.'

SIXTY-FOUR
DIANE

Nine Days Earlier, Inverness

When Diane comes home from work, there are suitcases sitting by the door.

She looks up to see Cameron coming down the stairs. His chest is bare. He's been working out a lot lately, and he's getting increasingly buff. If he keeps this up, she's going to have to buy him some new shirts. Not that she minds. It's damned sexy if she's honest.

Her thoughts are derailed by Cameron's serious expression.

'What are these for? Are you coming to Asha's wedding after all? Because it's only a week. You won't need this much stuff. And it's a bit late to RSVP. You already said you weren't coming.'

His expression turns dark and he responds through gritted teeth. 'Will you stop talking a minute and give me a chance to speak for once?'

She blanches a little at his tone. 'Go on then, out with it.'

'Shall we go and sit down?'

'No, here is fine. I'm going to go and take a shower in a minute.'

She leans against the wall and waits for him to say whatever it is that's on his mind.

'Di, I wasn't going to do this until you came back from the wedding but I just can't wait any longer. I need to tell you how I feel.'

She tilts her head. 'About what?'

He steps forward and takes both of her hands in his. 'You know I'll always love you, but things just aren't the same as they used to be. I don't feel the same way I once did.'

She wriggles free of his hands. 'What the fuck are you going on about?'

She waits for him to crack up, to laugh, for friends to burst out from behind the doors and shout – 'Surprise!' For him to buffer and rewind.

He draws a breath, and she feels the bottom drop out of her world.

'I'm just not happy any more. I think we need a bit of space. Don't worry, you can stay here. I've found somewhere else. I really think time apart will be good for us.'

'And... and then you'll be back?'

'Honestly, I don't think so. I-I've been thinking about this for a while.'

'You what?'

'Okay, I'll be honest with you. You deserve that much. I've... I've fallen in love with someone else.'

Her eyes land on the letter opener lying on the shoe cupboard. Before she's even aware of what she's doing, her fingers are wrapped around the handle. In a flash, she closes the distance between them. He hardly has time to flinch before the tip of the blade presses against his gut, piercing through fabric, skin and muscle in one fluid motion. His eyes widen, shock freezing his face.

He staggers backwards, sliding down the wall, his hands fumbling to stem the blood seeping through his shirt. She watches in horror, and the hallway grows unnervingly still. The only sounds are those of her own heartbeat thundering in her ears, and the gasps escaping Cameron's lips as he fights for air.

It doesn't feel real. None of it does. She feels like she's having an out-of-body experience, looking down on them both as the weapon clatters to the floor. Blood gushes from his stomach. So much blood. He crawls on his hands and knees towards the door, and at first she is too stunned to react. He pulls himself up and grasps at the handle before she comes to her senses. There is a brief struggle. He lands a weak punch, but she knocks him backwards and the door swings back, trapping her hand.

She barely feels it. All she can think about is Cameron.

The colour is draining from his face as he lies dazed on the floor.

'I need to get to the hospital,' he croaks. 'Diane, baby. If you ever loved me...'

She laughs out loud at the absurdity of his words.

'Of course I love you. Why do you think I did this? You were going to leave me. You were going to split us up.'

'Diane. You're not thinking straight.'

He's said that a lot lately. As if she doesn't know her own mind. It's gaslighting at the worst level. She doesn't know why she didn't see it before.

He seems to be struggling for words, as if he too can no longer think straight. The dark red puddle is growing by the minute. She puts a foot on his neck.

'Who is it? Someone I know?'

He nods.

'A friend?'

He nods again.

'Who? Give me a name.'

She releases her foot, and he gurgles indistinctly. She can't catch what he's saying. Just the 'a' at the end. She narrows her eyes. Suddenly, it's all too obvious.

'It's Asha, isn't it?'

He has always liked Asha. Everyone does. And she knows that Asha is pregnant by a man other than Gordon. Is it Cameron's?

She hears the crunch of gravel on their driveway. There is a clattering sound as a leaflet flies through their letter box.

'Help me!' Cameron cries out.

She kicks his wound, and he splutters in a way that reminds her of a dying fish, gasping for air.

Then she paces around trying to think what to do. It's so hard to think straight these days. So very hard.

She goes into the kitchen. Asha's wedding invitation is pinned to the fridge door. She's supposed to be leaving today. She was looking forward to it. She walks back out to the hallway and takes another look at Cameron. His face is pale and he's staring blankly at the wall, not making any more attempts to move. What is he thinking about? Is his life flashing before his eyes?

Cameron is the love of her life. She knows it won't be long before she joins him. But not today.

There are a few things she needs to take care of first.

SIXTY-FIVE
DIANE

Now, Aberdeen

Diane lies in her hospital bed, the sterile walls pressing in around her. The steady hum of machines is a constant reminder that the operation was a success and she's still here, still alive. Her body feels distant, a hazy blur of disconnected sensations. The pain is gone, muffled by the drugs coursing through her veins, but in its place is a kind of numbness. The relief is almost overwhelming. It's such a pleasure not to be in pain. But she still feels as if she's in some kind of limbo.

There is a knock at the door. Diane lifts her eyes to see a nurse peering in at her. The harsh light from the corridor spills into the room.

'You've got a visitor.'

A policeman steps in. He is tall with a head that tapers flat at the top, like he's been carved out of a turnip. His dark eyes are unblinking and he approaches slowly, as if assessing the state she's in, weighing her, measuring how much danger he's in.

'Diane? Did you kill Gordon Kirkness, Asha Kirkness, Judith Henderson and Ethan Champion?'

Her brain flickers through all the names, but it's like watching an old film reel, the images out of focus, disconnected, jerky.

She sees their faces: Gordon, bald and beaming; Asha the last time she saw her, the dead princess with the frozen smile; Judith, squealing as her face hits the windscreen; Ethan returning fire, then gargling as hapless Asha blows his brains out. Even cooler than a Tarantino movie. Will he dine out on that story in the afterlife? Asha gasping, appalled at what she's done. But it's too late. She can't take it back. Asha, looking at Diane, thinking she's finally going to end her. Diane, reaching for Ethan's gun. But she doesn't have to do anything, because Asha's already shot. Seems like she doesn't even know it, until she looks down and sees all the blood. Asha, retreating, stumbling backwards, falling to the ground outside the cottage. Diane going to check she's really dead. Closing the door behind her. Collapsing back into her chair. Wondering how long it will be until she too feels the gentle release of death.

'Diane?'

She looks at the policeman. She is already bored with being questioned. She decides she's not going to give him anything. Not unless he answers her questions first.

'Who was it who set off the flare? No one would tell me.'

He sighs. Perhaps he senses that if he tells her what she wants to know, she'll reciprocate. 'It was Broderick Henderson. He arrived back to the island to find the body of Gordon Kirkness on the beach. He then returned to his cottage to find the place ransacked and his wife missing. He radioed for help, but we were already on our way.'

Diane nods. Broderick. Of course it was.

'How did you find Cameron so quickly?'

'Your neighbours reported a bad smell coming from your flat. So, we broke the door down and found your husband. Fortunately for us, the wedding invitation was still pinned to the fridge. So, Diane? Did you kill Gordon? And Asha and the others?'

She racks her brain, trying to remember.

'I've had this feeling since Cameron died, like nothing I do is of any consequence, because without him, nothing's real. It's like I'm living in a simulation.'

He leans in, his tone stern yet sympathetic. 'Well, I can assure you it's all real, Diane. There are five dead bodies to account for. And up until now you've never so much as got a speeding ticket. So, I would really appreciate it if you would help me out here. Help me understand.'

SIXTY-SIX
DIANE

Then, Haarlorn

On the night of Asha's wedding. Diane sits with Pete for a few minutes, once he's fallen asleep. He is still in his wedding suit, though his tie is loose, his shirt collar gaping open. A faint snore escapes his lips. She is about to leave, when she spots the disgusting bird carcass on the floor by his bed.

'What the hell!'

He must have retrieved it when he thought she wasn't looking and brought it inside, for reasons known only to him. It has a funky smell to it, and she is loath to touch it, but wouldn't it be funny, she thinks, to leave it in Sarah's bed?

In the old days, of course, she would have done this to Asha. But tonight she has other plans.

As she bends down to pick it up, she sees something else under Pete's bed.

A rifle.

What is this doing here? She saw the way Pete was looking at Gordon earlier. Did he steal it for self-protection? She will have to talk to him about it in the morning. He needs to put it back before anyone realises it is missing.

She picks up the bird and plops it down on Sarah's pillow, because she wants to give her friends one last laugh, then she ducks into Ethan's room and sits there as if she's been there all night. He seems pleased to see her, and they soon fall back into old habits, chatting and laughing. But all the time she is listening, waiting for Sarah to scream.

And when she does, it's just beautiful.

She plays her part well, rushing in like she's had nothing to do with it. She even offers to help dispose of the thing and lets Sarah sleep in her bed. No one has any idea it was her.

A little later, Asha and Gordon drop round. Diane studies Gordon as he walks over to Ethan. He has the gentle giant routine down pat. He smiles easily and knows exactly what to say. But she can't help but wonder if it's all an act. She remembers how Asha's dad took against him instinctively, and Pete was terrified when he first clapped eyes on him. He said he looked like the man who abused him, but without the internet, Diane has no way of knowing if Gordon has in fact lived in Orkney all his life, or if he spent a few years down south. If so, it might be best to let Pete keep the gun after all.

Gordon is having a word with Ethan, presumably about his speech. It's interesting to watch. Although Gordon is speaking calmly, Ethan looks quite scared. Well, serves him right, now she thinks about it. That speech was bang out of order.

Asha has brought a box of cake left over from the wedding. It's a melty chocolate sponge, rather than the traditional fruitcake, because Princess Asha hates raisins. She and Asha chat for a while, but every so often, Asha looks over at Gordon and breaks into a huge grin. Diane watches her curiously. She doesn't look like someone who is having an affair. She looks hopelessly in love. And it occurs to her that perhaps she's got it wrong. Maybe Asha isn't the person Cameron has fallen for.

Has she been too quick to jump to conclusions? Maybe he wasn't talking about Asha after all.

She heads into the kitchen to get herself a drink.

Asha follows. Diane pops open a bottle of wine and pours them both a glass. Asha is really drunk already but she's only too happy to have another. She goes on and on about what a great day she's had. She pauses for a moment, pulling a little silver compact out of her pocket. She pouts at her own reflection as she repaints her bright red lipstick.

'It's your wedding night,' Diane says, watching her. 'Aren't you supposed to be consummating the marriage?'

Asha grins. 'Already taken care of. My life is so perfect right now. But I deserve this, don't you think? Isn't it awesome, when you find that special someone to share your life with?'

Then her eyes widen, and she claps her hand over her mouth.

'What am I saying? That was so insensitive of me, going on about me and Gordon. Now you have to promise me you won't go back to that cheating rat.'

Diane tilts her head. 'Back up a minute. What are you on about?'

Asha sways. She really is wasted.

'He's such a sleaze!' she says, as if it's all a big joke. 'Don't you remember your wedding day?'

Ice freezes in Diane's veins. 'What about it?'

'Well, remember how Pete and I left early? That was because Cameron followed me into the loos and tried to snog me.'

Diane stares at her, unable to believe what she's hearing.

'I ran out, straight into Pete, and he offered to see me home. I didn't tell him what happened, but he can be very perceptive. He's a really good guy, you know?'

'But if this is true, then why the hell didn't you say anything?'

Asha rests a soothing arm on her sleeve. 'I would never ruin your wedding day. Every bride deserves to have her moment. I figured he was just drunk.'

Diane shakes her head and storms off to the bathroom, tears streaming down her face. Bile burns her throat as she empties the contents of her stomach into the toilet, leaving her drained and weak. This is even worse than she suspected. Asha has known what Cameron is like since their wedding day, and she has chosen to say nothing. Has she done this to protect Diane, as she claims? Or is there a part of her that has enjoyed this knowledge? She must have thought of it every time she spoke to her and Cameron. She must have looked at him and remembered. If she really cared about Diane, she would have found a way to let her down gently. Instead, she has chosen to hold this back. To let Cameron carry on with his vile ways, and to allow Diane to be hurt more deeply than she ever thought was possible.

She breathes in and out slowly.

Ethan has conked out on the sofa, and Asha giggles as she places her veil on his head. Diane watches as she and Gordon walk off hand in hand. They don't head back to their cottage, but down to the beach for a moonlight stroll. Diane turns and heads back to Pete's room. She takes the gun from under his bed and checks the chamber. Ever since she killed Cameron, she's had a feeling like nothing she does really matters any more. Nothing will make her feel better. Well, it seems she was wrong.

Now she knows exactly what will make her feel better.

A LETTER FROM LORNA

Dear Reader,

I want to say a huge thank you for choosing to read *The Wedding Party*. If you enjoyed it and want to keep up to date with all my latest releases, just sign up at the following link. Your email address will never be shared and you can unsubscribe at any time.

www.bookouture.com/lorna-dounaeva

The Wedding Party was inspired by Orkney, a place where I am lucky enough to live. Haarlorn, the fictional setting, is a blend of several real islands, with their sweeping cliffs, unpredictable seas, and close-knit communities that can be both nurturing and claustrophobic. The idea of being trapped on an island, unable to escape, felt like the perfect backdrop for a psychological thriller. At its heart, though, *The Wedding Party* is about people, particularly the complexities of old friendships. It explores the way time can erode trust and magnify secrets, creating drama, tension and fear. In this story, the setting and relationships are inseparable, each adding to the sense of unease and entrapment.

If you enjoyed this book, I would love to hear from you. You can connect with me on social media.

I'm on Facebook, X, Bluesky and Instagram. I'd love to hear your thoughts or answer any questions you might have.

Thank you again for reading.

Warm wishes,

Lorna

- facebook.com/LornaDounaevaAuthor
- x.com/LornaDounaeva
- instagram.com/lorna_dounaeva
- goodreads.com/lornadounaeva

PUBLISHING TEAM

Turning a manuscript into a book requires the efforts of many people. The publishing team at Bookouture would like to acknowledge everyone who contributed to this publication.

Audio
Alba Proko
Sinead O'Connor
Melissa Tran

Commercial
Lauren Morrissette
Hannah Richmond
Imogen Allport

Data and analysis
Mark Alder
Mohamed Bussuri

Cover design
Jo Thomson

Editorial
Harriet Wade
Sinead O'Connor

Copyeditor
Janette Currie

Proofreader
Liz Hatherell

Marketing
Alex Crow
Melanie Price
Occy Carr
Cíara Rosney
Martyna Młynarska

Operations and distribution
Marina Valles
Stephanie Straub
Joe Morris

Production
Hannah Snetsinger
Mandy Kullar
Ria Clare
Nadia Michael

Publicity
Kim Nash
Noelle Holten
Jess Readett
Sarah Hardy

Rights and contracts
Peta Nightingale
Richard King
Saidah Graham